CONQUEST

THE FOUR GROOMSMEN OF THE WEDPOCALYPSE
BOOK 1

LILIAN MONROE

Published by Method and Madness Publishing PTY LTD
PO Box 168 Subiaco, WA, Australia 6008

Print ISBN: 978-1-922986-32-0

Cover Design by Sybil at PopKitty Designs
Editing by Shavonne Clarke at Motif Edits
Proofreading by Paige Kraft (paigekedits.com)

WANT THREE BOOKS DELIVERED STRAIGHT TO YOUR
INBOX?
HOW ABOUT THREE ROCK STAR ROMANCES THAT WERE *WAY*
TOO HOT TO SELL?

GET THE COMPLETE *ROCK HARD* SERIES:
WWW.LILIANMONROE.COM/ROCKHARD

WELCOME TO THE WEDPOCALYPSE

ONE

AMELIA DARCY WAS ready to crawl out of her skin. Red ants marched through her veins, leaving burning anxiety in their wake. They traveled the length of her body in an unending loop, through every artery, vein, and capillary, around and around and around.

Because he was *late*.

Huffing in a failed attempt to clear her mounting frustration, Amelia spun on her heels and continued wearing a line through the thin red carpet of the church's narthex. The single strap of her bridesmaid dress draped strangely over her shoulder. Why had her sister chosen an asymmetrical design? At least with two straps, the feeling would be mirrored on both sides of her body, which would be acceptable. Amelia hadn't been comfortable since she put the thing on.

She wouldn't even think about the color; that would only make her anxiety worse. Earlier, when Amelia had slipped on the lilac silk garment and caught sight of herself in the mirror, she'd fully recoiled. Against her pale, desaturated skin and her pale, desaturated hair, the pastel purple shade produced a distinctly corpselike effect. Even her eyes, which she'd always thought were her best feature, looked sunken, their pale gray irises turning dull as worn pewter. The makeup artist had tried to glue false eyelashes on her lids, cheerily claiming they'd brighten her face right up, but then Amelia had twitched and blinked so much the whole endeavor had been aborted. So she still looked like she belonged outside in the church's graveyard instead of the bridal party, except now with slightly irritated eyelids.

But today was Maggie's wedding day, and Amelia would wear a sparkly leotard and dance the cha-cha backward if it made her sister happy. It didn't matter what color her dress was, or how many straps it had, or if that number was one too few.

Wedding planning hadn't been fun, exactly, but Amelia had thrown herself into it. She'd made phone calls, coordinated vendors, ordered decorations, planned and attended a hellish bachelorette party, helped set up the church and the reception venue, and completed countless other tasks—all in the name of sisterly love. She'd taken her role as Maggie's maid of honor seriously.

The best man, on the other hand?

Not so much.

He hadn't shown up to the rehearsal dinner, hadn't helped with any of the preparations, and now, the only time that *actually* mattered, he was late. Two more minutes, and she'd lead the bridal progression down the aisle on her own. He could slink in whenever he arrived and watch from the back pew, for all she cared. If he showed up at all.

The strap on her shoulder slipped, so she yanked it back up. Stupid thing.

She'd strangle him when she saw him. Months—*months!*—of planning, and now the whole wedding hinged on the arrival of some mysterious best man. Nerves morphed into anger, and Amelia wanted to scream. She'd make him sorry for being so late. That was a promise. She'd strangle him with his own tie and enjoy every gruesome second of it.

Her feet stomped as she made another lap. And another. And another. Her teeth gnashed so hard a headache started pulsing near her temples.

A door creaked open behind her. Amelia whirled, only to let her shoulders drop in disappointment.

A dark-haired man poked his head out of the room where the bridal party waited. He lifted a brow. "No sign of him?"

"No." Her answer was curt. Her lips compressed, as if she could make the missing best man appear by drawing her mouth into a perfectly straight line. It didn't work.

"All right. I'll let them know." Marlon St. James didn't seem worried about his brother's tardiness. He certainly didn't seem surprised. Even the groom hadn't worried when she'd scurried to the altar to inform him his best man was missing in action.

Emory had given her a little half-smile and said, "He'll show. He's flying in this morning, probably hit traffic."

Amelia didn't share Emory's confidence. A scowl etched itself over her brow as she spun around to do another lap. She hadn't been able to get a straight answer from her sister's other bridesmaids when she asked about the best man. Sly looks and rolled eyes were the usual response to the mention of his name. Maybe a snort and a wry, "You know how he is."

But she didn't know how he was. She'd never laid eyes on the man. All she knew was he was *late*.

Murmurs swelled in the church as guests grew restless. She'd wait one more minute, and then they'd start without him. She'd apologize to Maggie and Emory afterward, but really, it was—

Hinges groaned to her left. Amelia turned toward the sound, only to be struck dumb by the vision unfolding before her.

The church's arched doors split down the middle, letting in golden sunlight through the widening gap. A man stood in the center, a hand on either door, silhouetted by the sun's honeyed rays. He pushed the doors all the way open to step through them then straightened, standing as tall and proud as a king returning from war. Or maybe a fallen angel, seeking vengeance.

Or a missing best man, finally deigning to make an appearance.

Leo St. James stepped into the church, the sunlight limning the edges of his body in gold while casting the rest of him in black, impenetrable shadow. He looked impossibly large. For no reason at all, Amelia's heart rattled.

The doors squeaked on their way shut and bit by bit, the best man was revealed to Amelia's hungry stare.

Because that's what was growing inside her—hunger. A ravenous ache pulsed in the very heart of her as she saw the strong lines of his face, his heavy-lidded green eyes, his softly masculine lips. There was a sort of disheveled grace to him, a quality that made him seem more than perfect. Like his appearance was a veneer her mortal gaze wasn't supposed to penetrate, his flaws purposefully chosen to make him seem simply human.

Slowly, sunlight disappeared behind heavy timber doors until a final groan and a click sounded. The best man watched her, a brow quirking at her perusal.

Suddenly she realized she'd been gaping. Her spine snapped straight. "You're late," she clipped.

His gaze didn't leave her face. "Am I?"

"And you're a mess."

Leo looked down at himself and seemed surprised to see the state of his clothes. "So I am," he muttered. "Got changed at the airport."

Edging dangerously close to mania, Amelia tried to wrangle her fleeing wits. She felt lightheaded and strange. He was very beautiful. But—so what?

He was also late, and that was nearly unforgivable. It was Maggie's wedding day, and nothing—especially not *him*—would ruin it. Even if this was "how he was." Whatever that meant.

Stomping toward Leo, she ignored the incessant thumping of her heart. He looked even worse—better?—up close. Rumpled. Deliciously so.

Before she could divine what they were doing, Amelia's hands rose to the bow tie hanging undone at Leo's neck. She couldn't fasten the bow until the top button of his shirt was clasped, so she clicked her tongue and pulled at his collar. He rocked forward when she yanked the fabric, letting out a short, low grunt.

From the corner of her eyes, Amelia caught the curl of his lips.

Smiling! At a time like this! Strangling him would be too kind. He deserved to be tickled to death. Or stretched out on a medieval rack and submitted to the most horrid water torture imaginable. Or...or...have every one of his long, full eyelashes plucked out.

Her fingers trembled as they dipped near the hollow of his throat to do up the button. Stubble rasped against her knuckles, and a sharp jolt of heat traveled through her middle.

"This is...unexpected," he said, voice dropping to a low baritone that did interesting things to Amelia's inner thighs. Amelia's inner thighs needed to get ahold of themselves. "Are you sure we should be doing this in a church? You haven't even told me your name."

Fury was a rocket launching in her chest. Explosions created a cloud of dust and debris in her veins as anger took off inside her, because he didn't even seem sorry for being unforgivably late. He was *flirting*, at a time like this! Leo St. James, professional annoyance. Who did he think he was? Showing up at Amelia's sister's wedding, looking like a disheveled prince, then *joking* about it!

The. *Nerve*.

The man couldn't even dress himself, and he was trying to be cute with her?

"Oh, please," she hissed. "Spare me." She scowled at him, flicking her gaze upward to meet his eyes. It was a mistake. As soon as her gaze clashed with his, she saw the gleam that lived in his emerald-green irises. It promised everything dark and dirty, and Amelia wanted to let herself fall into those promises and never emerge again. Her anger was snuffed out in an instant as a wave of unfamiliar lust took over.

Strange. It wasn't like her to feel this way about men—not even the pretty ones. Flustered, yes. Anxious, definitely.

Aroused? No way.

Her body's reaction swung her back to anger, and she gripped the feeling with both fists. She was angry at him for being late. Angry at the bridal party for putting her in this position. Angry at herself for finding him attractive.

Maybe the stress of her sister's wedding was getting to her. Or it was the lack of sleep over the past six months. Her work had been intense, after all. Starting a business usually was.

A small shake of her head, and her mind felt slightly clearer. Today was her sister's wedding, and this absolute lump of a pretty boy was threatening to throw the whole thing off-schedule. He needed to get himself together, then she'd hold his arm and walk down the aisle ahead of the rest of the bridal party with a smile plastered on her face. Nothing else mattered.

She tugged the collar to straighten it, then set herself to tying the bow tie. It was the same soft lilac as her dress, but against his tawny skin, the color looked rich and creamy. Of course it did. Her frown deepened, and Amelia used the moment to settle her unstable emotions. She tied the fabric carefully, straightening the corners until a perfect purple bow stared back at her.

All the while, Leo's gaze pressed like a weight. He stood

very still to endure her ministrations, arms at his sides, chin lifted out of the way. But she felt it—the heaviness of his stare. He didn't have anywhere else to look but at her, she reasoned, but it still made her want to squirm.

It was no surprise that Amelia would feel put out by a beautiful man's gaze. She wasn't exactly beating men back these days. She'd been focusing on her career; she hadn't had time to date. Never mind the fact that being this close to a man made Amelia feel like she had a bird trapped in her chest and noodles for limbs. Best to avoid these sorts of situations altogether. She wasn't known for being a man-eater. More like a man-evader.

Sipping in a short little breath, she frowned at his vest. It, like the jacket and pants, was a navy so dark it was nearly black. His white shirt bunched awkwardly between his vest and pants. He'd have to re-tuck it.

She pointed at the offending area. "Fix this. It looks like a deflated muffin top," she blurted—and there was the other reason she hadn't had much luck with men. Words sometimes fell out of her mouth without warning, and often they weren't exactly delicate. She'd come to learn that her lack of filter wasn't an attractive trait. There were many, many data points from failed dates and awkward interactions to prove it.

But Leo didn't seem bothered. In fact, he leaned ever so slightly closer to her, so she could smell the scent of soap rising from his skin. "I was led to believe that fixing my clothing was your job," he answered, and for a moment, Amelia felt off-balance. It was the velvet quality of his tone and the way his scent wrapped around her like a drugging cloud. Then she registered the laughter in his voice.

Despite herself, Amelia's eyes snapped up to his once more. He was *mocking* her. Thunder rumbled in the distance, and Amelia knew it was her temper.

She just wanted this day to go right. For Maggie. For beautiful, kind Maggie with the luminous smile. Her sister deserved this. She'd found Emory, and they'd fallen in love, and now they'd have a perfect wedding day. Amelia would make sure of it.

This was what she *did*. She identified problems, then parsed the data into something useful. Whether it was a complicated data set for a client, or a wedding venue scheduling for today's event, or ordering supplies for seventy intricate handmade centerpieces (which included twenty-five hundred and ninety individual components, ordered from four different vendors), Amelia could sort any problem into a tidy, efficient solution.

She'd made sense of the wedding preparations, and now it would all go off without a hitch. No matter what the man before her did or said.

Leo narrowed his eyes, seeing something written on her face. What, she didn't know. Maybe he could hear the thunder just as clearly as she could. Ozone crackled in the air between them, like that breathless, heavy moment before a strike of lightning.

With a gusted breath, Leo turned, and a belt jingled. Amelia averted her gaze from his broad back, blood rising to her cheeks. It was half humiliating, really, to be blushing at the mere sound of a belt buckle clinking. No wonder men saw her and took off running in the other direction. Middle schoolers had more poise than she did.

Leo spun around and spread his arms, a roguish grin holding up the corners of his lips. "Satisfied?"

Ugh. "Annoyed."

His smile grew, as did the trembling in Amelia's thighs.

Leo tugged his jacket sleeves and arranged his cuffs just so. He combed both hands through his hair, and the gently curled light-brown locks fell into the kind of perfect disarray that betrayed an expensive haircut.

Rings glinted on two fingers: the thumb of his right hand, and the index finger of his left. They were simple gold bands that shone in the low light of the room and drew attention to his hands. Beautiful hands for a beautiful man. He lifted his gaze to hers and arched a brow.

"Good enough," Amelia grumped, even though the more truthful statement would be *drop-dead gorgeous* or *positively edible.*

"Do I get to learn your name now?" The gleam was back in his eyes.

Nerves gripped Amelia in a tight fist. Giving him even her name was handing over more power than was wise. A man like Leo St. James would take one look at her and crush her vulnerable heart. She felt the urge to protect herself, but Amelia was a rational being, and she knew it was only her name. He'd learn it eventually. She forced the syllables out. "Amelia."

"Amelia," he repeated, like he was sipping fine wine and detecting all kinds of hidden notes in it. Touching a hand to his chest, he said, "Leo."

"So I've heard," she said, and something undefinable flitted across his expression. His smile widened, but his eyes grew shuttered.

Amelia frowned. Odd.

No time to figure it out. She had a wedding procession to lead, and she wasn't letting Leo St. James out of her sight for a second until Emory and Maggie were husband and wife. She reached out and grabbed Leo's wrist, tugging him toward the room where the rest of the bridal party awaited, not trusting him to follow without physical encouragement.

Then he shifted, and his hand slipped against hers. She made to pull away, but he intertwined their fingers before she had the chance to escape.

He was... He was *holding her hand*.

It was a shock to the system, intimate in a way she hadn't expected. That broad, warm palm pressed against hers. His long fingers curled and notched between her knuckles. The heat of it. The sheer *size* of it.

She paused halfway to the side door and stared at their joined hands. His golden tan against her pallid skin looked... wrong. Foreign, somehow.

It made her feel very, very hot.

SHE WAS AN ENIGMA. A snippy, terse enigma that made Leo want to needle her. He knew she'd hate him holding her hand, so he made sure to grip it firmly. If, in the process, he enjoyed the soft give of her flesh against his calloused palm, well, that was only a happy coincidence.

She'd known about him; surely she was aware of his reputation. A smart woman would run in the other direction, unless she was looking for a hard ride with no promise of anything more. His name was synonymous with casual, no-strings-attached fun.

But *her* name...

Amelia was a name suited to a soft flower of a woman, someone delicate and girlish. The creature staring at their clasped hands was anything but. She was all angles and frowns and pinched lips. It fascinated him, especially as she hadn't reacted to his reputation in one of the familiar ways. Women were usually intrigued or disgusted by him—or both. At least until the light of morning broke over the horizon, and then women were usually gone.

Amelia only seemed irritated.

He wanted to push her. Just a little bit.

She stood in front of him, looking down at their hands, her brow wrinkled, and he was caught up in the sight of her. He wanted to smooth the line between her brows with his thumb. Instead, he lifted a finger and drew it across her exposed collarbone. Her skin was soft; it felt so thin over the protruding bone. Tracing the line all the way to her shoulder, he let his fingers memorize her shape. So angular. Hard and delicate all at once.

At his touch, she let out a gusting breath as a little shiver trembled through her body. Her eyes closed, briefly, like she couldn't help herself.

"What about this?" Leo asked, gratified to see the flush rising up her neck to stain her cheeks. "You can't criticize my suit when your dress is missing an entire sleeve."

Her scowl was a thing of beauty. It made him laugh as an

unfamiliar feeling shot through him. Bubbly—he felt effervescent at the sight of her glower. He wanted more.

"Come on," she said in that husky, peeved voice of hers, and she dragged him across the room to a heavy wooden door.

She wasn't beautiful, exactly. Her face was too pointed and her eyes too wide to be called anything but striking. Still, she captivated. There was something discoverable about her beauty, like it might reveal itself to him bit by bit, given enough time. Tall enough to reach his nose in her three-inch heels, she walked like she had no time to lose, dragging him along by the hand she'd allowed him to continue gripping. Pink gloss shone on her lips, and he wondered how they would taste to lick. He was caught like a fly in her grouchy web, and he had been since he'd opened the doors and seen her standing in a shaft of sunlight. She was so fierce. So... *nettled.*

Leo wanted to find all the places on her body that would make her soften for him. He was just imagining drawing the zipper of her dress down to the base of her back—wondering if she'd shiver again if he traced his fingertips down her spine— when they reached the door at the side of the church's anteroom.

She opened it with a violent tug, and he was confronted with a pack of familiar faces.

Suddenly, he remembered who he was. Who *she* was.

He dropped her hand.

She went still beside him for a short second, then clapped her hands together. "All right. Places, people!"

"Leo." His brother Marlon nodded as he came to his feet off

an uncomfortable-looking, straight-backed chair. Marlon tugged his suit jacket down and ran a hand through his jet-black hair.

"Leo," Tori said with distinctly more venom. She hooked her arm through Marlon's and pointed her nose in the air, the same expression she'd worn for him since their two-week tryst in college years before. It bored Leo that she still cared enough to hate him. She'd known what she was getting into when she knocked on his door that first night, and it wasn't wedding bells and happily-ever-afters.

Tori, Rinn, and Lauren were the three bridesmaids in Maggie and Emory's party—and they were definitely in the "disgust" camp when it came to Leo. They made it obvious with their sniffs and slitted glances. He'd endured years of this, and in some corner of his mind, he thought he should be insulted, or at least amused. It only bored him. But could he blame them? He'd earned their disgust with his own actions. He didn't deserve any better.

Still, it was Emory's wedding day, and rumination wouldn't help anyone. He did what he always did when faced with the consequences of his reputation and painted a sly grin on his lips. Spreading his arms like a showman at a circus, he pitched his voice in just the right way to get a reaction. "Hello, ladies."

Three sets of eyes rolled in unison, and the men snorted. Beside him, he felt Amelia's curious gaze, but, coward that he was, he couldn't face her. He should never have touched her.

Marlon, looming taller than everyone, gave him an impenetrable stare. Leo's brother was quiet, and he might see too much. Leo averted his gaze just in case. Behind Marlon, Cormac and Archer attended to their assigned bridesmaids after giving him a slight chin nod in greeting. They wore the same navy suit as Leo. The women were dressed in the same shade of pastel purple, those silky asymmetrical gowns that hugged their chests and flared out at the hips, fluttering down just below the knee.

Tori, Rinn, and Lauren all looked distinctly more comfortable in their dresses than Amelia did, but he still thought she wore it best. He had the impression the dress vexed her, which delighted him. That probably made him an ass. Well—more of an ass than usual.

Behind the group, a vision in white appeared. Maggie's beautiful face split into a smile at the sight of him. She extended her arms and wrapped him in a hug, brimming with her usual mothering energy. It was one of the things that made Maggie so special. Not only was she a vision, but she was also incredibly *kind*. In other words, not the type of woman Leo would ever pursue. He'd always known she was too good for him.

"Glad you could make it," she said, as if he'd ever miss the occasion. Her voice utterly lacked the hot, raspy quality that Amelia's had. But that made sense—Maggie had no angles and hardness. She was all gentle curves and soft femininity.

She squeezed him again and turned her lips to his ear as she continued, lower, "If you hurt my sister, I'll lobotomize you with a fireplace poker."

Ah. So she'd noticed that he'd walked in holding Amelia's hand. Leo gave her his most dazzling smile as she pulled away to meet his gaze. "Aye aye, Captain."

Her answering smile was more of a baring of teeth. So, the mother hen had spurs, and after all these years, he was finally discovering how sharp they were. Good for Emory; he needed a woman who could keep him honest.

Mothers and fathers of the bride and groom rounded out the party, and everyone did one final primp before the procession began.

"Here," that maddeningly raspy voice said from behind his shoulder.

Leo turned to see Amelia holding a single white rose, its stem trimmed short. She motioned to his suit jacket, then met his gaze. Her eyes were liquid mercury. He wanted her desperately.

"Thanks," he grated as she pinned the rose to his pocket. Her fingers were long and slim, dexterous as she worked the pin's mechanism. She gave his chest a little pat. *Pat, pat.* Like she was knocking against his heart with the very tips of her fingers.

Then Amelia curled her fingers into her palm and hesitated only the briefest moment before she took his offered arm.

They had a wedding to celebrate.

TWO

AMELIA HATED BEING the center of attention. Behind a computer screen was where she was most comfortable, parsing thousands of lines of data into clean, beautiful conclusions. She liked numbers more than she liked people, and leading a bridal procession wasn't something she'd do for anyone but her sister. As they approached the nave of the church, the rustle of fabric grew loud. Pews groaned as guests shifted to watch, and the weight of two hundred stares felt heavy on Amelia's skin.

Feeling her stiffen, Leo placed his free hand on top of hers. His palm was warm, and it sent little shivers darting through her blood. Her heart thundered, and she didn't know if it was the touch or the nerves or the anticipation of seeing her sister married. She glanced up and saw him flash a wide smile at the assembled guests. What would it be like to walk through the world with that much confidence?

Leo's fingers curled around hers and he turned to meet her gaze. "You ready?"

She nodded and let her lips curl into a wobbly smile of her own. Leo squeezed her fingers gently and kept his hand on hers as they began to move. Then they walked down the aisle and took their places. Emory took her hands and kissed her cheek, then he shook Leo's hand and clapped him on the back. He did the same to each of the four bridesmaids and groomsmen, his face full of quiet joy.

Amelia watched him, so she saw the moment he spotted Maggie. Emory's face lit up in a way she'd never seen before, his blue eyes shining bright, his spine straightening. Love poured off him in waves, and Amelia knew this man was meant to be with her sister.

She followed his gaze to the end of the aisle, where Maggie held onto their father's arm, aglow. Music swelled as Maggie made her way toward her husband-to-be, and Amelia's emotions grew with every step her sister took.

It was impossible not to smile at the sight of her sister floating down the aisle. Her dress was an elegant trumpet shape, with lace and tiny pearls overlaying every inch. Her blond hair shone, the glossy waves held back with jeweled pins. Maggie's lips curled into a smile that betrayed nothing but utter happiness. Her eyes were already wet with unshed tears. She was so beautiful, and she deserved every bit of joy coming her way.

But when Emory took her hands, Amelia felt a tiny, shameful twinge of jealousy. It had no venom; she definitely didn't want *Emory*. But after so many years on her own—so many years telling herself she didn't care about men or relationships—Amelia finally admitted to herself that she'd like to have a man look at her the way Emory did her sister.

The bride and groom took a step closer to the altar, and she met the green gaze of Leo St. James. He tilted his head slightly, like he could read every thought passing through her mind. His lips curled into a half-smile, and he arched a brow in question. She saw it, then, how he used his smile like a weapon. She didn't like it aimed at her.

Amelia couldn't help the scowl that tugged her brows. Oddly, that only made Leo's smile widen, his eyes twinkling at her from the other side of the altar. What did a man as attractive as him have to do with her? Shouldn't he be looking at one of the other bridesmaids? They were as glamorous and beautiful as Maggie.

Flustered, she shifted her gaze back to her sister. The ceremony began, and an hour later, after many tears and heartfelt words, her sister was a married woman.

STIRLING, New Hampshire was a town of ten thousand people and almost as many wedding venues. Amelia followed the bride and groom outside the gothic church, trailed by their many wedding guests. Outside, the sun shone. Flowers were in full bloom, lining baskets and beds all along Main Street. It was a perfect Saturday in early May, with a soft, warm breeze fluttering every petal, leaf, and hem in sight.

Amelia wobbled down the church's steps, gripping the handrail on her way down. Her emotions had run the gamut over the past few hours, and she was utterly exhausted. She made her way to the clump of bridesmaids at the bottom of the steps and leaned against the handrail. The groomsmen followed.

There were photos to take. The rest of the guests made their way to the reception venue, which was a short, five-minute walk away in a nearby hotel.

Amelia let herself be led to the side of the church, where a beautiful garden made for the perfect backdrop for photos. A stream wended through the trees at the back of the church and through the garden, burbling along, oblivious to the wedding party gathered on its banks.

"Okay, bridal party! Maid of honor and best man in the center," the photographer called out, waving Amelia forward. "Everyone else, fan out."

Click, click, click. Her smile held on by its fingernails until Leo, who stood beside her, let his hand brush her lower back. Then her smile collapsed completely as she glared at him.

"Say cheese, maid of honor!" The photographer looked up from his camera, then took another dozen photos with various combinations of people. This went on for an eternity.

When the groomsmen were the focus, Amelia found herself engulfed in a cloud of pale lilac and strong perfume. The other bridesmaids tittered around her while Maggie and Emory stood aside, arms around each other. At the sight of them, surrounded by blooming flowers and singing birds, their eyes only on each other, the same twinge of loneliness pierced Amelia's heart. But now was not the time to feel sorry for herself. Banishing her dark thoughts, she turned back to the gathered bridesmaids.

"So," Tori said to Amelia, a funny gleam in her eyes. "You've finally met Leo."

"Pestilence, you mean," Lauren cut in.

The three of them covered their mouths and sniggered.

Amelia frowned. "What are you talking about?"

"You haven't heard?" Rinn asked. She was the shortest of the bunch, her dark hair and skin set off beautifully by the lilac dress, damn her. When Amelia shook her head, she continued, "Leo St. James has a reputation."

"Ever since college," Tori added.

"His nickname was Pestilence," Lauren explained, "because he gave our *entire* graduating class chlamydia."

"Slept with *everyone*," Rinn said, spreading her hands wide for emphasis. "There was one party where he slept with *five* women in the same night. They all got the clap."

"Even Tori got stung," Lauren added, eyes teasing. "Although their relationship lasted longer than most of his others."

"Worst two weeks of my life. His skills were way overrated," Tori grumbled, and an unpleasant sensation traveled through Amelia's middle. It was similar to the feeling she got when she looked at Maggie and Emory's happiness—but sharper.

"You slept with Leo?" she asked, voice low. Then she frowned. "And it was *bad*?"

Laughter erupted from Rinn and Lauren. Lauren leaned in. "She's revised her version of events. At the time, she thought he was amazing."

"I was delusional," Tori grumbled. "He gave me chlamydia!"

"Either him or Gerard Hill." Rinn arched a brow and tweaked her dress to adjust the fall of the skirt. She grinned at Amelia.

"It wasn't Gerard," Tori hissed. "It was Leo."

"Mm-hmm," Lauren said.

The photographer called out, and Amelia stood beside her parents to take a photo with them and Maggie. Her head spun, eyes drifting to where Leo stood under the branches of a maple tree.

"How's my girl?" her father asked softly, putting his arm around Amelia. "The church looked amazing."

She tore her gaze away from the best man and smiled at her father. "Thanks, Dad."

"Now," he said, reaching around to put his other arm around Amelia's mother. "We've talked about it, and you're going to relax for the rest of the day." He glanced behind his wife to smile at his eldest daughter. "Isn't she, Maggie?"

Maggie smiled beatifically at Amelia. "I want you to have fun today. You've helped me so much during the planning, and you deserve to enjoy the day just as much as I do."

"I will."

"Good." Maggie smiled again, then let her gaze drift to her husband. Then the photographer called out more directions, and Amelia pasted another smile on her face.

She felt Leo's gaze, then, like her body was attuned to him. *Pestilence*, they called him. Did he really give his whole college chlamydia? It didn't surprise her that he was a player. After all, he'd flirted with Amelia, of all people, within seconds of meeting her.

"Okay," the photographer called out. "We got it! Now wifey and hubby, you're with me. We're going to go to the top of Stirling Hill for some shots." He put his camera in its case and waved them forward.

Maggie squeezed Amelia in a tight hug. "See you at the reception in an hour. Let me know if you need anything."

"Will do," Amelia lied. She wouldn't bother her sister while she was taking wedding photos—no way. Her father and mother led the way to the hotel, hands clasped. They'd just celebrated thirty-five years of marriage, and the way her dad looked at her mom, Amelia knew they were on track for thirty-five more.

"You can relax now," a deep voice said beside her. "The hard part's over."

She glanced up at Leo. The sun warmed his complexion, casting shadows under his cheekbones and lighting up the green in his eyes. She didn't know what to think of him, and it didn't help that her brain seemed to malfunction anytime she looked directly at him. No wonder she hadn't had a boyfriend in six years; even being this close to an attractive man made her body feel like it belonged to a stranger.

Tori, who was walking ahead of them, glanced over her shoulder and scowled.

"Who says I'm not relaxed?" Amelia answered Leo, lifting her chin up.

His laughter was warm and a little bit teasing, and it wrapped around her like a silk ribbon. His hand brushed her lower back as they stepped onto the sidewalk, sending a trail of fire through her veins.

This man was dangerous, with or without the risk of a sexually transmitted infection. Best to stay away from him altogether.

He didn't seem to get the memo. He walked beside her all the way to the Stirling Hotel where the reception was held, only leaving her side when they entered the big revolving doors to join the other groomsmen across the lobby. Most guests were in the lobby bar, talking and laughing as delicate music floated through the air. Amelia had spent the morning directing workers in the lobby bar and the hotel ballroom, setting up decorations and attending to last-minute tasks while Maggie got ready to be married.

Now, her work was on full display. She took a deep breath at the sight of the easel holding a board with Maggie and Emory's names at the mouth of the lobby bar, the entrance framed with an arch of flowers. Beyond it, she saw the small arrangements of flowers on the high-top tables, plates of appetizers being passed around by bow tie-wearing waiters, and the busy bartenders pouring drinks.

"Oh, Amelia," her mother said, bustling up to wrap her youngest daughter in a tight hug. "It looks incredible."

Warmth spread through Amelia's chest, chasing away the fire Leo had laid there. "Thanks, Mom."

"Come and have a drink. You heard Maggie and Dad; you need to relax now."

"I will," she promised. "I just have to check on the ballroom first."

Her mother huffed but relented.

Amelia crossed the lobby to the reception desk and smiled at the older gentleman behind the desk. "Hi, Renny."

The hotel manager gave her a wide smile. "Everything's set up," Reynold told her as he handed her the tablet she'd stashed behind the desk. "Kitchen's on schedule, and the bar is ready, as you can see." He gestured behind her. "It looks great, Amelia. I wonder if I could hire you full-time for wedding set-ups. We'd blow the Old Road Hotel out of the water."

She grinned at the mention of Renny's bitter rival in the wedding venue business. "No way," she told him. "This was a special occasion for my sister. I'm never planning a wedding again."

"Not even your own?" the older man smiled at her. "One of those groomsmen seems to be glancing over here pretty often." He wiggled bushy eyebrows.

It took all of Amelia's self-control not to glance over her shoulder. It was silly to hope that it was Leo looking over at her. Completely ridiculous. And, really, marriage? If Maggie's friends were to be believed, two weeks was as long a relationship as Leo had ever had. It was certainly more than Amelia had managed in the past half-decade.

All this wedding planning had gone to her head.

"Yeah, yeah," Amelia said, unlocking her tablet to pull up the master checklist she'd created months ago. "Did you get the seat covers we rushed over this morning?"

"We did. They're all in place. I can take you to the dining room if you'd like to take a look."

Amelia smiled at Reynold. "That would be great."

She followed the older man across the lobby as guests laughed boisterously in the lobby bar. The sound of merriment faded as they made their way down the hallway to the main ballroom. Round tables draped with white tablecloths filled the space, with a big dance floor at the front of the room. The DJ's table stood in the corner, and the man behind it lifted an arm to wave at Amelia.

She waved back with her free hand. He bent his head to plug another cable into a speaker, then moved to his laptop with a deep furrow between his brows.

Amelia turned to her tablet and scrolled through her check-list. The centerpieces were in place, bursting with flowers in all shades of purple. The seat covers were tied with elegant bows, the swags of fabric were draped around the walls of the room, DJ, dance floor, lights, name cards, seat map...

Good, good, good. Everything was in place.

Amelia let out a huff, her shoulders dropping. For the first time in three weeks, she felt like she could take a breath. A wide smile tugged at her lips as she met Reynold's eyes. "It looks amazing, Renny."

The kindly old man smoothed a hand over his thick gray hair, then did the same to his mustache. He nodded solemnly at her. "Couldn't have done it without you," he said as he gave her a nod. "And as soon as the cake gets here, we'll be all set."

Amelia froze. Blinked. Inhaled. "The...cake? What do you mean? Where's the cake?"

Reynold frowned, his mustache quivering. "I...well... I was going to ask you the same thing."

Her heart stopped as she scrolled down the list, reading every item twice. Her eyes were deceiving her. There was no way. After everything, after all the hours, after every painstaking detail...

Amelia had forgotten to pick up the wedding cake!

THREE

IT WAS ONLY because Leo had been keeping one eye on the bar's entrance that he saw Amelia sprinting across the lobby toward the front doors. Her purple dress and white-blond hair trailed behind her as she ran, heels clomping on the tile floors so loudly he could hear them over the music and chatter filling the space.

He didn't even tell the other groomsmen where he was going. He just tore off after her without a word, catching sight of her as she disappeared through the hotel's revolving doors.

It didn't make sense to follow her like this. He didn't even know where she was going. But it was an urge he couldn't resist; he sprinted around the side of the hotel into the parking lot, catching up to her as she skidded to a stop beside a white four-door sedan.

Amelia's head snapped up, silver eyes flashing. "What are you doing?"

He circled to the passenger seat. "I was going to ask you the same thing."

They stared at each other across the hood of the car, and Leo could almost sense the annoyance growing in her. It was better than the panic that had filled her gaze a moment ago. Her light brows slashed downward. "Go back inside."

"No can do."

Her scowl intensified.

Leo didn't know why it pleased him so much, but it did. It wasn't that he wanted Amelia to be annoyed, it was just that her gaze was currently pointed solely at him, and that was a lovely feeling. She planted her hands on her hips, but the effect lost a lot of potency because all he could see of her was her head and the tops of her shoulders.

He tried the door latch. "It's locked."

"Of course it's locked," she grumped. "Why would I leave my car unlocked?"

"Where are we going?" Leo smiled when her eyes shot fire across the hood of the car.

"*We* are not going anywhere. *I* am going to pick up my sister's wedding cake."

"I'll help."

She inhaled and opened her mouth as if to protest, then snapped it shut again. Her gaze narrowed, and Leo met it squarely. Finally, Amelia relented. "Fine." She dug through her purse and found her keys, pressing the button on the fob to unlock the doors.

When they slid inside, Leo caught a hint of her scent, a mixture of notes that weren't exactly feminine except for the fact that she wore them. He clipped his seatbelt and tried to rein himself in.

What was he doing? Why was he here?

He wasn't the kind of man who ran after a woman he didn't know. Or even a woman he *did* know, for that matter. But he'd seen Amelia sprinting, and he had to follow.

She'd looked at him when they were in the garden taking pictures. It was a contemplative look, sent his way when she'd been surrounded by the other bridesmaids. They were filling her head with stories of him, no doubt. Leo felt the urge to defend himself, to explain that his reputation wasn't true.

But—it *was* true. Wasn't it? He hadn't had a real relationship since his freshman year in college. He liked keeping things casual, and he wasn't shy about inviting a woman to warm his bed. Even now, his phone vibrated in his pocket. It was probably a text from someone who had heard he was back in town. Either that, or it was Marlon asking him what the hell had gotten into him.

Leo settled into his seat and let out a long breath. He shouldn't have chased after her. A woman like Amelia deserved better than he could give her. She was right to be suspicious of him.

But he was here now, and he might as well help her with the cake.

Without a word, she started the car, and it quickly became apparent that Amelia Darcy drove like an absolute raving maniac. They tore out of the parking lot in a squeal of tires and burned rubber. He grabbed the handle above his window and let out a low grunt as she turned onto Main Street and put her foot on the accelerator to get through a yellow light. They drove for five minutes, making their way across the small downtown area, hitting a Stirling-sized snarl of traffic near the clock tower, which finally cleared once they crossed the bridge into the quieter part of town.

Amelia turned onto Hemlock Drive and jumped the curb as she slid into a parking spot outside a bakery called The Sweetest Thing.

Leo let out a huff, glad to be alive. "Remind me never to get in a car with you ever again," he said as she opened her door.

She lifted a brow at him and sniffed, regal and haughty. "You invited yourself, buddy."

He laughed, delighted. Following her into the bakery, Leo was assaulted by scents of cinnamon, sugar, and fresh-baked bread. He'd trade it all for the scent of Amelia's skin any day.

Then Amelia let out a little squeak and bumped into him as she tried to leave the bakery again.

He caught her shoulders and spun her around. "What's wrong?"

Her face was red. She shook her head. "Nothing."

Leo leaned over, using a curled finger to tilt her chin up. "Tell me."

Her snort was short and sharp. She glanced over her shoulder and spun around again, red staining her cheeks. "Ben is working," she whispered.

Leo frowned, fighting the urge to curl an arm around her shoulders. "Who's Ben?" he whispered. "The barista? You want me to punch him?"

Amelia looked at him like he was insane. "What? No!"

"I will, you know," Leo promised.

"Don't punch him. Don't punch anyone! Why are we even talking about this?"

"What did he do to you?"

"Nothing!" She huffed, shaking her head. "He doesn't even know my name."

"Amelia?" the barista called from behind his hissing espresso machine. "Amelia Darcy? Is that you?"

"Is Amelia here?" a woman's voice called out from the back of the bakery. She appeared a moment later, her red hair gathered beneath a hair net. She smiled at the back of Amelia's head. "Oh, good! I was just about to call you."

Slowly, Amelia turned, and Leo dropped his hands from her shoulders. She lifted her chin and smiled at the woman. "Hey, Camilla." She turned to the barista. "Hi, Ben."

The barista gave her a nod, then glanced at Leo for a beat. He turned back to Amelia. "Hey. Coffee?"

"Um, we don't really h-have t-time..."

Stammering? Amelia? The woman made of fire and brimstone? Leo frowned at her, then at Ben the barista. Now he *really* wanted to punch him.

An uncomfortable feeling passed through Leo's gut, and when Ben stared at Amelia for a few seconds too long, the feeling intensified. Then Amelia smiled at the barista, and Leo wanted to flip the nearest table.

Which was...odd.

Leo didn't have strong feelings about women. He didn't *care* about women, unless they happened to be beneath him. He knew exactly what he could provide to a woman: a few fun hours and an entertaining story to tell her friends when it was all over. A woman like Amelia deserved a lot more than that.

But he still didn't want her blushing and smiling at another man.

"You're here for the cake," Camilla guessed. She was a tall woman with a wide smile and kind blue eyes. "It's boxed up and ready. I'll grab it for you."

"Thanks," Amelia said, drifting closer to the counter.

Camilla hesitated, eyeing Amelia, then Leo. Her shrewd gaze shifted back to Amelia again. "When's the last time you ate? Did you have breakfast?"

"Cam," Amelia huffed. "I'm fine."

"You forgot breakfast, didn't you?" Her gaze met Leo's once more. "Has she eaten?"

"How would he know?" Amelia asked, jabbing a thumb over her shoulder at him.

Camilla's eyes narrowed. "Amelia, I love you, but you will not deflect this question. Have you eaten anything today?"

Amelia's jaw hardened for a moment, then her shoulders slumped. "No," she admitted.

Camilla harrumphed, sounding like an eighty-year-old man. She disappeared for a moment, reappearing with a steaming-hot cinnamon bun dripping with gooey icing. Sliding the plate across the counter, she slapped a couple of napkins beside it and crossed her arms. "Eat."

"I need to get back to the wedding," Amelia said, but her eyes were on the cinnamon bun.

"*Eat.* I'm not giving you the cake until you eat something."

Amelia's scowl was back, and she lifted her gaze from the

bun to glare at Camilla. Leo grabbed the plate and drew her gaze back to the steaming confection. He walked over to a table, set the plate down, and pulled a chair. Amelia glanced at him, then at Camilla, and threw up her hands in defeat. "Fine! I'll eat!"

"Make her a coffee before you leave for the day," Camilla said to Ben. "You." She pointed to Leo. "Make sure she eats the whole thing."

"It's as big as my head!"

"Half of it at least."

Amelia grumbled, but she slid into the chair and ripped off a piece of cinnamon bun. When the soft, steaming dough hit her tongue, she let out a noise that made Leo's groin tighten. Her eyelashes fluttered closed, and she slumped in her seat, chewing with such bliss on her face that Leo suspected she'd temporarily left their current plane of existence.

Leo moved slowly, sitting down across from her, watching the way her cheeks flushed pink as she swallowed. He tried to ignore the blood rushing south, tried to tear his gaze away from the look of ecstasy on Amelia's face. Eyes still closed, Amelia licked the tips of her fingers one by one, then finally opened her eyes and reached for the cinnamon bun again.

Heart pounding, Leo watched her bring the dough to her mouth again, that same orgasmic expression spreading over her features as she swallowed another bite. He wanted to put that look on her face himself. Craved it. He wanted to eat *her* like she was a confection placed on the table before him. He wanted to peel that dress she hated so much off her body and taste every hidden corner of her skin.

"It's so good," Amelia said in a dreamy voice he'd never heard before. Then she blinked and seemed to come back to herself, meeting Leo's gaze. She cleared her throat and straightened, pushing the plate toward him. "You should taste it. No one bakes as well as Camilla."

Leo didn't want to take even a crumb of that cinnamon bun away from Amelia, because that meant one less bite that she could eat with that pleasure-drunk expression on her face.

A cup clattered as it landed on the table in front of her. Amelia jumped, her face growing red. "Thanks, Ben."

"Want anything else?"

She shook her head, then watched him walk back toward his espresso machine. Leo frowned, then tore a piece of cinnamon bun off for himself. When that drew Amelia's gaze back to him, he felt a dirty, shameful bit of satisfaction. *That's right,* he thought. *Keep your eyes on me. Not him.*

She watched him take a bite, arching her brows expectantly.

Cinnamon, sugar, butter, and soft dough filled his mouth with the taste of heaven. He let out a surprised grunt, which made Amelia grin. She looked like a mischievous sprite with that expression on her face, a fairy that had convinced him to partake in a forbidden feast. He was already doomed.

"Told you it was amazing," she said, then tore off a piece of dough for herself.

"I'm heading out!" Ben waved at Camilla behind the desk, then shifted his gaze to Amelia. "See ya, 'Melia."

Amelia waved, chewing, her cheeks turning pink again. Leo scowled. Why was some scrawny coffee slinger making her blush so much?

The bell above the door jingled, and Leo leaned back in his chair. "You like him, or something?"

"What?" Amelia kept her eyes on the cinnamon bun.

"That guy. Ben."

Amelia finally glanced up at him and rolled her eyes. "What do you care?"

That meant yes, which made jealousy blast through him in a wave of heat. Curling his fists against the onslaught, Leo took a controlled breath. Then he loosened his limbs and shrugged. She was right; what did he care? It wasn't like he could chase after Maggie Darcy's little sister. Emory would kill him, if Maggie didn't do it first.

Leo knew the kind of man he was, and he knew he'd never outrun the reputation he'd earned. Amelia Darcy was far, far too good for him.

"Why haven't you asked him out?"

Amelia snorted. "Please."

"What?"

She clicked her tongue. "Right. Because *that* would go over well."

Confusion momentarily overshadowed Leo's jealousy. "What's that supposed to mean? Why wouldn't it go over well?"

"Um, hello? Look at me?"

He did. He still didn't get why that would stop a guy like Ben from being interested, because from where Leo was sitting, Amelia looked like a goddess. He especially liked the grumpy little frown that tugged at her brows. "You look fine to me," he grated.

"How flattering," she deadpanned. "I, like every woman, aspire to be called 'fine.'"

Then, eyes dropping back to the cinnamon bun, her expression cleared. Amelia gave him a look of pure mischief and grabbed a knife and fork from the container at the edge of the table. "I'm going to commit a cardinal sin," she admitted, eyes dancing, "and I don't want to hear you give me any shit for it."

Leo watched as she carefully cut through most of the swirls of the cinnamon bun, peeling it open with her utensils like she was a surgeon performing a triple bypass. The gooey center of the bun offered itself up to her, and she used the fork to pluck the middle swirl out of its nest.

"This is the best part," she explained, then popped the whole thing in her mouth. Icing dropped onto the corner of her lips, but Amelia was too deep in her own personal cinnamon-flavored heaven to notice. Leo listened to the little moans that emanated from her throat and sat, rapt, unable to tear his gaze away from her.

She was a woman incapable of hiding her feelings. Annoyance, anger, ecstasy—it was all written right there on her face. She couldn't hide her thoughts if she tried. For a man like Leo, who hid behind a mask every hour of the day, the sight was almost irresistible. A tug pulled at his gut, drawing him ever closer. He wanted her to open her eyes. He wanted to see something other than animosity written on her face when she looked at him. He wanted to make her laugh.

That little smear of white icing on the corner of her lips called to him. Before he could stop himself, his hand moved up, fingers sliding over the soft silkiness of her cheek. Startled eyes fluttered open at the touch, but Leo was in too deep to care. His thumb brushed the frosting off her lip, giving Leo the barest hint of how pillowy-soft Amelia's lips would be to kiss.

When he brought his thumb to his own mouth, she stared at him, wide-eyed, and it wasn't anger or annoyance heating her gaze; it was lust as violent and raging as his own.

And that's when he heard the jingling of the bakery door's bells, a mere second before a booming male voice reached his ears.

"St. James!" his boss, Fred Goodhew, bellowed behind him. "You can't hide her from us any longer." A gregarious laugh. A slap on Leo's back, followed by a tight grip on his shoulders. Fred shook Leo as he squeezed his shoulder, cackling delightedly.

Leo dropped his thumb from his mouth, the sweet taste of cinnamon and icing turning sickly on his tongue. He glanced up at the middle-aged man standing beside his table. Fred Goodhew was built like a retired linebacker: solid, but softened with age. His salt-and-pepper hair was receding slightly at the temples, and his clean-shaven complexion looked slightly battered by years of sun and wind and hard living. He was dressed immaculately, as was befitting of a billionaire in charge of a luxury party planning empire.

The man was all smiles, but he suffered no fools. And Leo was a very, very big fool.

Fred was staring at Amelia, who looked like a deer about to go *splat* against the hood of an oncoming car. Beside Fred, a younger woman clung onto his thick arm and smiled down at Leo and Amelia. Her chestnut-brown hair was pulled back from her face in a high bun, and she wore her designer dress like it had been made for her, which, knowing whose arm she clung to, it probably had. Her left arm was in a bright-pink cast that matched her purse exactly, held in a sling of the same color.

Another clap on the back from his boss sent Leo rocking forward.

"Well?" Fred prodded. "Aren't you going to introduce us to your fiancée?"

FOUR

HIS *WHAT?*

The cinnamon bun in Amelia's mouth turned to glue. It stuck to the roof of her mouth and coated her tongue, an immovable substance that in no way resembled Camilla's creation. Concrete cured to something softer than the dough currently filling Amelia's gob. She stared at the couple looming above their table, then turned her startled gaze to Leo, waiting for him to correct the man's obviously bonkers assumption.

His fiancée. Right.

Amelia began chewing again, but still Leo said nothing. He met her eyes, like he was trying to communicate something important to her. What, she had no idea. Her cheek still tingled where he'd touched her, which was another thing she'd have to address once the obstruction in her mouth was cleared.

Gnashing her teeth, she gave Leo a death glare. Her best,

most aggressive death glare. Leo would do well to scurry and hide, her gaze was so potent.

But he didn't scurry. He didn't hide.

Instead, Leo painted a wide, attractive smile on his face, and reached over to put his palm over hers. He squeezed her fingers when she would've pulled back, then brought her fingers to his lips. Then he *kissed her hand*. What—how—who?

What the hell was wrong with him?

"Caught us," Leo said, that stupid, fake smile still stretched over his lips. "Fred, this is Amelia. Amelia, Fred."

Still looking like she was a squirrel storing nuts for winter, Amelia chewed like her life depended on it and finally swallowed, but—

"Amelia!" Fred put his meaty paws on her shoulders and gave her a loud kiss on each cheek. "You have no idea how good it is to meet you." He smiled genially and tilted his head toward Leo. "This one has kept you hidden away for so long, I was worried you didn't exist!" He frowned. "But I thought your name was Cat—Kitty—um—"

"Stage name," Leo smoothly provided.

Stage name? What world was Amelia living in? What the hell was going on?

Fred nodded, apparently accepting that idiotic explanation.

She opened her mouth to answer, but all that came out was an outraged squeak. Her squirrel transformation had gone so far, now she sounded like one too.

"We like to keep my personal life and professional life separate," Leo interrupted before Amelia could find her tongue. "So it works for us."

She glared at him. "Wait. No. I'm not—"

"I hope you're here for the retreat," Fred interrupted, his dark-brown eyes intent on hers. His gaze skimmed her outfit, then Leo's, and he snapped his fingers. "The wedding. Of course. But you'll stay in town for our company retreat, correct?"

Amelia would throw herself off the Stirling clock tower before she went to a company retreat posing as Leo St. James's fake fiancée.

"Where are my manners?" Fred curled an arm around the woman beside him, his expression softening. "I have a fiancée of my own now. Leo, Amelia, this is the love of my life, Nadia. Although getting her to accept my proposal was a mission."

Nadia laughed. "Through no fault of my own!" She shifted her purse, and a tiny dog's golden head poked out. Cooing softly, Nadia scratched behind the pup's ears. "It was this little monster's doing, wasn't it?"

"Butter made his feelings about me very clear," Fred added wryly. "At least the cast comes off in a couple weeks."

Amelia watched them, mind whirling with ways to extricate herself from this situation. But she couldn't do that without getting Maggie's cake.

Leo was no help. He just smiled at the couple and asked, "The cast?"

"Oh, when Fred proposed, Butter was with us, of course," Nadia explained. "Fred got down on one knee, and the sun was setting, and everything was so perfect."

"Until the squirrel," Fred answered darkly.

Nadia clicked her tongue. "You have to admit, Fred, it was

good to see Butter moving so well! Ever since his surgery, he hasn't been as active."

"The leash broke two of your fingers, baby."

"Well, yes, but Butter was so speedy. Weren't you, honey? Your leg isn't bothering you at all anymore, is it?"

"Then you fell and broke your arm," Fred continued. "I had to finish the proposal in the ER."

Nadia laughed. "I said yes, didn't I?"

Fred swept his hand down Nadia's back and kissed her temple. "Made me the happiest man in the world. Show them the ring, baby."

Nadia thrust her right hand at them, making mooneyes at Fred. The ring slid down her finger to nudge slightly against her knuckle, and Nadia repositioned it with reverent fingers. "It's a vivid pink diamond that Fred chose to match my favorite Birkin." She lifted her Hermès purse for emphasis, then smiled at Amelia. "I decided to wear it on my right hand until the cast comes off. I just couldn't bear to not wear it until then. Don't you think Fred chose perfectly?"

Amelia shifted her gaze from the honkingly large pink stone on Nadia's finger to the bag slung carelessly over her arm. Both were bright pink. That bag, she knew, was worth more than her car. Probably more than ten of her cars, and Nadia was using it to carry her dog.

"He chose perfectly," she repeated robotically, while her brain scrambled for a way out of this.

The truth. The truth was all that was needed to extricate herself from this situation. Leo would be humiliated, of course, but what did she care about that? Leo was the one who dumped her in this mess in the first place. He deserved to be humiliated! Who did he think he was?

She took a deep breath. "Listen. I'm not sure why—"

"But where's your ring?" Nadia cried, grabbing Amelia's left hand. She tugged, thrusting the hand toward Leo. "Explain, mister."

"Yes," Amelia bit off. "Explain, mister."

"It's being cleaned," Leo lied smoothly, taking Amelia's hand from Nadia's grasp and pressing his lips to her knuckles once more.

Despite everything that had happened since his blasted thumb had stroked her mouth—every lie he'd told in the last few minutes—the touch of Leo's lips on her skin still made her go utterly still. Heat swamped her middle as he brushed his lips over and back across her knuckles as his eyes held hers, as if he knew precisely the effect his touch had on her brain.

Anger detonated somewhere deep below the surface of Amelia's consciousness, but her body still remained frozen as he pressed a kiss to the back of her hand, then tucked her fingers against his palm and gave her a soft smile.

This man—this man was *out of control!* What the hell was his problem? Amelia glared at him, but the only reaction he gave her was a twinkling in his brilliant green eyes.

"Well, we have a wonderful four days planned," Fred said, "and the whole team will be glad to finally meet St. James's mysterious fiancée. You'll be there, of course."

"Of course," Leo cut in smoothly, just as Amelia said, "No."

Fred patted Leo's shoulder, then curled an arm around his own fiancée's waist. "We'll leave you two lovebirds to it," he said, then headed for the counter. Amelia spun around and met Camilla's wide-eyed stare, but the baker had to paint a professional smile on her lips to take Fred and Nadia's order. How much of that had Camilla witnessed? All of it, probably, which meant an inquisition was incoming as soon as Amelia was done with her sister's wedding.

"What the hell was *that*?" Amelia hissed.

"Oh, there's the cake," Leo said smoothly, and he stood up to grab the tall cardboard box holding Maggie and Emory's wedding cake.

"Drive carefully!" Camilla called out, then gave Amelia a look that said, *We will speak of this soon.*

And they would. Amelia would tell her everything, right after she skewered Leo through the guts with one of the dowels supporting the cake's upper tiers.

"We'll see you on Wednesday!" Nadia called out, waving her fingers. "The retreat is going to be *so* much fun." She gazed at her ring, tilting it under the bakery's bright lights, then wiggled her finger at Amelia again. "We can compare rings!"

The dog yipped for emphasis, then disappeared back into the bag.

"Ha," Amelia managed past the mounting fury tightening her throat.

Oblivious to the gory death in his near future, Leo held the big cardboard box with tender hands and asked, "Grab the door, will you, hun?"

Hun. Amelia reminded herself that she shouldn't upend Maggie's wedding cake on Leo St. James's head, even if he deserved it. She opened the door and held it for him, then headed for the back seat of her car. She secured the box with a seatbelt, then gently closed the door and whirled on Leo.

"Not here," he said, tilting his head toward the bakery windows. "They'll see."

"Oh, we wouldn't want them to see, would we?" Amelia snarked. "But wait. I don't care!" She thrust her arm toward the bakery. "What the hell was *that?*"

"We should really be getting back to the wedding. Maggie and Emory are probably at the reception by now."

"Oh, no. No, no, no. You're explaining yourself to me right now."

But Leo was circling the car and opening the driver's side, which mean—

"How did you get my keys?"

He flashed her a smile and got behind the wheel. Amelia gaped, and the boiling magma of her temper finally erupted. She ripped the passenger door open, and its hinges squealed in protest. She fell into her seat and glared at him, her breath whistling as she inhaled through her teeth. There were so many words fighting to come out that none of them did. She looked at his stupid purple bow tie and wished she'd strangled him when she had the chance.

"You—"

Leo met her gaze, then let his eyes roam over all of her face. "You're beautiful when you're furious," he said softly, then cleared his throat like he hadn't meant to say that out loud.

And—well—

Ugh!

"I am *not.*"

A brow arched, and Leo's gaze met hers once more. "That's what you want to argue about? That you're not beautiful when you're angry?"

"I want to argue about a lot of things," she gritted out through clenched teeth. "Like, for example, what the hell just happened in there."

"We should really get back. The cake—"

"Oh, spare me." Amelia turned in her seat and clamped her hands on her knees, then brought them up to slap against her face. She felt like a giant had grabbed her by the ankles and shook her like a piggy bank, hoping her brain would fall out of her ears in fat gold coins. She couldn't make sense of her thoughts.

But they really did need to get the cake to the hotel. Leo waited until her seatbelt was clipped to gently ease himself into the street.

"Keep an eye on the cake," he commanded, like this was his car and his cake. The arrogant turd of a man. Argh!

Amelia ground her teeth and glanced at the back seat, because despite everything, she didn't want to ruin Maggie's wedding cake. It was secure and survived the first turn that took them onto the bridge that linked this side of Stirling to the town's central district.

Reaching back to put a hand on top of the cardboard box, Amelia took a few deep breaths. She didn't want to upset Leo while they were carrying such precious cargo, so she forced herself to stay silent until they pulled into the hotel parking lot and Leo turned off the engine.

Then, Amelia removed her hand from the cardboard box in

the back seat and knotted her fingers together on her lap. She took a long, deep breath.

"I can explain," Leo said quietly.

She blinked and took another breath, lest her anger take over and she use his seatbelt as a garrote, which was exactly what he deserved. "Please," she finally answered pleasantly. "That would be wonderful. In your own time." She made a careless flick of her hand, for emphasis, hoping he could smell the sarcasm and bitterness pouring off her skin.

Leo's shoulders fell as he combed a hand through his perfect haircut, but Amelia didn't feel a twinge of pity. Oh, no. She wasn't letting him off the hook that easily. This man had just pretended to be betrothed to her! He'd lied to his boss!

The worst part of it all was Amelia felt oddly humiliated. Was it a joke? A prank? A man like Leo would never stoop so low as to be with Amelia. She had no game. She spent her days behind a computer screen, sorting through data for hours on end. She had it on good authority that she was terrible in bed, and it wasn't like any other man had ever disproved that theory by begging her for sex after the first time or two.

Her ex had been *very* clear. Her skills between the sheets were abysmal, and nothing she had tried had ever been an improvement. She was sitting beside a man who had allegedly given his entire college chlamydia because he had *so* many women dying to sleep with him, and she knew for a fact that her own skills ranked somewhere far below terrible.

But she wouldn't cry. No way. She wouldn't give Leo the satisfaction. If this was some sick joke, it would bounce right off her.

"I've been telling everyone at work I'm engaged for the better part of a year," Leo admitted quietly. The car's engine clicked and rattled as it cooled down, filling the silence that followed his words. He let out a huff and turned to meet Amelia's gaze. "It turned into this whole...*thing*. Everyone became obsessed with it, and the more I tried to deflect, the more they tried to figure out who she was. Fred and my coworkers would try to convince me to bring my fiancée to work events, and I'd dodge the invitations. This week is the annual work retreat, and Fred was really putting the pressure on me. Partners are always invited, so he said I had no excuse."

"So your solution was to lie to him? What happens when I don't show up on Wednesday?"

He scrubbed his face then let his hands drop on top of the steering wheel, which reminded Amelia that she was angry that he'd somehow hijacked her car keys and was driving her car. Although, she had to admit, the cake probably had a better chance of survival with him behind the wheel. She wasn't a bad driver, but the ride had definitely been smoother with him at the helm.

But that wasn't the point!

The point was, he was an arrogant, lying bastard, and she wanted nothing to do with him.

"I panicked," Leo said. "He was right there, and I'd just been touching your face, and if you weren't my mysterious fiancée, it would look like I was cheating on her. And everyone already thinks I'm some kind of manwhore—"

"Pestilence," Amelia said, then clamped her lips shut.

The bitter laugh that fell from Leo's lips was an awful

sound. He leaned his head back against the headrest. It hit with a soft thump. "Yeah. I wondered if you'd heard about that."

"So it's true?"

Leo's gaze turned shuttered, and his lips curled into a flirtatious smile. "It's all true, sweetheart. I'm as bad as they come."

Amelia rolled her eyes and reached for the door. She wasn't going to sit there and listen to that. It sounded a hell of a lot like self-pity. Whatever reputation Leo had in college, it was none of her business. They were both in their thirties now, and plus, they should be inside the hotel celebrating Maggie and Emory's wedding. This whole situation was ridiculous, and it had nothing to do with her. So there. The end.

But before she could slip out of the car, Leo's hand dropped onto her thigh. She froze at the warmth of it, the soft squeeze he gave her flesh. "Amelia—" He pulled in a ragged breath then let it out, finally meeting her gaze. His eyes held an edge of hurt, or panic, or something deeper and older that she couldn't read. "Come to the retreat with me."

His voice came out as a whisper, but it might as well have been a shout for how badly it made Amelia jump. She flung his hand off her thigh and slipped out of the car. "Absolutely not," she said into the open door, then slammed it shut.

Another door opened, and Leo's stupidly beautiful head popped up on the other side. "Please."

"Are you kidding me? No!"

"I'll pay you."

"I don't need your money." Her business was finally generating enough income to live on, and she'd endured countless sleepless nights over the past months and years to get it to that point. She didn't need to rely on anyone else for anything, and that's how she liked it. She'd only ever relied on one man, and he'd torn her to pieces. She wasn't going to let that happen again —financially, emotionally, or otherwise.

"I'll... I'll..." Leo cast around him, like he could find the right offer written somewhere in the parking lot. He dropped his shoulders and met her gaze again.

"Grab the cake," Amelia said before he could say anything else. "And give me my car keys."

Leo held her gaze for a long moment, determination hardening the line of his jaw. He actually meant to convince her about this stupid scheme. Well—he'd have a long way to go. Amelia wasn't going to pretend to be anyone's fiancée. No amount of money would ever convince her. No glittering green eyes. No attractive hands. No knuckle kisses.

No way, no how.

They headed inside and left the cake in the hotel's kitchen. Guests were still gathered in the lobby bar, and Amelia checked her messages. Her sister was on the way back, so it was time to move everyone to the ballroom for Maggie and Emory's grand entrance.

Thank goodness. That gave her an excuse to act busy and forget about whatever the hell had just happened. She found the bridesmaids gathered together at one of the high-top tables, and the four of them began gently guiding everyone to move to the ballroom.

Leo watched her for a moment, and she felt his gaze as intensely as she'd felt the touch of his thumb on her lip. A tiny, rebellious part of her wondered what she could get out of him in exchange for her attendance at the work retreat. That part of her whispered that maybe there was something between them. Maybe he felt the sparks as much as she did. Maybe...

She clamped down on the whirling thoughts, banishing them to the void. A man as attractive and irresistible as Leo St. James had his pick of women. He wouldn't pick some sexless harpy who happened to be a little too independent and opinionated to be attractive. She was patently incapable of stroking men's egos, and Leo's ego looked like it required endless attention.

He wouldn't get it from her.

But as Amelia entered the ballroom, she glanced over the shoulder and met his jade-colored gaze. She knew one thing: Leo hadn't given up on the prospect of bringing her to his company retreat. Not even a little bit.

FIVE

SPEECHES, food, dancing, happiness—it was all too much for Leo. He found himself stealing glances down the long table at the front of the room to the maid of honor's chair. She ignored him so thoroughly, it was almost impressive.

Even more impressive was the way she managed the proceedings, consulting her tablet every once in a while and darting around the room to make sure everything was in order.

Maggie and Emory didn't appreciate her nearly enough. Their wedding was perfect, and Leo saw that it was because Amelia didn't stop working for a second. She didn't even eat her meal. A waiter whisked it away, untouched, so the cake cutting could proceed. Once the cake cutting was done, Amelia was at the bar, making sure they had everything they needed, organizing a delivery of limes when she noticed they were getting low. A minute later, he saw her by the DJ's table, deep in conversation, trusty tablet in hand.

"Careful," Marlon's deep voice said from behind Leo's back.

Leo spun around and arched a brow at his brother. "I don't know what you're talking about."

"Amelia Darcy isn't one of your women, Leo."

"'One of my women?'" he repeated, rearing back. "What's that supposed to mean?"

Marlon studied him from beneath thick, dark brows. He let out a long sigh and scrubbed the stubble on his cheek, finally shrugging one large shoulder. Taller than Leo by a couple of inches, Marlon took "dark and brooding" to another dimension. "Emory won't like it if you touch his new sister-in-law."

Leo glanced across the ballroom to where his best friend was deep in conversation with some aunt or another. He scowled. "I'm not touching anyone."

"You're thinking about it."

"How do you know what I'm thinking?"

"Never seen you run out of a room as fast as when you saw Amelia darting across the lobby."

"You know what? I've heard enough of this." Leo made to step around his brother, but Marlon stopped him with a hand on his shoulder.

"Leo, you know I'm right. Amelia deserves better than a quick fuck in a hotel stairwell."

Shame burned Leo's throat, because Marlon knew him better than anyone. How many events had he been to where he'd ended up in a stairwell, or a closet, or a hotel room? It wasn't outside of the realm of possibilities that Leo would be looking at Amelia like she was his next conquest.

Except she *wasn't*. He didn't want to drag her to a dark corner and—

Okay. That was a lie. He definitely *did* want to drag her to a dark corner and have his way with her, but that was different. He wanted...

He didn't know what he wanted! He wanted Amelia to eat another cinnamon bun somewhere he could hear the little noises she made. He wanted to finally make her laugh. He had an unbearable itch under his skin anytime he looked at her, and the only thing that fixed it was when she met his gaze.

There was something wrong with him.

"I'm not going to sleep with her," he growled at Marlon.

Marlon dropped his hand from Leo's shoulder and dipped his chin. "Good."

"I'm not an animal."

"Debatable."

"Fuck off, Marlon."

Marlon laughed, then clapped his brother on the back. "Just making sure you've got your head on straight."

"Yeah, yeah," Leo grumbled, then walked toward the dessert table—*away* from the corner of the room where Amelia stood.

Because Marlon was right. Leo's reputation had been well-earned, and he knew just how much he deserved a woman of Amelia's caliber: not at all.

It didn't matter if he was attracted to and intrigued by her. She deserved better than someone who only had his body to offer. Leo was good in bed, but he wasn't relationship material. He'd learned that many times over.

Long tables were draped with thick white tablecloths and

covered with all manner of sweet things. There were cake pops, bite-sized brownies, mini cupcakes, tiny cream puffs, little jars of creme brûlée, and a few well-presented trays of fruit. Many of the desserts had been picked over, but Leo still grabbed a plate and started wandering down the table, grabbing a few choice pieces of fruit and a center-cut brownie.

"Not an edge man, I see," Amelia said as she sidled up beside him, plucking a corner piece of brownie for herself.

Leo should've walked away, but instead, he found himself turning to face her. He looked at the gooey brownie on his plate, then at her crispy corner piece. "I'm not a heathen."

"I beg to differ," she said. "Only uncultured swine eat the middle pieces. The edges are obviously superior both in flavor and in chew."

"If I wanted chew, I'd have beef jerky."

She pursed her lips, which Leo suspected was to hide a smile, then took a bite of her corner piece brownie. Bliss overtook her features for a moment, and she made one of those beautiful noises that seemed to have a direct connection to Leo's cock.

"I really shouldn't eat this," she said, brushing crumbs off her fingers. "But I'm so hungry."

"Well, you didn't eat your dinner."

Her gaze sharpened as she lifted it to his. "Keeping tabs on me, were you?"

"Just being a dutiful fiancé."

Amelia's shoulders dropped an inch. She glanced over her shoulder, then wrapped a slim hand around Leo's wrist, just below his cuff. Her skin was warm and smooth, and he let himself be led out of the room.

This was exactly what Marlon warned against, but what was Leo supposed to do? *She* was leading *him* away.

Okay, that was a weak excuse. He could break the hold any second and walk away—but he'd die before doing that.

Amelia stopped in an empty hallway and faced him. She dropped his wrist and crossed her arms, narrowing her eyes at him. "We need to talk about what happened at the bakery. I've been thinking about it, and I really don't think you took me seriously enough when we left. I'm not going to pretend to be your fiancée. Ever. In fact, I think it's pretty crappy of you to put me in that position in the first place."

Leo didn't need another reminder of what a piece of shit he was. This was exactly why Marlon had cornered him and warned him off. Had the situation been reversed, he would've done the same.

He ran a hand through his hair and let out a breath, still holding his little plate of desserts between them. "Yeah. I'm sorry."

Amelia blinked at him, her gray eyes widening slightly. She rocked back on her heels and blew out a breath. "Fine. Good. I'm glad we had this talk. Enjoy the rest of the wedding."

He watched her walk away, still feeling the ghost of her touch manacled around his wrist.

THE NEXT DAY, Amelia dragged her sorry self out of bed at seven o'clock and made it to a bootcamp in the park, arriving only three minutes late, which had to be some kind of miracle. Her feet were covered in blisters from her stupid lilac high heels, and her body felt like she'd run a marathon. Her mind— her mind was a mess. Thankfully, Maggie was her only sister, and Amelia would never have to go through the hellishness of helping to plan a big wedding for anyone else. Ever.

The bootcamp trainer, a big, buff man named Chet, made her do ten pushups as a punishment for her tardiness, which was a bit extreme, even though she deserved it. But she did the pushups from her knees, then found Camilla and their friend Lucy near the back of the pack.

"Hey, girl," Camilla said, beaming. "Ready to sweat?"

"How are you so chipper?" Amelia grumbled. "It's unnatural."

"I run a bakery," Camilla answered. "I'm up at two o'clock in the morning to start making bread. This is my midday." She grabbed a big weighted ball and tossed it to a bleary-eyed Lucy, who stumbled back at the impact.

The shrill, piercing sound of a whistle interrupted their conversation. "Okay, ladies!" Chet called out. "Let's form two lines. We're going to start with some bear crawls."

"Bear claws?" Amelia said hopefully, looking for one of Camilla's bakery boxes that might be stashed behind the nearby tree.

"I wish," Lucy grumbled while Camilla laughed.

The three of them dragged their way through the workout, then collapsed on the grass. This was a four-times-a-week routine for them on Sundays, Mondays, Wednesdays, and Fridays. It had been Camilla's idea, obviously. The nutter.

Still, Amelia always felt better by the end of the workout. Except today. Today, she still felt angry and off-balance. When the rest of the group had wandered off to get a coffee at the little coffee truck parked at the east end of the park, Camilla sat up and leaned back on her palms.

"So," she said, arching a brow at Amelia. "Are you going to tell us what the heck was going on yesterday?"

"Were you really out on a date with Leo St. James?" Lucy turned onto her side, her black hair plastered to her forehead. "You know he's a huge player, right?"

"It wasn't a date," Amelia said, sounding a little snippier than intended. "We were picking up Maggie's wedding cake."

"He was ready to vault over the table and ravish her," Camilla cut in. "Only that Fred Goodhew walked in."

"He was *not*." Amelia felt hot all over. She scowled at her friends, who beamed at her. "He's not interested in me at all."

"He said you were his fiancée."

"*What?*" Lucy bolted upright, eyes wide. "Since when?"

"Since never! He lied!" Amelia huffed, then started at the beginning. By the time she told the girls about her interlude in the hallway at the wedding, they both had thoughtful expressions on their faces.

"I wonder how much he's willing to pay," Lucy mused.

"Stop it," Amelia grumbled. "I'm not doing it."

"Wish he'd said I was his fiancée," Camilla cut in. "I could use the cash."

Amelia collapsed on the soft grass and threw an arm over her face. She was sore, and tired, and she had three clients waiting on her to update their sales and KPI dashboards with this week's numbers. Running her own business was rewarding, but she hadn't expected it to be quite so relentless. As her friends chattered to each other above her, Amelia remembered the way Emory had looked at Maggie, and she realized she was lonely.

Even here, feeling the morning rays warm her skin and the dewy grass prickle her back, with her two best friends close enough to touch, Amelia was alone. She should be happy; she had everything she'd ever worked for. Her data analysis business generated more than enough money to live, and she had a nice little nest egg. She'd made it.

But...

The moment in the bakery played on repeat—those few seconds when Leo had dragged his thumb over her lips. She brought her fingertips to the spot, as if her own touch could mimic the fire that had blazed across her skin when his hand had made contact with her lips.

Yes, it was loneliness seeping through her veins like poison. It was the old refrain in her mind, that familiar voice telling her that she was unlovable. She was a terrible kisser. She was a dead fish in bed, except when she tried too hard, which was apparently worse. She never did anything right when it came to men, so after a while, she'd cut them out of her life entirely.

While she built her business, it had been easy to throw herself into the project. There was so much to do, and no time to think about men and sex. She had *goals*. Ambitions. Direction.

Now, she felt oddly aimless. Going home to sit in front of her computer to deliver her work to her clients didn't hold the same appeal. Grinding for grinding's sake was pretty depressing when there wasn't an end goal.

She dropped her arm down to her side and let out a deep breath. "I think I want a boyfriend," she announced.

Lucy and Camilla stopped talking and stared at her. Lucy was the first to move. She reached over and squeezed Amelia's forearm, softness suffusing her features. "Yeah? That's good! You haven't wanted to date in so long. You think you're ready to put yourself out there again?"

Camilla squealed excitedly. "Have you signed up for any apps?"

"Ugh," Amelia replied. *That* was not an enticing prospect.

Lucy made a sympathetic noise. "You don't need to use an app if you don't want to. The right guy will come along, Amelia."

"Someone who understands you," Camilla added. She brightened. "What about Ben? You think he's cute, right?"

Amelia groaned. "Remember when I asked him for his number when he first started working for you? He was confused and gave me the bakery number, then explained the lead times for baked goods. He thought I wanted a cake, Camilla. He didn't even understand that I was trying to flirt with him. It was humiliating."

"That was two years ago." Camilla beamed, undeterred. "You just need to get back on the horse and try again."

"We've barely spoken more than two words to each other since then other than me asking him for coffee and him grunting out an acknowledgment. And I turn as red as a tomato whenever he's in the same room as me."

"Aww," Lucy added, utterly unhelpful.

Bitterness sluiced through Amelia's stomach. Ben *was* cute. She'd love to go out with him. She knew he worked as a barista part-time while he tried to develop a mobile app game. He was smart and brainy and loved data, just like Amelia.

But he wasn't interested in her.

Amelia stared at a fluffy white cloud on a journey across the sky. "I'd settle for someone who doesn't find my personality revolting. He doesn't have to understand me. Someone who doesn't care about sex too much, so they're not disappointed by me."

There was a short silence, then Camilla let out a growl. "I'd like to find Josh and wring his stupid little neck."

Amelia bunched her lips to the side, snorting at the sound of her ex-boyfriend's name. They'd broken up six years ago. It had been rough, but a lot of time had passed. "It's not just him," she said. "I haven't been on a date in over a year, and before that, they were all disasters. I'm just not good at it. Dating. Guys. Sex. I'm just not...attractive."

Yesterday, she'd felt attractive for a moment, with Leo. He'd even told her he found her beautiful, though he obviously said it to annoy her. But then she'd seen how easily he lied about her being his fiancée, and she began doubting everything.

"You are amazing, and beautiful, and kind, and smart, and the best friend ever," Lucy said, still gripping Amelia's forearm. "You're sexy as hell in your own spreadsheet-loving, data-analyzing way."

"And don't ever forget it." Camilla nodded once, like it settled everything.

Amelia felt that sliver of space between her and her friends grow. She wanted them to understand that it wasn't that easy for her. She couldn't flirt. She couldn't act all doe-eyed and cute. She just wasn't... It just didn't work for her! Guys were simply not interested.

To her horror, tears pricked her eyes. She squeezed them shut to hide the evidence until Camilla let out a low whistle.

"Sit up, Amelia. There's a Grade-A hottie jogging toward us. You want a boyfriend? You want to flirt? Here's your chance. That horse is galloping your way, and you just got to get up there and ride it, baby."

Amelia snorted, sitting up and scanning the park to see who Camilla was talking about. "What, I'm supposed to just wave my arms, and he'll come begging me to saddle—"

"Hey," Leo said, jogging to a stop in front of them. "I thought that was you."

He stood before them wearing a pair of black athletic shorts and a sheen of sweat. The sun stroked his muscular body like even its rays loved to touch him. He glistened, the muscles over his ribs shifting as he reached up to push a strand of damp hair off his forehead. His eyes were as green as the grass beneath Amelia's body, and they were currently occupied studying the lines of the sports bra that dug into her chest.

"Did you just do a workout?" he asked after a pause, which Amelia belatedly realized she'd spent shamelessly ogling his sweaty, beautiful body.

She rolled her tongue back into her mouth. "If you could call it a workout," she answered, shading her eyes with a hand. Gosh, he was gorgeous. Shadows played over his chest and abs, highlighting all the carved lines of his muscles. She hadn't realized people could actually have bodies like that outside of movies and magazines.

"What would you call it?" he asked, a grin playing over his lips.

"Torture," she answered.

Lucy and Camilla watched the exchange like a game of tennis, their heads shifting from one to the other. Camilla cleared her throat, and Leo blinked, looking at her for the first time.

"Leo, you remember Camilla, from the bakery," Amelia said, her voice slightly dazed. She introduced Leo to Lucy, and he shook their hands.

Then his gaze landed on Amelia again. "You give any more thought to my proposal?"

Her eyes narrowed. "Listen, I—"

"We're going to The Shed tonight," Camilla cut in, standing up to grab her little duffel bag, pawing for her phone. "You should come. Amelia will be there. Let me give you her number."

Amelia started. "What? No."

"Camilla..." Lucy hissed.

Camilla made a little motion with her hand near her hip, like she was telling them both to calm down. Leo watched, calculations happening behind his eyes. Then he took Amelia's number from Camilla and promised to come to The Shed that night. He jogged away and the three ladies watched him go in silence.

Well, she wasn't sure what her friends did, but Amelia

watched him go. The view was even better from the back. Apparently, people had muscles there too. All she'd ever seen on her own back were those little bulges above her bra strap.

When Leo disappeared from sight, Amelia remembered she was outraged and rounded on Camilla. "What the hell?"

"He is *perfect*," Camilla said, falling to her knees to grab Amelia's hands.

"What are you talking about?" Lucy screeched. "He's a player! I've heard all about him. He was a party animal in college, and then he started working for Goodhew almost right after graduation. They plan insane, luxury events for the rich and famous, which means all he does is party for work. He's probably drowning in poon—"

"'Poon?'" Amelia arched a brow.

"He's the *last* person Amelia should date. She needs someone who will treat her right, not bang and dash." Lucy harrumphed.

Amelia opened her mouth to respond, but she realized what she wanted to do was defend Leo. There was a lot more to him than just partying...but what did she know? She'd only met him yesterday.

But Camilla's eyes were shining as she shook her head. "No, ladies. He's not perfect for Amelia to date. He's the perfect guy to teach Amelia *how* to date."

Amelia frowned. "What do you mean?"

"What's the one thing a man like that is good at?" Camilla asked, then didn't wait for a response. "He's good at flirting, seducing, and sealing the deal."

"Those are three things," Amelia grumbled.

Lucy sat back, a thoughtful expression on his face. "You think he can help Amelia find a boyfriend. But Leo isn't known for relationships. How is he supposed to help?"

"Amelia doesn't need help with the relationship part. She's thoughtful and caring and amazing. Any guy would be lucky to have her as a partner. But she needs help getting guys to *realize* how amazing she is." She pointed down the path where Leo had disappeared. "He can help with that."

"You might be onto something," Lucy said, tapping her index finger on her lips.

"Don't I get a say in this?" Amelia climbed to her feet and planted her hands on her hips. She scowled at her two friends, but despite herself, the seed of Camilla's suggestion germinated.

Leo *would* be able to teach her how to make herself more attractive to the opposite sex. After all, seduction was seduction. He had oodles of experience attracting women. He knew what worked and what didn't. Plus, if they were going to pretend to be engaged, they'd have lots of time to go over the basics.

Amelia turned the suggestion around in her mind and considered that maybe he'd be able to give her advice of a more carnal nature. Her ex-boyfriend, Josh, had been very clear about how bad her bedroom skills were. Leo St. James had had sex with five women in one night! He'd probably bedded a thousand women. He could write a handbook on sex—he *would* write a handbook on it! Amelia would make sure of it! She'd have her own personal sex book, and no one would ever accuse her of being too enthusiastic, or not enthusiastic enough, or too wet or too dry or too stiff or whatever other complaint Josh had

had about her. She would be a sex queen. She just needed to collate the right data to figure out how to do it.

"Yeah," Amelia heard herself say. "This could work."

In exchange for her presence at Leo's work retreat as his loving fiancée, Amelia would squeeze every bit of information she could out of him. The man was a veritable treasure trove of knowledge on sex and seduction.

Data analysis required data, and Amelia would mine Leo for all he was worth.

SIX

"ABSOLUTELY NOT." Leo ground his teeth, lest a more forceful answer fall from his lips.

Amelia met his gaze, looking as fierce and determined as ever. He loved that little pinch of her lips. It made him want to run his thumb over her mouth just to feel it soften against his skin.

And she wanted him to teach her how to attract some other guy? *Fuck* no.

"Leo," she said, smoothing her little cocktail napkin on the table before her. "Listen. It's simple. You need me, and I need you."

"You don't need me to learn how to be attractive, Amelia."

"Ah, see, that's where you're wrong." She stuck her index finger in the air. "I *do* need your help with that."

Jaw clenched, he cast an eye over the sheer, loose, cream-colored blouse she wore. The top few buttons were undone, and he caught a glimpse of something lacy underneath. The blouse was tucked in the front of her jeans, which were tight enough to make him want to peel them off. Her little brown booties had clip-clopped over the bar's polished concrete floors when she'd walked toward him five minutes earlier.

"You're plenty hot, Amelia," he growled.

She blinked, then narrowed her eyes. God, he wanted her. Not *once* had she engaged in the usual flirtation with him. She hadn't giggled or playfully smacked his arm. She hadn't tried to gaze at him seductively or start any of the usual dance steps that usually led him to a horizontal position with a woman. Every time she spoke to him, he almost forgot who he was. With Amelia, he wasn't Pestilence. He wasn't the shameless flirt. He was just Leo.

She made him feel like a better man than the one he knew he was.

"Be that as it may," she said, smoothing her cocktail napkin again, and again, and again. "This is my offer. I'll go to your work retreat and pretend to be your fiancée if you help me improve my dating and seduction skills."

Stubborn little minx. Fine. She wanted to play this game? He'd entertain it. He leaned back in his chair and picked up his glass. Ice clinked against the walls of it as he tilted it this way and that. "That's a very vague target," he said. "How will we know the objective has been achieved?" The next words, he had to force out. "Is there a specific man you have in mind to seduce?"

The pulse jumped in her neck. Her cheeks flushed a pretty shade of pink, and Leo's heart began to pound. There *was* a man. Was it that barista? That scrawny little jerkoff? He should have punched him when he had the chance.

"No," Amelia finally answered. "There's no one specific. But, well, recent experience has indicated that my skills are lacking across the board. So, I've created a rubric." Her expression brightened on the last word, and she pulled out the tablet she'd used to run Maggie and Emory's wedding from her purse.

"A rubric."

"A curriculum, if you will." She swiped up on the tablet and tapped a few times. "This is what I'd like to learn."

Leo pulled the tablet toward him, watching Amelia swallow nervously, then dropped his eyes to the device. "I'm surprised you don't have a full binder with labeled tabs and everything. You seem like the type of person who would have a color-coded binder."

"Don't be ridiculous. It's the twenty-first century. An electronic copy is far superior. I have a color-coded spreadsheet."

He bit back his grin and looked at the file. "'Section One,'" he read. "'Flirting.'"

She leaned closer, and he caught a bit of her scent. Something fruity and sweet, different from Saturday—her hair? Shampoo?

Determined to see this charade through, Leo ignored the way his body tightened in response to the smell and read through the line items in the first section. "'Topics of conversation. Laughing and/or giggling. Physical contact—how much and where? Eye contact—how much is too much? Bedroom eyes.'" He huffed, looking at the woman beside him. "What is this shit? You don't need this! 'Bedroom eyes?' Seriously?"

She straightened, and Leo knew he'd offended her. She closed the cover on the tablet and shoved it back into her bag. "These things might come easily to you, Leo, but not all of us have such a *lengthy* resume of conquests."

She made to leave, her cheeks fully red now, but Leo caught her arm. "Wait. *Wait*, Amelia. I'm sorry."

"This was such a stupid idea. Forget it."

She wouldn't look him in the eyes, and he hated it. "Hey," he cajoled. "I'm sorry. It's just—you're an attractive woman, Amelia. I can't believe that you think you need me to tell you any of this." Still holding her arm, he slid his hand down and brushed his thumb over the pulse point of her wrist. Her skin was so soft. Touching her like this, even when she wouldn't look at him, settled something inside him. Ever since he'd held her hand before the wedding, he'd craved the feel of her skin against his. He knew he didn't deserve her, knew he should stay away— but he couldn't help himself. He brushed his thumb over her wrist once more, studying the fine tremor that passed through her body.

"You can stop saying that, you know," she said softly.

"Saying what?"

She flicked her gaze toward him, then rolled her eyes. "I know I'm not some sexpot, okay? I'll never be a bombshell, but I still think I deserve to find someone who cares about me."

Her words made his chest ache, which was odd. He didn't like that feeling at all. He tugged her closer and spun her around, gently touching her hips until they were face-to-face. She stood between his spread knees, watching him suspiciously.

"All right," he gentled. "Why don't we see what we're working with?"

Her suspicious look intensified, and Leo had the urge to laugh. Not in a mocking way—not at all. But she was so cute and leery of him, every skeptical thought written right there in her quicksilver eyes. "What do you mean?"

"Hit me with your best bedroom eyes." He made a little "come at me" gesture with the fingers of both hands.

"What—right now? Here?"

He glanced around the bar. The Shed was somewhere between a dive and a sports bar, and it was about half-full of beer drinkers and pool players. There were about a hundred screens showing various sports dotted on every wall. Camilla and Lucy were watching them from the corner booth without even trying to hide it. He turned back to the woman in front of him. "Yeah. Here."

"I can't just...turn them on. I'm not even sure I *have* bedroom eyes." She frowned at him. "That's why it's in the curriculum."

Leo dropped his lids to half mast and let Amelia see a mere fraction of all the things he wanted to do to her.

She threw her hands up like a shield. "Whoa! Jesus!"

He laughed and reached up to tug her hands down, gently circling her wrists with his fingers. Touching her was an impulse he wasn't quite able to leash. He tugged her a bit closer and laughed again at the sight of her grumpy face.

"That's unnatural," she complained, not pulling her hands away from his grasp. "You're a freak."

"That's not very nice."

"Yeah, well..." She huffed, then bit her lip. "How did you do that? All of a sudden you looked..."

The flush that warmed her cheeks made Leo want to look at her like that again and see where the evening took them. He dropped her hands and took a sip of his drink to try to get himself back under control.

Marlon's voice floated through his mind, and Leo knew he needed to keep some semblance of distance from her. Amelia wasn't interested in him. She was never going to be interested in him. He wouldn't do her the disservice of pursuing her, only to inevitably leave her disappointed when he couldn't be the man she deserved.

Being with her might make him feel like he was a better man, but he still knew the truth. He was Pestilence. He was a playboy. He was good in bed, but not much else.

"All right." Leo spoke slowly, his eyes focused on the task of centering his drink on its coaster. He cleared his throat and glanced at Amelia. "Your turn."

Her brows were slightly darker than her hair, and they lowered at his words. "But...how? What were you thinking about when you did that?"

Ha. That was something Leo would never, ever tell her. Not when she deserved so much better. "Just think about something that turns you on."

"Like what?"

"You're asking me what turns you on?"

"Well—no. I mean..." She huffed, shifting her gaze to the side. "I don't know what turns me on."

He paused, then asked, "You've had sex before, right?"

Amelia pursed her lips. "Well, yeah. But my sex life hasn't been..." She let the sentence drift off, then dragged her gaze back to meet his. She looked lost and a little overwhelmed.

Leo shifted in his seat and put his hands on his knees. She still stood between them, wearing that sheer blouse, looking entirely delicious. "Okay. Let's try this. Just look at me."

"Just look at you?" Her frown deepened.

"Yeah. Just look in my eyes and try not to think of anything. You don't need to be turned on, but—wait. No, not like that. Not like you want to stab me." He laughed. "Amelia, just, clear your mind. Just look at me normally. Now you look suspicious—no."

She let out a rough little growl, tearing her gaze away from his.

Leo reached up and turned her chin back to face him. "Hey. Come on." He spoke softly, stroking her cheek with his thumb, then forced himself to drop his hand.

"This was a stupid idea."

Her eyes were pools of silver, and for the first time, Leo saw a hint of vulnerability. It made his chest ache. "Forget the bedroom eyes. They'll happen naturally when you're interested in someone."

"If that's true, how did you just turn them on like you were flicking a switch?"

Because I want you so badly I can barely think of anything else.

He rolled his shoulders and gave her his best lady-killer smile. "I'm just that good, baby."

Amelia clicked her tongue, but the corner of her lips kicked. The dull thumping in his chest eased off the tiniest bit.

He grinned, then said, "You just need practice. Any one of the guys at this bar would be lucky to spend five minutes talking to you. All you have to do is go up to one of them and strike up a conversation."

Amelia stared at him for a beat, then gently shook her head. "Leo, you saying 'just strike up a conversation' is like saying 'just build a rocket ship and go colonize Mars.' It's not that easy."

"Sure it is." He looked up and saw a familiar face leaning against the bar. Although everything in him rebelled, he made himself say, "There's your barista friend. Just go up to him and say, 'Hi...'"

"Ben."

Ugh. *Ben.* "Say, 'Hi, Ben. Nice shoes.'"

Amelia stared at him for a beat like he'd suddenly started speaking Finnish. "I'm supposed to tell him he has nice shoes?"

"It doesn't matter what you say. It's just a little compliment you can use as an icebreaker. He'll say thanks, and you can ask him where he got them, and then you're off. Easy."

The words seemed to take a while to penetrate, but Amelia finally let out a long breath. She straightened her shoulders and gave Leo a curt nod, then glanced over her shoulder at the bar. "Okay," she said. "I can do this."

"You definitely can."

"I'm doing it."

"You're going to kill it."

"Off I go."

"Go, Amelia, go."

Her lips curled a tiny bit more, and she threw him an unreadable glance. Then she spun on her heels, huffed out a harsh breath, and started stomping toward the other man.

It killed Leo to watch her walk away. It felt like a little piece of him being torn out of his body. It was *wrong*. She should be beside him, shivering at the touch of his thumb against her wrist. She should be flicking her gray eyes up at him in exasperation, giving him her little grumpy frown.

He watched her hips shift with every step she took away from him, downing the rest of his drink. She walked with purpose, like an army advancing in war. The barista hadn't spotted her yet, but he'd see her in the next three seconds. Leo gripped his glass and tried to regulate his breathing. Five more steps until she was beside him. Three. One—

Amelia made a hard left and scurried around the gently curved bar. A sign for the washroom hung above her head as she turned to look at Leo. She slapped her hands on her cheeks and made a silent screaming face, like she was McCauley Culkin in *Home Alone*, then hurried down the hallway and out of sight.

Leo laughed. Relief swamped him so fast he could do nothing but try to breathe through the feeling.

He couldn't continue this. She was too cute. Too charming. Too damn perfect.

After tonight, he'd figure something out with Fred—he'd come clean about the fiancée thing or cook up a suitable breakup story. He couldn't keep spending time with Amelia and pretend that he didn't want to drag her to bed. She was far too good for him, and Leo wouldn't sully her life by being the guy who fucked her and left her the next morning.

A buzz in his pocket drew his attention. Then, a few seconds later, another buzz. He pulled his phone out and frowned. There was an email from Fred's assistant and a text from Fred himself.

Fred: Nice to finally meet your lady, son. I've had Percival put both your names up for the scavenger hunt on Thursday, and I've upgraded your room to the forest-facing side of the residence. You know we're a family here. Glad you finally understand that.

Leo read the text three times while despair settled over his skin like a slick of oil. He leaned back in his chair and groaned, dropping his head in his hands.

Fred's insistence on family wasn't just corporate lip service. Their team was small; less than a hundred people made up the core group of Goodhew's company, with another few hundred contractors and temporary employees. They planned lavish parties all around the world, so networking and relationship-building was a key part of the work. Being one of Fred's event directors was a highly sought-after position that paid well and had endless perks.

Despite what people said about him, Leo didn't just party for a living. He built relationships with small vendors all around the world and coordinated them to throw parties on private islands, exclusive venues, even one event on a private jet. Clients came to Goodhew because they knew the company could cater to the weird and wacky, as long as their money was good.

Leo had worked very, very hard to get the position as a permanent employee in Fred's company. It was only his third year on the full-time roster. Even being asked to the annual retreat was an achievement in itself. Only the top performers got an invite.

If Fred Goodhew found out that Leo had lied his way there by pretending to be engaged, he'd lose his job. No question. A decade of work would disintegrate in seconds.

Reading the text message over again, Leo tried to see a way out, but none came to him. This job was the one thing he excelled at. It was the one thing in his life that he could point to and feel proud of. His personal life was in shambles, his family life was nonexistent, and his friends—although they were good guys—thought he was just a party animal with a healthy sex drive and a phobia of commitment.

His job *meant* something to him. He couldn't just give it up.

"Did something happen?"

Leo jumped at the sound of Amelia's voice. She'd popped into existence near his elbow and was currently frowning at him like she could read every shameful secret written right there on his face.

He slipped his phone into his pocket and shook his head. "No. Everything's fine, except for the fact that you chickened out."

A groan slipped through her lips, and Amelia slumped against her stool. "I know. Pathetic."

"Good thing you've got a master flirt to learn from." He painted a grin on his lips, but his heart wasn't in it. Desperate, he scrambled to find some way out of this. Maybe he could cook up a family emergency, and skip the retreat altogether?

No. Fred wouldn't buy it. He'd already committed, and Fred knew he wasn't close with his family.

Amelia saw right through him, of course. She straightened, frowning, and asked, "Are you sure you're okay?"

"I'm sorry to drag you into this," he said.

She snorted, then gave him a one-shouldered shrug. "I'm not. It's obvious I have a lot of work to do if I'm going to find a boyfriend."

She'd find one. Leo knew it. She'd find a guy who had a steady job and a big heart, and she'd probably marry him within a year. Because once she cracked open her shell even the tiniest bit, it wouldn't take long for someone to realize how special she was.

But that man wouldn't be Leo. It couldn't be.

"We'd better get started," he heard himself say. Extending his hand toward her, he popped a brow. "You get a date with Ben the Barista by the time the retreat is over, and we'll be square. That's got to be worth four days as my fake fiancée, right?"

Amelia's teeth sank into her lower lip as she considered his expression, then his outstretched hand. She slipped her palm against his and pumped once, a witchy smile curling her lips. "I guess we're about to find out. You've got a deal, St. James."

Now, all Leo had to do was keep his attraction for Amelia buttoned up and hidden away. He'd keep his job, she'd get a date, and they'd go their separate ways.

In one week's time, all of this would be behind them, and they could both move on.

SEVEN

AMELIA STRETCHED her lower back and glanced out the window. Her spine crackled and popped as she moved it, and she knew she'd been sitting too long. The angle of the sun's rays told her it was midafternoon, which meant she'd been working for nearly seven hours straight.

If she was going to be busy with Leo's work retreat from Wednesday afternoon to Sunday morning, she had to get three of her clients' projects finished before then. She'd made progress, but Monday was quickly slipping away from her. She only had tomorrow and a few hours Wednesday morning to get all her work done before the madness began.

Last night at The Shed had been...illuminating. She felt less embarrassed by her lack of flirtation skills than she'd expected. Leo had a way of making her feel at ease, even when she'd completely failed her task to go up to Ben and strike up a conversation. He didn't seem to be worried about her ability to get a date at all, and his confidence was reassuring.

It wasn't that she was insecure, exactly. Amelia felt good about herself. She was smart, capable, and it wasn't like she was an ogre. Amelia had no problems with the way her face and body looked. Although—

She pulled out her tablet and added a section to her curriculum: Clothes and Makeup. Her wardrobe was full of tees and tanks, a nice top or two, jeans, denim shorts, and athleisure wear. She didn't exactly scream sexy and available, but Leo would be able to tell her how to update her look for maximum enticement.

That done, she hummed to herself as she made a late lunch, her mind occupied with a thorny problem with a certain client's data set. The small business wanted to figure out how to boost their repeat customer orders, but they hadn't been able to analyze any of their data because the back end of their online website was a mess. She'd spent four hours manually cleaning the data today, but she still couldn't figure out the best way of displaying it so that—

A knock rattled her front door. Padding over to it on sock-clad feet, she glanced through the peephole before pulling it open.

"Hi, Mrs. Gordon."

"I'm sorry to bother you, dear," the white-haired woman on her doorstep said. She was stooped over and leaning heavily on her cane, her wide brown eyes remorseful. "I know you're busy."

"Not at all! What's up?"

The old woman lived next door in an apartment that was filled top to bottom with knickknacks. She was spunky yet kind, and Amelia loved having her as a neighbor. Mrs. Gordon sighed. "I forgot to buy Her Majesty's wet food last time I was at the store, and with the elevator out of order and my old legs struggling to make it up three flights of stairs..."

"I'll go to the store for you!" Amelia smiled. "No problem. It's the grain-free stuff in the vacuum packs, right?"

"That's right. Here. Get as much as that can buy." She pushed a few bills into Amelia's hands and curled her fingers over the crinkled money. "And next time my grandson is in town, I'll have him take you out to dinner as thanks."

"Oh, that's okay," Amelia said as she slid her feet into the nearest shoes, laughing awkwardly. Mrs. Gordon's grandson was nine years younger than her and more interested in skipping his college classes to go to his fraternity's keggers than dating a thirty-one-year-old data analyst who preferred Saturday nights spent with spreadsheets over shots.

"Will you stop pestering her?" a gruff voice said from across the hall. Mr. Petrovski stuck his head out of apartment 306. The old man's ice-blue eyes looked out from a network of wrinkles. His bushy white-and-silver brows quivered as he frowned.

"I'll stop bothering her when your ratty mongrel stops trying to diddle Her Majesty," Mrs. Gordon spat, whirling around faster than Amelia thought she was able. The old woman hobbled across the hall and lifted her cane like she wanted to whack it against the old man's shins.

"Mongrel! A *mongrel*! My Winston!" The door slammed just in time for Mrs. Gordon to hit it with her cane, then opened again. "He'd stay away from your beast if she didn't come to my balcony and start rubbing her rear all over the window. She's nothing but a two-bit hussy. I wonder where she learned *that*."

Mrs. Gordon lifted her cane again, and the door closed. She scowled at it for a moment, then straightened, picking a bit of lint off her shirt. She met Amelia's wide-eyed stare and lifted her chin. "The grain-free version, dear. Don't forget. It has the yellow label."

"Got it." Amelia made a mental note to call maintenance again. She lived in an apartment building constructed in the 1970s that was only a five-minute walk away from Main Street. It was a fantastic location and the rent was cheap, but the building itself was falling apart. That was probably why she'd gotten such a good deal on a two-bed apartment. The elevator had been out of order for three days, and she didn't want to know what would happen to her feuding neighbors if it went on much longer. They were clearly going stir-crazy, and Mrs. Gordon's cane packed a wallop, judging by the dent it'd left in Mr. Petrovski's door.

Grateful for the break—and wanting to get away from the walking stick before Mrs. Gordon decided to do more target practice—Amelia grabbed her purse, locked her door, and headed out into the sunshine. Spring was beautiful in Stirling, but the town welcomed most of its tourists in autumn, when the leaves turned a thousand different jewel shades and painted the landscape with their vibrance. For now, the town was bustling with locals but still relatively quiet.

Amelia stepped onto the sidewalk and nodded to a couple pushing a stroller, then turned left and headed toward town.

Smiling to herself, she decided to stretch her legs and enjoy the weather. She did a loop behind the gothic church where Maggie and Emory had been married on Saturday and followed the riverbank to the main bridge that joined both sides of the town. From there, she crossed over and wandered toward Camilla's bakery. Camilla would be closing up soon, and she'd have almost-stale pastries Amelia could devour.

The houses here were a bit smaller than the further outskirts of town, mostly colonial-style residences with well-kept yards and white-painted window sashes. She paused to admire a flowering tree and waved at the woman pulling weeds in her garden bed, happy that she now worked for herself and had the flexibility to enjoy these moments. It had taken a lot of effort to strike out on her own, but she finally felt like things were coming together with her business and career.

Amelia was good at accomplishing goals. When she put her mind to something, it got done. As the sun warmed her shoulders and the multitude of flowers around her filled her nose with their lovely perfume, she felt a rush of confidence.

How hard could it be to find a partner? Leo had shown her just how easily he turned on the charm. That proved it was a skill, and it was learnable. She wasn't unlovable, she just hadn't built the skills to attract a mate. But now, she'd found the perfect teacher. She smiled to herself, tilting her head to listen to a bird twitter.

"Amelia?" Turning toward the voice, Amelia was startled to see Ben approaching at a jog. He must have finished his shift at the bakery, because he was coming from that direction. He grinned at her, pushing a strand of blond hair off his forehead. "Hey."

"Hi," she said, and her voice mostly came out normal. That was a relief.

In the sunlight, Ben's hair glinted, but he didn't have the kind of otherworldly beauty she'd admired in Leo. His smile widened, and Amelia was surprised to feel only the slightest thump in her chest. She looked down, confused with herself. Where was the rush of emotion? Why wasn't her tongue suddenly three sizes too big for her mouth?

She felt entirely normal in his presence, which was decidedly *not* normal for her. She'd had a crush on Ben for two and a half years. Why did he suddenly seem so...human?

"Um," she said, scraping her mind for something to say. Her eyes alighted on his footwear, and she remembered last night's lesson. "Nice shoes."

"Oh, these? Thanks! My mom picked them out." He stuck out his leg and tilted his foot so she could admire his footwear from another angle.

"Your mom still buys your shoes?" Amelia blurted, frowning, then tried to recover by smiling extra wide. "Lucky you! She has great style."

He nodded, then took a deep breath. "I saw you at The Shed yesterday."

Her eyes widened. Had he seen her marching toward him and then veering off at the last minute? Oh, no. Oh, *no*! How mortifying!

But Ben just smiled at her and said, "You were with someone, so I didn't want to bother you." He cleared his throat while

Amelia tried to process his words, then continued, "Was he... Are you... Was that your boyfriend? He was at the bakery with you the other day too."

She blinked. "Who, Leo?" She laughed. As *if* Leo would deign to be anyone's boyfriend—least of all hers. "No, not my boyfriend."

"Oh, good." Ben smiled wide again.

"Good?" she repeated, increasingly baffled.

"Well, no, I mean..." He huffed, and Amelia was amazed to see someone else fumbling with their words. Was this what she looked like when she spoke to guys? How awkward! How *fascinating*. She felt like an anthropologist getting a rare glimpse of heretofore unobserved human behavior: her own, reflected right back at her. Ben recovered by pulling out his phone. "Do you use Picstagram? I don't think we're connected yet."

Picstagram was a social media platform that had taken the world by storm. Everyone was on Picstagram...and Ben was wanting to connect with her there?

"Oh. Sure!" A rush of pleasure swelled in Amelia's chest as she pulled her own phone out. They exchanged information, and Ben gave her another sweet smile. He waved and walked away, wishing her a nice day.

She clutched her phone to her breast. A million butterflies fluttered in her chest, tugging her lips into a smile. Ben had asked her for her social media! He wanted to connect with her!

That...had never happened before. As soon as Ben was out of sight, she let out a little squeal and did a dance on the spot. This *had* to be a good sign. And Leo was right—all she had to do was tell him he had nice shoes!

This flirting stuff was *easy*. After a few days under Leo's tutelage, she'd be a pro.

Phone still in hand, she let her thumb hover over Camilla's name...then kept scrolling. Before she could think too hard about it, she found Leo's number and called him.

He answered on the second ring. "Hey, Amelia." His voice was deep and smooth, and hearing it felt like sex. Amelia's thighs spasmed, and she leaned on the brick wall next to her for support. Whoa. He sounded like he was breathing hard, which was also extremely hot. Another spasm took Amelia's lower body.

How did he *do* that?

She shook her head. "I have news," she announced. "You were right!"

A deep chuckle reverberated through the phone, and a shiver traveled the length of Amelia's body. She closed her eyes.

"Where are you? I just finished a workout, and I was going to grab a smoothie. How about you tell me in person?"

"*Another* workout? Didn't you just do one yesterday?" It was kind of hypocritical, seeing as Amelia usually worked out on Mondays too. She'd skipped it today in order to get her work done.

Leo laughed again, like she'd been joking. "Meet you at the smoothie place on Maple Street in ten?"

"Sure," she said, and turned in that direction, ignoring the little thrill in the center of her ribcage at the thought of seeing Leo again. She was just happy about the Ben thing, that was all. Her excitement had nothing to do with Leo.

. . .

LEO SUCKED his mango-flavored protein shake and frowned at Amelia. He swallowed and forced himself to take a moment so his voice would come out halfway normal. It still sounded like a rough growl when he said, "He asked you for your Picstagram profile?"

"Yeah." Amelia beamed. "Isn't that great? And you were right! All I had to do was tell him he had nice shoes." She tilted her head from side to side. "I mean, what wasn't so great was that his shoes were kind of ugly, and he said his mom picked them. I'm all for a good mother-son relationship, but a man in his thirties should feel confident enough to pick his own shoes. But maybe I'm just being a judgmental jerk? I don't know! I'm too excited."

They sat outside the smoothie shop, a little hole-in-the-wall place not far from the gym Leo had joined for his stay in Stirling. Their table and chairs were wrought iron, and the afternoon spilled over them in golden puddles. It was a beautiful day, but Leo felt only dark clouds gathering above his head. "He only wanted your Picstagram profile, not your phone number?"

Amelia paused, her smile slipping slightly. "Um. Yes? Is that a problem?"

Leo shrugged. "It sends a certain message."

Sunlight gleamed over her hair and skin. She wore cutoff jean shorts, white sneakers, and a white tee. Her hair was in a bun on top of her head, and her tortoise-shell sunglasses were nestled in her blond locks in front of the bun where she'd pushed them after flopping onto her chair. She looked hot as hell.

"What message?"

"That he isn't serious enough to get your number."

"Huh?"

"Getting a phone number means he wants to date you. Looking at your Picstagram profile just means he wants to check out what kind of pictures you put online, and maybe send you a message late at night to see if you bite."

"Oh." Pursed lips bunched to the side as she shifted her gaze to the middle distance. Then, Amelia shook her head. "Whatever. I haven't had a guy ask me for my phone number since my ex-boyfriend did in college, and your advice worked. I'm going to take it as a win, which means we need to figure out your side of the deal. This fiancée business."

Leo didn't want to talk about the fiancée business. He wanted to find Ben and ask him what the hell he thought he was doing. He wanted to shove Ben off the Main Street Bridge and watch him belly flop against the water. He wanted to build a time machine so he could go back and punch the guy when he had the chance. Instead, he said, "I asked you for your phone number."

She blinked, looking up from the tablet she'd pulled out to make notes. "What?"

"You said no one's asked you for your phone number since your ex-boyfriend in college. But I did."

"Leo," Amelia said with a teasing smile. "Camilla told you to take my number, remember? You didn't ask for anything. It was thrust upon you."

His brow wrinkled. "Oh. Right. Well, I was going to ask you for it."

A snort. "Yeah, okay. Never mind that. Let's get our story straight. What have you told your boss about me?"

Leo winced. "Ah..."

The look Amelia gave him was sharp as steel. "Ah, what? Does this have something to do with that stage name thing?"

"I might have told them you're a singer. I had to think of a reason they'd never met you, and that was the first thing that came to mind. You're always touring with the band."

She just stared at him.

"Your band is called the Nymphomaniacs."

She stared harder.

"You're really good at whistle tones, like Mariah Carey."

The metal chair tumbled to the ground as Amelia pushed to her feet. She glared at him, breathing heavily. "Are. You. *Kidding me?* What happens when someone asks me to sing?" She turned her back on him, then whirled right around to glare again. "The Nymphomaniacs? Are you for real? Is this a joke?"

He frowned. Why was she being so unreasonable? "I had to come up with something on the fly. There had to be a reason you were never around, so it had to be a job that required a lot of travel."

"Flight attendant!" Amelia threw her arms out to the sides. "There. Was that so hard?"

"Flight attendant," he scoffed. "Who'd believe that?"

She blinked at him, shaking her head. "This is insane. You're insane. *I* must be insane for agreeing to this."

"Look. It's not a big deal. Just tell them you need to save your voice and you can't sing for them. Oh, and your stage name is Kitty Catelli."

Anger blazed from her eyes. "Absolutely not. Kitty Catelli? How'd you come up with that? Let me guess: Someone asked you for my name and you panicked, and then a cat walked by?"

Leo pinched his lips, turning his palms up. "Well…"

"Oh my God." Amelia took a deep breath and let it out slowly. "Leo," she said, then pinched the bridge of her nose. "What if someone googles me? What if they look up The Nymphomaniacs and see that a) the band doesn't exist, and b) I'm not in it?"

"Well, you're a private person," he answered reasonably. "You don't like having your photo all over the place. I've told them that already. It's totally fine." He didn't get what the big deal was. The cover story was fine.

She leaned her hands on the table and stared at him. "I'm a singer in a *band*—a band that presumably is trying to make money by promoting their music—and I don't like having my photo taken? How is that believable *at all*? Why would I have a stage name if I don't have an online presence anywhere?"

Hmm. He saw her point. Still. "Look, Amelia, it's not a big deal. Everyone bought it. You won't have to sing anything. I'll cover for you."

Her chest heaved as she inhaled, eyes blazing. "No. I'm not doing this."

She made to leave, but Leo jumped out of his chair and caught her around the waist. He tugged her close, trying to ignore the way she felt warm and sweet beneath his palm. "Wait. *Wait*, Amelia."

"No." She scowled at him. "I'm not doing it."

"Hey, I've already helped you with Ben. You owe me." It

felt slightly dirty to say the words, but he couldn't let her slip away.

"I don't owe you shit."

God, she was hot when she was like this, all stubborn and angry. Leo's arm was still around her waist, and he spread his hand so it spanned her lower back. She felt like heaven to touch.

But he couldn't have her. Amelia was a business owner. She was intelligent. She was beautiful and stubborn and driven, and she deserved a whole lot better than a guy who'd answered to the name Pestilence for the last three years of his college degree and hadn't quite shaken the reputation ever since. What could Leo possibly provide that Amelia would want, other than a night of hot sex?

He knew his value, what little of it there was. He knew Amelia deserved a lot better.

But Leo was also selfish, and he couldn't stand the thought of not having her beside him at his company retreat. So, he used the only tool at his disposal. "What are you going to say to Ben when he messages you?"

Her hands had curled into his shirt and her knuckles pressed against his stomach. He wondered if she'd even realized she did it. "*If* he messages me," she corrected.

"He'll message you."

Blond brows tugged together, and a line appeared between them. She bit her lip and looked up at him. "I don't know."

"I'll help you through it. You'll have a date with this guy by the end of the week."

She dropped her gaze to his shoulder and pinched her lips. "You're the worst."

Leo couldn't help the smile that curled his lips. She'd come to the retreat with him. He had more time to spend with her. "Yeah. I am."

She pointed a finger at him. "I'd better be able to attract the love of my life by the end of the week. That's the only way this is going to be worth it."

"I'll teach you everything I know."

Amelia snorted. "Fine. I have to go buy cat food for my neighbor." She pushed against his stomach and stepped back, then lowered her sunglasses to her eyes, shading them from view. But her lips were expressive enough that he knew her eyes were shooting daggers at him. Then she whirled around and walked away, and Leo watched her until she disappeared around the corner.

THE DOOR to apartment 303 opened to a very suspicious-looking Mrs. Gordon. Amelia lifted her reusable bag full of vacuum-packed, grain-free cat food and gave the elderly woman a closed-lipped smile. "Hi, Mrs. Gordon. I have Her Majesty's food and your change."

Mrs. Gordon glanced over her shoulder before opening the door a smidge wider. "Thank you, Amelia," she said, reaching for the bag with one hand and holding her palm out for the change with the other. "I'll put these in the fridge and give this bag right back."

Amelia kept her foot on the door to prop it open and leaned against the jamb. She watched the older lady hobble away, her cane safely tucked against the console table by the front door.

The table held a variety of items, including porcelain figurines, carved coasters, a blown glass bowl, and two hefty silver candlesticks.

"These are nice," Amelia said, picking one of the candlesticks up as Mrs. Gordon came back into the room with Amelia's empty cloth bag. "Are they new? I don't remember seeing them before."

"Hmph." Mrs. Gordon thrust the bag into Amelia's chest and grabbed the candlestick. She placed it back down exactly where it belonged. "They're not new. I just took them out of storage."

"They're lovely," Amelia said, just as a door opened somewhere deeper in the apartment.

Brows rising, she glanced behind the older woman's shoulder. In the four years she'd been Mrs. Gordon's neighbor, she'd never heard any guests come in and out of the old lady's apartment, other than her grandson. She knew the old lady had a sister, but she was pretty sure the rest of Mrs. Gordon's relatives lived across the country and never visited. She'd never see anyone come in or out of here, in any case. The rowdiest resident of the apartment was Her Majesty the cat.

"Okay," Mrs. Gordon said. "Bye-bye now." She shoved Amelia out and slammed the door.

Standing on her neighbor's welcome mat, Amelia's lips curled into a smile. She glanced across the hall at number 306, wondering if Mrs. Gordon's guest was a certain grouchy cat owner. Tiptoeing across the hall, she listened at Mr. Petrovski's door. No sounds reached her ears.

"Two-bit hussy, indeed," she mumbled, grinning, then

headed back to her apartment. She sat down at her desk, wiggled her fingers, and got back to work. It was only hours later, when the clock told her it was nearly midnight, that Amelia leaned back and checked her phone.

Leo had sent her a message with an attachment detailing the schedule for the company retreat. There were cocktail-attire dinners, a scavenger hunt, and a thousand other activities she'd have to attend while pretending to be the lead singer of The Nymphomaniacs.

Was all that hassle worth probing Leo's brain for a few days? Was she making a huge mistake?

...or was it worth the short-term pain to finally get over her insecurities and find a life partner? Leo had succeeded in getting Ben to ask for her contact information with a single sentence. Surely that kind of knowledge was worth the risk?

EIGHT

ON TUESDAY EVENING, Amelia pushed away from her computer and rubbed the heels of her hands into her eyes. She'd finished her work, but she'd barely left her desk all day. Her body was sore and creaky, and she spent a few minutes stretching out the kinks that had knotted her muscles over the past two days. She'd missed a family dinner at her parents' place to see Maggie and Emory off on their honeymoon and had to beg off hanging out with Camilla and Lucy this morning. She knew she wouldn't make it to bootcamp tomorrow morning, either.

This was the downside of being an ambitious small business owner: there was no one else to pick up the slack. She had to rely on herself to get the job done; otherwise, she wouldn't get paid.

Sighing, she bent over at the waist to stretch her hamstrings, only coming up when her buzzer rang. Walking across the room, Amelia frowned when she looked into the small, grainy screen that showed her a view of the front door. Leo stood on the stoop, leaning against the wall with one hand.

She stared at him for a beat, then pressed the button to speak. "Yeah?"

"It's me," he said, like it was completely normal for him to show up at her building. He lifted a white plastic bag. "I brought Chinese for dinner."

At some point over the last twenty-four hours, Amelia must have slipped through a crack and fallen into an alternate universe. What was happening? "How do you know where I live?"

His lips curled, and he looked so attractive Amelia wobbled on her feet. "I have my ways."

"It was Camilla, wasn't it?"

He laughed. "Let me in, Amelia. I brought food."

"You can't just bribe me with food to get your way, Leo," she grumbled, but she buzzed him up and flicked the lock on the door. Then there were a few panicked seconds where she gathered a dirty pair of socks and three mugs out of the living room, then scanned the space to make sure she hadn't forgotten a bra on the lampshade or a thong on the sofa cushions.

Then the door opened. He didn't even knock.

"You should lock your door," he said.

She planted her hands on her hips. "I unlocked it for you, you doorknob."

He grinned his beautiful, heart-stopping grin and crossed the space to deposit his offering of Chinese food onto the kitchen table.

Amelia watched him, unsure about how it felt to have him in her space. He moved with a powerful sort of grace, and he took up a lot of room. He cast an eye around her apartment, and she suddenly felt exposed. She had pictures of Lucy and Camilla, her sister, and her parents displayed all around the apartment. The kitchen was tidy except for the three dirty mugs she'd just placed in the sink. The door to the office was open, and she could see the mess on her desk from across the room.

"You hungry?" Leo asked.

She suddenly realized she was starving. "Yes."

That seemed to please him. He started hunting through the cupboards until he came out with two plates, then went searching for utensils, as comfortable in her space as if he lived here.

She couldn't decide if she loved that thought or hated it, but she was drawn to the kitchen table by the scent of steaming food in Styrofoam containers. They ate in silence until their plates were cleared and Leo leaned back in his chair.

Amelia narrowed her eyes at him. "What are you really doing here?"

His gaze roamed over her face, and he lifted a shoulder. "Thought we should talk about tomorrow, and maybe attack another module of your syllabus. We only have a few days to find the love of your life, after all."

"Hmm," Amelia answered noncommittally. Then she nodded to her phone, which was on the arm of the sofa in the other room. "I got the schedule for the retreat you sent. It seems intense."

"There are a lot of activities," he agreed. "It's a multi-day party that Fred throws for the top employees and their partners. It happens every year, and getting invited is a huge honor. It's the one party a year that we don't have to plan."

"So, if they find out we're not actually engaged, it'll be a big deal."

"Very."

Amelia nodded. "Okay." She watched Leo for a moment, then asked, "Why did you lie about having a fiancée?"

A sigh slipped through his lips as his gaze drifted from hers. He played with the edge of a Styrofoam container for a moment and finally shrugged. "Fred cares a lot about family. His company caters to all these A-list celebrities and wealthy people, and we plan all kinds of crazy events for them. But at its core, our team is pretty small. The business is built entirely on relationships and reputation. He's built a name for Goodhew to the point that the waitlist to have a party organized by us is years long. When he says that the company is like family, it's not just corporate bullshit. He really means it."

"And you didn't think being Mr. Pestilence would jive with that."

A bitter laugh. "No. I didn't." He combed a hand through his hair and lifted his gaze to Amelia's. "This job is important to me. I wouldn't ask you to do this if it weren't."

Amelia held his gaze, then nodded. She could respect that. Leo sometimes put on his charming smile and dazzled people into thinking he was a carefree guy, but Amelia had seen glimpses of something deeper. She'd seen it in his desperation in the parking lot, when he tried to convince her to pretend with him, and in the way he comforted her before they started the bridal procession down the aisle.

Their conversation at The Shed had shown her just how easily he slid on a mask for the benefit of others. To him, bedroom eyes weren't a result of arousal; they were a means to an end.

It made her want to see the real Leo. In spite of his reputation, the fact that he could probably get any girl he chose, and his painful good looks, Amelia wondered if Leo felt as lonely as she did.

"Okay," she finally replied. "I get it. I won't mess this up for you."

He blew out a breath. "Thanks."

They spent a few minutes going over a backstory, which turned into talk about Leo's work. Leo ended up telling her about a party he threw on a private island in the South Pacific, where they had to fly everyone in on helicopters and planned to get them out via boat, and then realized they hadn't brought enough fuel, and some drunk partygoer had thrown the satellite phone in the pool and ruined it. He had her clutching her stomach with laughter as he explained the harrowing journey across the water in his tiny metal boat to get to the nearest island where he could contact the right people to get fuel to the island —all before the guests realized anything was wrong.

They'd moved to the sofa, and Amelia had one leg curled under the other, her elbow resting on the back of the couch as she listened. She huffed and shook her head. "I would have panicked. Everyone would have known there was a problem."

"Your poker face needs work," he conceded. "When I

walked into the church on Saturday, you looked like you were ready to kill me."

"That's because I was."

His warm chuckle wrapped around her, teasing her own lips into a smile. Then he reached into the pocket of his jeans and pulled out a small ring box. "Here."

She caught the box and flipped it open, brows arching. "Wow." A glittering princess-cut diamond stared back at her from its bed of black velvet, the delicate white-gold band carved in a filigree pattern. It looked vintage and cool and very expensive, even though the stone didn't look particularly large. It was beautiful. "Where did you get this?"

Leo shifted in his seat, then shrugged. "Rented it from a jeweler. I have to give it back next week."

"A jeweler let you rent a ring like this?" She lifted it out of the box and watched the light play through the stone. "I didn't even know you could rent jewelry."

"We go way back," Leo explained. "Try it on."

She put the ring on. It was a little bit loose but still felt secure behind her knuckle. Her throat was suddenly tight. "It's beautiful."

"Good," Leo said. "Your turn. Why do you think you need help finding a boyfriend? From where I'm sitting, all I see is an attractive, successful woman."

Her cheeks flushed. "I guess I just get weird around guys. I start overthinking what I'm saying. I stumble over my words. Sometimes, they ask me about work and I go off on tangents about dashboard software and I only stop when they keel over, dead of a boredom-induced heart attack."

And then there was sex. She knew she was bad at it, so anytime a guy touched her, she'd freeze up with nerves and awkwardness. Was she making too much noise? Moving awkwardly? Did her boobs look weird in that position? Had she forgotten to pluck those stray hairs that grew around her nipples? Was it going to hurt? And then oh, yes, it *did* hurt! Should she ask to stop? Would her partner be mad?

It was exhausting. She didn't know how people actually enjoyed being intimate when there was so much to worry about.

Leo's face softened slightly, his green eyes reading something in her face that she wasn't sure she wanted him to know. "Tell me about dashboard software," he said, voice velvety and low. "I promise not to keel over."

She clicked her tongue. "Stop it."

"I mean it. I don't even know what dashboard software is. Tell me."

"Well," Amelia answered slowly. "All data analysis really starts with a problem, or multiple problems. So the creation of a dashboard is just a way to present solutions—or information—relating to that problem. I think a lot of people who are good with numbers get too bogged down in them, and they forget that the layperson needs information available at a glance. So with dashboards, we can—" She frowned as Leo shifted on the sofa, leaning his head back as he stretched his long legs out. He folded his arms over his stomach. His eyes were lazy as they held hers. Amelia huffed. "See? I'm boring you."

"I'm not bored. I'm just getting comfortable."

"This is the problem. I start talking, and I don't know when to stop."

Leo reached over and grabbed her hand. He tugged it, threading his fingers through hers. "A guy worthy of you will love listening to you," he said, "even if you're talking about dashboards, or numbers, or the best textile to use for socks."

"Bamboo, obviously."

He laughed. Green eyes glimmered as they met Amelia's, and he didn't let go of her hand. "What's the next topic in your color-coded rubric?"

She tugged at her hand, but he held it fast. "I'd have to check."

"Bullshit. You remember every cell of that spreadsheet."

It took all of Amelia's willpower to hide the smile that wanted to burst through. She bit her lip. "Clothes and makeup," she finally admitted.

"Your clothes are perfect. Your makeup is great. Next item."

Sitting up, Amelia clicked her tongue and glared at him. "That is *not* an adequate response! How is that supposed to help me?"

Leo gave her a heavy-lidded look, brow arching the tiniest bit. "Am I the expert or not? Your clothes are hot. Your face is beautiful. You looked great with makeup on at the wedding and you look great now."

He'd called her beautiful again. Not knowing how to respond, she frowned harder.

His voice was soft and low when he continued, "You shouldn't change them just for a guy. Take my advice or leave it, sweet cakes."

"Okay, no. You're not calling me sweet cakes."

He still hadn't let go of her hand. "What's the next item on your list? We're burning through them. This is easy." Another grin.

Oh, he thought he was funny, did he? Amelia hummed to keep her frustration at bay. "Next is kissing."

Leo froze beside her. His hand turned to granite around hers. Then, as though he were speaking through gravel, he asked, "Kissing?"

"I've been told I'm a bad kisser. It's an area requiring improvement, so I'd like to learn how to be better."

Another pause stretched, and Amelia turned to meet Leo's gaze. His jaw was hard, and his eyes were focused on her lips. "Kissing," he repeated.

"Yes. Kissing. Have you heard of it?"

"Who told you you were bad at it?" His eyes remained on Amelia's lips, and heat began to swirl in her lower belly.

She shrugged, finally succeeding in pulling her hand away from his. "It doesn't matter."

"I think it does."

She stared at the wall, face heating. "No, it doesn't. Someone said it to me, and I have reason to believe they're telling the truth. So, assuming you've kissed thousands of women and have built up the skills to be good at it, you're the perfect person to give me tips."

"Tips."

A huff fell from Amelia's lips, and she turned to stare at him. "Are you just going to repeat everything I say?"

"I don't think giving you a few pointers will help you learn how to be a better kisser."

"No? Well, I guess you've outlived your usefulness. I won't

have to go to your retreat, after all. So your presence here is no longer welcome." She popped a brow and crossed her arms. "Feel free to leave."

The look Leo gave her was nothing short of predatory. He sat up on the couch and turned to face her, one hand on his knee, the other on the back cushion. "First of all, I don't believe that you're a bad kisser. Someone put all these ridiculous ideas in your head, and once I find out who it is, I'll deal with him separately."

A shiver traveled through Amelia at those words, starting behind her belly button and spreading outward. She sat very still, caught in Leo's gaze as it darkened with every word.

"Secondly," he continued, "if you're going to get better at kissing, the last thing you need is a bunch of *tips*." He spat the last word.

Amelia couldn't move. "No?" It came out as a croak.

"No. You need practice."

Amelia's bravado was quickly failing. Her heartbeat hammered in her chest as she fought to keep her face still. Sitting next to Leo when he stared at her like that was like being in a cage with a lion. One wrong move and he'd tire of toying with her, and that'd be the end of Amelia. Danger filled the air until she was afraid to twitch. But she tried to process what he'd said to her.

His words finally penetrated. She exhaled, disappointment piercing her chest. "You want me to find guys to practice kissing on?"

Leo blinked, and a muscle jumped in his cheek. "No, Amelia," he replied darkly. "That's not what I want."

The lion was padding over and back across the cage, its eyes steady on hers. They sat like that, unmoving, for long, silent moments. Amelia tried to think of something to say, but she knew anything that came out of her mouth would be the wrong thing.

Then Leo rumbled, "Come here."

"I don't think—"

She squeaked as Leo's hands wrapped around her waist and pulled her across his lap. He plopped her down so she was draped across his thighs, her back resting against the arm of the sofa. His hand slid from her waist to her leg, leaving a trail of fire in its wake. When his palm touched the bare skin below her athletic shorts, Amelia inhaled sharply. He left his hand on her flank, his thumb pressing into the top of her thigh to hold her in place.

"We're going to practice right now," he informed her.

"Oh." That soft sound was all she could manage, because Amelia couldn't think of anything except the warmth of his palm against her skin and the coiled power in his body.

With his free hand, Leo cupped her jaw. His thumb stroked her cheek as he studied her face, his gaze flicking between her eyes before dropping to her lips. "Okay?"

Was this taking their little game too far? Was kissing Leo a bad idea? Was it everything Amelia had wanted since the moment Leo had pushed the church's doors open?

Those were questions for Future Amelia. Right now, she just dipped her chin. "Okay."

She thought he'd crush his lips against hers and kiss her in an explosion of passion. She closed her eyes and braced herself, only to feel the softest brush of his mouth against hers. Surprised, she let her lips fall open, and Leo took advantage. He kissed her lower lip then nibbled her upper one. He pulled away and kissed a line down her jaw, then moved back to her mouth.

All the while, the thumb on her thigh stroked softly, over and back, a soothing metronome marking the beat of the moment.

When his tongue swept between her parted lips, she met it with her own. A delicious melting feeling happened behind her navel, and Amelia found herself clinging to his shirt to pull him closer. He made a noise, low in his throat, that made Amelia pull away.

"Was that okay?" She frowned. Had she been too aggressive? Josh used to hate when she did that.

But Leo wasn't turned off. His voice was a low growl when he said, "Fuck yes, it was okay." He tangled his fingers into her hair and angled her head back so he could drop kisses down her neck, following the line of her thudding pulse. A whimper escaped her lips, and Leo responded by tightening his hold on her hair.

It felt so good. For the first time in her life, Amelia was in the arms of a man and her mind was blissfully blank. She tangled her own fingers into his golden-brown locks and pulled him back up to her mouth. Instead of being repelled by her assertiveness, Leo responded by kissing her harder and longer than he had before. He groaned into her mouth and set liquid heat tumbling through her veins.

"You can kiss," he told her, lips against hers. "I knew you'd taste amazing."

She nipped his bottom lip and tugged him closer. That seemed to drive him wild, because he gripped her jaw and redoubled his efforts. This was more than a kiss. It blasted Amelia into the stratosphere. Lust burned her from the inside out.

The hand he'd kept on her thigh moved to her breast. He shaped and fondled her curves, making noises that stoked Amelia's flames ever higher. A gentle tweak of her nipple over her clothes had her gasping, and Leo's lips shaped into a smile against hers.

She'd never been kissed like this before. This was a full-body experience. She'd never felt as attractive, as free. Leo touched her like she was beautiful. He made her feel like he appreciated *her*—the real her—like she was special and desirable and sexy. Her hips began to make small circles, moving of their own accord—

Amelia pulled away, suddenly stiff. What was she *doing*? She couldn't do this with Leo! He was supposed to help her get a boyfriend—someone who wasn't him! This was a simple business exchange.

It was all well and good for the player of the century to kiss her; he wouldn't get attached. But Amelia had never been kissed like that. She'd misinterpret everything—hell, she was already feeling like Leo cared about her. He didn't care! He was just here to get her to play along with his stupid fake fiancée scheme. And after one kiss, Amelia felt like she'd found The One.

Pathetic.

"Hey." His hand cupped her chin and tilted her face so he could study her. "You okay?"

She nodded and forced herself to smile. "Yes. That was great, thanks. I see what you mean about practice."

Amelia made to move off his lap, but Leo circled his arms around her waist. He held her in place. "Wait. What just happened?"

"Nothing. That was great. Thank you for the demonstration. I see that I'm not as bad as I thought." She peeled his hands off her waist and stood, brushing the front of her shirt down with a few rough movements. "Cool. Well, I should get to bed, and you should go home. We have a big day tomorrow."

She could feel his eyes on her, but Amelia forced herself to walk to the front door. Her legs were unsteady, and she bumped into an armchair on the way. When she got to the door, she held it open and finally met his gaze.

Leo's face was utterly blank as he watched her for a beat, then dipped his chin. In a toneless voice he said, "I'll pick you up at three p.m."

The door closed behind him, and Amelia made sure to throw the deadbolt. It slammed home with a loud *thunk* in the empty apartment, and Amelia let out a shaky breath. The ring felt heavy on her finger, and she pulled it off with shaking hands. She studied the glittering stone and regretted every decision that had brought her to this moment.

Then she took a long, cold shower.

NINE

FRED GOODHEW'S mansion stood on the outskirts of Stirling, nestled in a leafy, forested estate only accessible via a wrought-iron gate at the end of a long drive. Leo slowed as he drove the car onto his boss's property, his mind still spinning from what had happened the night before.

Amelia hadn't said much to him today. What was there to say? He'd acted like a horny asshole, and she obviously regretted kissing him. If he were a better man, he'd regret it too.

But he couldn't.

In fact, he couldn't stop thinking about it. He'd barely slept last night because his body had burned up for hours. He could still taste her on his tongue, could feel the way she softened and writhed atop him.

His hands tightened on the steering wheel as they made their way down the arrow-straight road, tree branches arching overhead, barrels of annual flowers dotting the drive at even intervals. It was his first year as an event director and the first time he'd been invited to the company party. He should've been happy about it.

Instead, he was ashamed.

"Whoa," Amelia breathed, shifting in her seat. She pushed a strand of hair behind her ear, and the ring on her third finger sent off multicolored sparks. The mansion came into view before them, a sprawling building with gray siding and a dark roof, its front door framed with four white columns. A round turret stood sentinel at the left side of the property, giving the building a strange, disjointed look, like multiple houses had been mashed together to create this gargantuan monster.

The circular drive led them around a spraying fountain shaped like two jumping fish, and they came to a stop in front of the grand front entrance. A valet in a crisp black suit stepped up and opened Amelia's door to let her out before circling to collect the keys from Leo. They were led up the steps to another staff member, who gave them both a shallow half-bow.

The man was in his fifties, with perfectly slicked-back silver hair. He wore an honest-to-goodness tailcoat with a starched white shirt and shiny, black, patent leather shoes. The only bit of color on his outfit was a pin with the Goodhew Inc. logo on his breast.

"Mr. St. James. Ms. Darcy," the man said, even though they'd never met. "Welcome to the Goodhew Estate. We hope you'll have a pleasant stay. My name is Percival. If you have need of anything at all during your time with us, please let me know." He led them inside the huge double doors, into an ornate foyer. "Your bags will be taken directly to your room. We have refreshments set up in the Blue Room. If you'll follow me."

Amelia's eyes were wide as she glanced at Leo. "A freaking butler," she whispered, wiggling her eyebrows.

It was the first hint of her personality he'd seen all afternoon, and Leo felt himself finally relax. Maybe she'd forgive him for acting like an ogre last night. Not that he deserved her forgiveness.

Percival the butler led them down a wide, marble-tiled hallway dotted with sculptural pieces and gilded paintings. Chandeliers glittered above them, sending twinkling lights flashing over all the luxurious furnishings. They turned a corner and the sound of conversation floated toward them. Halfway down the next hall, Percival stood aside and gestured to an open doorway.

The Blue Room was, indeed, blue. The walls were a soft periwinkle, and the two large couches that dominated the space were a rich, royal-blue velvet. Drapes of the same fabric and hue framed the gorgeous forest view, and tasteful vases burst with fresh flowers all around the room.

In contrast, the people milling around the space and lounging on the blue furniture stood out, wearing yellows and blacks and pinks, as if the designer had planned for people to pop against the monochromatic decor. It worked. The room was as striking as it was unique.

"St. James!" Fred boomed. "Amelia! Welcome!"

Arm firmly wrapped around his fiancée, Fred approached. Fred wore his usual button-down shirt and slacks, and Nadia was decked out in a fitted, knee-length dress in a pale shade of orange. Her cast, incredibly, had been changed to match her outfit.

They all greeted each other, and Nadia lifted Amelia's hand. "Gorgeous!" she exclaimed, admiring Amelia's ring. "The diamond is so small and cute! Adorbs!"

Leo stiffened slightly, but Amelia burst out laughing, clearly reading no maliciousness in the other woman's words. "I love it," she said, and it sounded like the truth. Leo felt a glow of warmth in his chest, which he tried his best to ignore. It wasn't a real engagement ring. It didn't matter if Amelia liked it or not.

Amelia nodded toward Nadia's hand. "Yours is a show-stopper."

Nadia admired the pink diamond on her hand, adjusting it on her finger. The weight of the diamond immediately slid to the side again. Nadia glanced at Fred. "He did well. I haven't been able to take it off for one minute, even to get it sized. It's just too pretty. I can't wait to get this silly cast off so I can wear it properly." She turned back to Amelia, brightening. "But tell me! Have you started looking for a dress?"

Shifting on her feet, Amelia cleared her throat. "Oh, um... Not yet, but my sister just got married, and she brought me along to all her appointments."

"And?" Nadia was obviously in her element, loving any and all mention of weddings.

"You know," Amelia said thoughtfully, "I loved the dresses with a sleek silhouette. They didn't work for Maggie, obviously, because she was getting married in May and she's much more dramatic than I am. But I love that Old Hollywood vibe."

Leo's brows jumped. He tried to picture Amelia in a dress

like that and had to wipe the drool from his face as a result. Her future husband was a lucky man.

"Oh, *perfect!*" Nadia squealed, clasping her hands. "It matches the ring! Vintage!"

"Much easier for us," Fred said as an aside, clapping Leo on the back. "We just show up and get married."

"Oh, Leo is taking a *very* active role in the planning stages," Amelia cut in, a wicked little glint in her eyes. "He'll be able to tell you all about every little detail. He'll talk your ear off about it. He has a color-coded spreadsheet and everything."

"Really?" Nadia swung toward him, and Leo had to force himself not to take a step back from the force of her interest. "I would love to see it! You *must* send it to me." She pointed to Leo's pocket. "Do you have it on your phone? Show me!"

Now he did take a step back. Clearing his throat, Leo shook his head. "I, uh, don't have it on me."

"You'll send it to me," Nadia proclaimed, smiling. She was obviously a woman who got what she wanted.

In his peripheral vision, Amelia grinned. Leo wanted to tackle her to the floor. She'd pay for that.

"Leo has always had a keen eye for detail," Fred cut in smoothly, just as Nadia looked like she was ready to start a full-fledged wedding inquisition. "He's highly requested by our clients," Fred told Amelia. "He's got real skill at understanding a client's vision, even when they're not exactly sure what they want themselves."

Surprised at the compliment, Leo straightened. Amelia peered at him from beneath her lashes, then smiled at Fred. "That doesn't surprise me at all. He's very perceptive."

Glancing at her, Leo tried to read her expression. It looked sincere. But that would mean she believed the praise Fred had given him, which was unusual. Most people thought he just partied for a living.

"I have to make the rounds," Fred said. "Here! Have a drink."

A waiter glided to a stop in front of them, bearing a tray with a selection of beverages. Fred and Nadia excused themselves and moved on to the next guest to greet, and Amelia and Leo turned to the waiter. Leo chose a glass of champagne, while Amelia was intrigued by the green juice the waiter pointed out. "Kiwi, ginseng, and apple," the man told her. "Energizing and delicious."

She tasted it, humming in appreciation. Leo couldn't help but watch her enjoy her sip. He craved that moment of bliss, wanting to witness it any time something touched Amelia's lips. Did she really think he was perceptive, or was she just playing the part of an adoring fiancée?

"So," a deep voice cut through his thoughts, "this is the famous fiancée."

Leo put his hand on Amelia's lower back and turned to look at the owner of the voice, already having recognized his bitter professional rival, Ari Ashfield. The man was six foot two, lithely muscled, and loved to snipe jobs out from under Leo's nose. He wore a fitted black shirt and pants, his dark eyes just as sharp as his tailoring.

"Ari," Leo responded coolly. "This is Amelia."

"The singer."

Amelia froze for a beat, then flashed a bright smile. "That's right."

They shook hands. His grip was firm.

"Give us a tune, then." Ari's eyes narrowed in challenge. "We've heard so much about your talent."

"Oh, I'm resting my voice." She lifted the green juice with one hand and touched her throat with the other.

A grunt, and Ari swung his gaze back to Leo. "Nice to see you finally performed well enough to get an invite to this thing. It was starting to get boring around here without you. I've done this so many years now, you know. It's good to have some fresh meat at the retreat."

Leo bared his teeth. Ari never let him forget that he'd been here longer, knew more people, and threw the best events—but they both knew the truth. It was because Ari liked to play dirty. He wasn't afraid to undercut his own coworkers to get hired for a job.

"Ari, darling, don't be such a prig." Vanessa Neale came floating toward them, statuesque and beautiful. Her dress was skin-tight and neon pink. She looked like a Barbie, except for the calculating gleam in her eyes. Her sharp-eyed gaze landed on Leo, then shifted to Amelia. Full, pink lips curled into a predatory smile. "I'm Vanessa. Leo and I go *way back*. We're *so close*, and I kept telling him to bring you around. *Finally*, you're here." Her gaze slid to Leo. "Took you long enough, silly."

There was a thick slathering of innuendo in her words, and Leo bristled. They'd never slept together, but Vanessa had made it clear she wanted to. If Leo had met her a few years ago, he wouldn't have hesitated. But this job was important to him. He wouldn't ruin it by sleeping with a coworker.

Plus, the thought of sleeping with Vanessa didn't appeal to him. She was beautiful, but... He couldn't put his finger on why he felt no attraction to her. Maybe he was just bored of the whole game. Flirting, innuendo, casual sex...it seemed so meaningless all of a sudden.

Amelia smiled at the other woman, something sharp in her eyes. "That's funny. Leo never mentioned you at all." Then she turned to Leo, lifted her hand, and stroked his cheek, letting her fingers drift up to push a strand of hair off his forehead. It was blatantly possessive, and Leo's knees nearly went weak. His eyes bored into Amelia, hands itching to grip her hips and drag her from the room so they could find some privacy.

He'd kill for her to do that again, for her to stake her claim over him in front of everyone. Between one blink and the next, he was hard as rock behind the zipper of his pants. She wanted him, and she couldn't hide it. She was as desperate for—

Stop, you idiot. It's not real. She's faking it. It's all an act.

Reeling himself back in, he curled an arm around Amelia's shoulders. "Vanessa runs the California office," he explained, voice only slightly raspy. He glanced at the two others. "Where are your dates?"

"Mark wanted to go check out the pool," Vanessa said with a wave of her hand. "He'll be around for dinner." Her eyes landed on Ari, and they shared a strange look. "And Ari came alone this year."

"There he is!" An older man came barreling into their little quad, clapping Leo on the shoulder. "St. James and the mystery woman!"

Leo huffed. "Amelia, this is Robert Lafontaine. He's our fixer. Anything goes wrong, Rob is there to make it right, as long as you don't ask too many questions about how."

Robert grinned, then leaned over and kissed Amelia on both cheeks, pulling back to look her in the eyes. "Glad Leo found someone who understands him," the man said. "I've been telling him to get his shit together for years."

"Oh, Robbie," his wife said, coming to join him with a glass of champagne dangling between her fingers. Trudy wore a gauzy, embroidered kaftan, her highlighted brown hair pinned back at her temples. "Stop bothering the lovebirds. Amelia, darling, Leo has told us all about you. You're a musician, yes? Kitty Cat, is that right?"

"Um." Amelia cleared her throat. "Kitty Catelli," she managed to say while maintaining a straight face. Leo wanted to kiss her.

More people flocked to meet Leo's fiancée, and Amelia began to look a little green. He'd underestimated the amount of curiosity his stories had generated. Their rep for Australia, Sean Walters, dragged his girlfriend over and the two of them had demanded to know if she could sing better than Mariah Carey. Then there were the two brothers who ran shipping and logistics, George and Gregory. They peppered Amelia with a dozen more questions about her band, pulling out their phones to try to look her up online.

She deflected and demurred, obviously uncomfortable with

outright lying. Leo kept his winces internal, regretting dragging her into this whole thing.

Finally, Cora Hale hobbled over, shooing all the others away. The payroll administrator was as fierce as she was short, her gray hair permed and set into tight curls. She wore a yellow pantsuit, a matching yellow purse slung over her arm. "Leave the poor girl alone," she said, swatting at the vultures pecking for bits of juicy meat. She used her purse like a cudgel. "Go. Shoo!"

Amelia gave the older woman a grateful smile when most of the crowd had dispersed. "Thank you."

"Of course, honey," Cora said. She grabbed Amelia's hand in both of hers, shaking and patting it, a smile tugging at her lips. "They're like dogs," she explained. "You just need a firm voice to tell them to buzz off."

Amelia laughed, and the older woman finally let her hand go. "What do you do at Goodhew?"

"Cora makes sure everyone gets paid on time," Leo said, smiling at the older woman. "The company would fall apart without her."

"You can say that again." Cora hiked her purse up and gave him a curt nod.

Leo slid his arm around Amelia's shoulders. Amelia leaned into him slightly, and some pinched feeling in his chest eased. "She's a genius with spreadsheets."

Amelia brightened. "I love spreadsheets!"

Cora laughed, but her eyes sharpened for a moment. "Interesting," she mused, patting Amelia's arm before shifting her gaze to Leo. "Found yourself a good one. Hang on to her."

"I plan to," Leo said, and it felt like a vow.

AMELIA'S HEAD SPUN. Thirty-odd people milled around the room, and she only remembered a handful of names. Grateful that Leo had stuck by her side, she sipped her third green juice—which was surprisingly delicious—and kept a placid smile on her lips.

These people just had to believe she and Leo were engaged. They didn't have to like her or think well of her. She just had to stand here and make their fake relationship believable.

It was easier than she wanted to admit. Every time Leo touched her, her body bent toward him like a sunflower following the light.

A clinking sound drew her attention to the far corner of the room, where Fred stood on top of a little raised pedestal. Nadia, his fiancée, was beside him, their arms wrapped around each other's waists. She looked up at her future husband with nothing but devotion in her eyes, and Amelia, uncharitably, felt another pang of jealousy.

It wasn't like her to feel this way. She was a keep-you-eyes-on-your-own-paper kind of person. But maybe the embers of lust that still warmed her blood after the kiss last night were muddling her brain. She couldn't help but be jealous of all the loving couples in the room, especially when it made it all the more obvious how fake things were between her and Leo.

"Welcome," Fred finally said, his voice carrying easily across the room. "Nadia and I are so grateful to welcome you to our home. Stirling was the town of my birth, and this property means everything to me. To welcome my most trusted employees into my home is an annual tradition that I hope to carry on for years to come. We have a few things to celebrate this year." He went on to describe the successes of the business, including truly staggering revenue and profit numbers, as well as some funny anecdotes about celebrity parties throughout the year. "This week is about celebrating your achievements. It's my thanks for another great year. To many more." He lifted his glass, and the assembled crowd did the same, repeating his toast.

Leo stood next to her, the warmth of his body radiating through her arm. A thrill shot through her middle when his hand slipped across her lower back, and she bit her lip to contain it. His touch was a drug.

The kiss had been wonderful, but she had to remind herself that this was all an act. An exchange of services. He was just teaching her how to get a boyfriend, not volunteering for the position. And she was pretending to be his betrothed. It wasn't the start of their love story. Far from it.

"There's another thing I want to celebrate," Fred continued, "and that is love." He lifted an arm and gestured to Amelia and Leo.

All eyes turned toward them, and Amelia froze.

"Our very own Leo St. James has finally brought his fiancée into the fold."

Polite applause filled the room, and Leo turned toward her. His hand slid from her lower back to her hip, warm and sure as he held her body. His eyes were serious as he stared into hers, gaze flicking down to her lips. Then, before she could react, he brushed his lips against hers and pulled away as the applause redoubled in volume.

Fred laughed from his dais, lifting his glass in acknowledgment. Leo tugged Amelia close to his chest, nuzzling his lips into her hair.

Amelia was being torn in two. Half of her loved the touch. Loved the kiss. Wanted so desperately for him to do it again...

And the other half reminded her that none of it was real. She wanted to kill Leo for putting her in this position.

The second half won. She elbowed Leo's gut, and he grunted, wincing, but caught her arm before she could do it again. "That wasn't very nice," he rumbled, and desire shot through Amelia's veins. His voice was an aphrodisiac. She was out of control. Her body was a runaway train.

"Neither was the ambush kiss," she whispered.

"Hardly a kiss," he murmured back, lips brushing her ear. "Unless you've forgotten what we did last night?"

Now he was mocking her again. "What if I have? It's not like it was memorable."

A low chuckle. He knew she was lying. "You're my fiancée, Amelia," he grated, his hand still wrapped around her arm, his breath coasting over her ear.

Amelia's lust didn't abate. She sucked in a deep breath and forced herself to smile, then leaned against her supposed fiancé, hoping the conflict raging inside her didn't show on her face. Her poker face was terrible, but thankfully everyone had turned back to the man on the dais.

"And on that note, I'd like to announce my own engagement. Nadia, baby—"

A scream tore out of Nadia's lips. Horror flashed across her features as she looked down at her right hand, slowly lifting it until it was at eye level. She trembled, frantic. After a long, confused moment when everyone frowned and watched her, Nadia dropped the arm and bent over, looking all around her. With a cry, she fell to her knees and ripped a nearby tablecloth off a table, sending glasses crashing to the ground.

"Nadia! What—" Fred tried to haul her back up, shouting at a nearby staff member to clean up the mess and get a doctor. Glass was everywhere. The smell of champagne filled the air. Murmurs surged through the room as guests tried to figure out what was going on.

Ari, nearest to the dais, backed away and slinked through the crowd toward the door. Vanessa frowned at Nadia, then met Ari's gaze. Ari tilted his head to the door, then slipped through. The two brothers—what were their names? They started with G, Amelia thought—pushed their way to the front of the crowd and called at everyone to watch the broken glass.

"What's going on?" Amelia asked quietly as Leo curled his arm around her waist to hold her close.

"I'm not sure," Leo answered as he set down his glass of champagne and clamped his other hand on her waist, shifting her away from the confused crowd.

Then, with a wail, Nadia's head lifted. "My ring!" she cried. "My ring is gone!"

TEN

A SHORT, chaotic half hour later, Amelia closed the door to their suite of rooms. The guest wing of the house had three floors, and their suite was on the top floor. Windows lined two walls, giving a view of the forest to the side of the house and the vast green lawn and pool behind.

The suite was beautiful. Decorated in dark green, cream, and rich warm wood, it was as calming as it was luxurious. They stood in a small living room that boasted two armchairs, a three-seater couch, and a fireplace with a big mirror on the mantel. There was a small desk beneath a wide window where Amelia would be able to do some work, and a little round table sat next to a coffee machine and breakfast bar.

Through two pocket doors, she spied the king-sized bed.

And her brain short-circuited.

Sleeping arrangements. There was only one bed. Of course there was. They were supposed to be engaged! How had she not considered this? She blinked, staring at the stacks of pillows and luxe bedding, and her mind spun out in a squeal of burned rubber and shredded tires. Her suitcase was placed next to Leo's, like they belonged together at the foot of the bed.

"I'll sleep on the couch," Leo said, clearly not suffering the same crash-and-burn thought process as Amelia, then slumped down into the piece of furniture he'd named. He scrubbed his face, and when he pulled his hands away, he looked worn out.

Tentatively, Amelia dropped into one of the armchairs. It was upholstered in soft brown leather, and the cushions sank down just the right amount as she leaned back. "What time do we have to be at dinner again?"

Leo checked his watch. "We have an hour and a half."

"You think they'll find her ring?"

"I hope so. It's worth twelve million dollars."

A strange, strangled noise fell from Amelia's lips. "Twelve —" She sucked in a breath. "Excuse me? Did you say twelve million dollars?"

Leo snorted, slumping on the couch. He kicked his foot up onto the coffee table and pushed his hair off his forehead, looking disheveled, undone, and delicious.

Amelia tore her gaze away. She had to get a grip on herself. Casting for something else to talk about, she asked, "What's the dress code for dinner?"

"Cocktail," Leo answered. He turned to glance at her, his face uncharacteristically serious. "Thanks for doing this, Amelia."

She shrugged. "You're helping me out too."

His gaze remained on her, so Amelia stood and wandered to

the window to try to get away from it. She opened the window, leaning against the frame to take a breath of cool evening air. It smelled sweet and fresh, and it tempered some of the heat rising from her skin. A stone wall jutted out to the left of the window where the building sprawled, but the rest of the view was unin-terrupted forest.

"What's the next topic in your spreadsheet?" Leo asked behind her.

Amelia hummed noncommittally as his question reminded her of their kiss. She'd have to be careful; last night had shaken her. It would be so easy to confuse Leo's advice for something more. She couldn't get attached to him when he so clearly was not attached to her. "I'd like to go over general advice for a first date. I don't know how to act when I'm out with a guy."

"You just have to be yourself, Amelia."

She turned to glare at him. "That hasn't worked so far."

"What if it's the truth?"

"If that were the truth, I would have been asked on a second date at some point over the past six years. Being myself isn't working."

"I don't know about that," Leo mumbled so low that Amelia thought she misheard him.

She arched a brow. "What?"

"Nothing. What usually happens when you go on a first date? Why do you think you never get a second one?" He stalked toward her, leaning on the other side of the window frame. Late-evening light carved his features and pulled out the green in his eyes.

Amelia blinked and looked out the window. He was too

handsome for his own good—or Amelia's. "There's no 'usually' about it. I haven't been on a date in over a year," she admitted. "When I started my business, I stopped dating. I was too busy, and I was sick of feeling unattractive."

"Okay," Leo said, voice neutral. "Tell me about the last date you went on."

Pinching her lips, Amelia let out an unladylike grunt. She didn't like talking about this stuff, but wasn't Leo the exact person who could help her? "The last date I went on was a guy I met on an app. When we exchanged messages, he said all the right things. Told me he liked ambitious women, said intelligence was a turn-on. Complimented my pictures, made decent jokes. We met up at a bar and it was all going great until he asked me what I did for work. I told him I'd just quit my job to start my own business, so I was really busy trying to get that off the ground. I probably rambled on for too long, but it was exciting. I'd just landed my first client, and I remember telling my date about that. It was like a switch flipped in him. Whatever it was I said was a complete turn-off. We'd ordered appetizers to have with our drinks, and he left before they even came out of the kitchen."

Leo shifted, leaning his forearm on the window frame to look out at the greenery beyond. A frown tugged his brows.

"Look," Amelia continued when he said nothing, "I'm not crippled by insecurity. I like my body. I like my brains. I think I'm a good person. But I just... I don't know! It's like guys don't see me and think, *I want to have sex with her*. There's no attraction." She stumbled on her words when Leo gave her a strange look, then soldiered on. "And the last few times I've made it to the kissing or heavy petting stages with a guy, I always end up overthinking it and messing up. I don't need you to tell me I'm pretty or pump me up with empty compliments. I need you to show me how to be attractive in a way that guys respond to. I need *help*."

A snort sounded, and Leo shook his head. "I'm not going to tell you to dumb yourself down just to attract some idiot who can't recognize your worth."

"Well, what am I supposed to do? If Ben texts me and asks me out—"

"When," Leo corrected.

Amelia rolled her eyes. "Fine. *When* he asks me out, how do I show him that I'm interested? How do I make sure he doesn't just ghost me because he doesn't feel a spark?"

Leo's jaw tightened. His hand curled into a fist for a beat, then he pushed himself off the window and turned to face her. He seemed to come to a decision and gave her a deep nod. "Okay. Let's do a little role play. I'm Ben the Barista."

"You can just call him Ben, you know."

"So, I'm Ben the Barista, and you're you. We've met up for a drink, and I'm telling you about my stupid job making coffee."

"Leo," she chided, the corners of her lips curling. "Be nice."

"Blah, blah, blah...something about latte art. I'm great even though I didn't have the balls to ask you for your phone number, and I probably spent three days stalking your photos online before sending you a one-word message." He waited expectantly, then rolled his wrist at Amelia. "Now, go. Your turn. What do you say to that?"

Amelia looked at him like he was insane. "What? You haven't even said anything for me to respond to."

"Wrong," Leo replied, lifting his index finger. "All you need to do is find an excuse to touch me—my arm, my hand, whatever —smile, and ask questions. Guys love talking about themselves. Ask me a question about coffee beans or grind size or whatever."

Amelia tilted her head. A cool breeze floated through the open window, ruffling the ends of her hair. Leo had shifted closer at some point, so she could smell the fresh scent of his soap. He obviously had a bone to pick with Ben, but she might as well play along. In a flat voice, she asked, "How do you know what grind size to use for the coffees you make?"

"Well, that depends on the freshness of the coffee bean and what you're using it for. Pour-over coffees need a slightly coarser grind, and—"

"Wait. How do you know this stuff?"

Leo clicked his tongue. "That was the perfect opportunity for you to pretend to be fascinated by every word coming out of my mouth, Amelia."

"Flirting is insane."

He huffed, tilting his head from side to side. "True."

"It seems really fake."

"Sometimes it is."

She bit her lip. "I'm not sure I like that."

He reached over and gently touched her forearm. "What about you? Tell me about your business."

A little buzz of warmth emanated from the place where he'd touched her skin. Her heart beat a tiny bit faster. What had he asked her, again? Oh. Right. "Well, a couple of years ago, I was working as a data analyst for a health insurance company, and I felt really restricted by some of their policies. I thought I could do a better job for my clients if I struck out on my own, so I…" Her eyes widened. She looked down at her arm, then up at Leo. He was grinning. "What the heck!"

Laughing, Leo flicked his fingers toward himself. "Your turn. Hit me."

"What, just touch you and ask you a question?"

"Sure."

He wore a navy button-down shirt tucked into dark-gray fitted pants. The top few buttons of his shirt were undone, and his collar was slightly crooked. With fingers that only trembled the slightest bit, she reached up and adjusted his collar. With a start, she realized she'd done the exact same thing the first time they'd met. She gulped and asked, "How many brothers and sisters do you have?"

"Just the one brother," he answered, body leaning toward hers as she pulled her hand away. "Marlon's two years older than me."

"Are you close?" She looked up and met his eyes.

Leo shrugged, eyes darkening. "Close enough. You?"

"Just Maggie." Her voice came out breathy, and Leo shifted closer still. The moment hung between them, and words fled from Amelia's mind. What was she supposed to be doing? Asking…questions… What questions?

All she could see was the fading sun warming Leo's skin and his green eyes burning as they met hers. He made a quiet, rough noise in his throat and slipped his hand onto her waist to tug her closer. His head angled and dipped, and Amelia knew they were going to kiss again.

She parted her lips as her pulse pounded through her body, drawing her awareness to all the places she wanted Leo to touch. Arm tightened on her waist, he brought his free hand up to cup her jaw. His hand was so big his fingers spread over the side of her neck and jaw, thumb coasting over her lips as he tilted her head up.

When Leo spoke, she felt his breath on her lips. His voice was a low, erotic rumble. "You are the most—"

"It was on my finger!" The hissed exclamation reached them through the window.

Amelia froze. Leo didn't let her go, but he turned his head toward the noise.

Fred's voice, tight with tension, came next. "Baby, are you sure you didn't take it off? Maybe in the bathroom?"

"I was next to you the whole time, Fred," came the whispered reply. "I didn't leave your side. I had it when we greeted Leo's fiancée, remember?"

Fred hummed. A dog yipped.

"No, Butter. We aren't going out in search for the perfect place to pee. You have to make do with this corner." Nadia sounded stressed, even when she tried to gentle her voice for her dog.

Amelia frowned, wondering why they could hear the couple so clearly. She angled her upper body closer to the window and saw Fred and Nadia leaning against the building, notched in a corner formed by the guest wing wall and the rest of the building. The dog was marking his territory against the stone wall.

It must have been an acoustic quirk that allowed Amelia and Leo to eavesdrop.

"The ring didn't slip off?" Fred sounded tense.

"We searched that room top to bottom, Fred. Someone took it," Nadia answered. "They took it right off my finger."

Meeting Leo's gaze with her own wide-eyed stare, Amelia put a hand against her mouth.

"I don't..." Fred cut himself off with a grunt. "I believe you, baby, but I just don't see how..."

"There's no other explanation. You know it was loose, and I didn't want to have it resized until my fingers healed. We scoured the room. If it had fallen off, we would've found it. I was in that room the whole time. My ring was *stolen*, Fred."

After a short pause, Amelia heard Fred huff. "We'll see how everyone acts at dinner. I'll have the staff keep an eye on the guests, and I'll make sure all movements in and out of the property are tracked. If someone came to my house to steal from me, I will find out." Rage filled his voice. "And if *any* of my employees are lying to me—for any reason—they'll live to regret it."

The sound of a quick kiss reached the third floor, and then the couple was gone. Amelia poked her head out the window to make sure, then quickly closed it and whirled to face Leo.

He was grim, and he only said one word: "Shit."

. . .

AMELIA FOLLOWED Leo out of the guest wing and down the grand staircase near the house's front door. They were directed past the Blue Room hallway and into an elegant dining room. A long table stretched in the middle of the room, surrounded by ornate chairs. About half the guests were already seated. Amelia took a seat next to Cora, and Leo settled on her other side.

"Good evening," Cora said with a kind smile.

"Hi." Amelia's own lips curled in response. She couldn't help it; she liked Cora. The woman radiated grandmotherly energy, and after everything that had happened earlier, it was nice to be seated between two people who didn't put her on edge.

"Beautiful place settings, don't you think?" Cora said, admiring her fork. The silverware was real silver, polished to a high shine. Cora tilted the fork this way and that to let the light bounce off of it.

"The whole house is incredible," Amelia replied. She shifted her gaze to Fred, who was seated at the head of the table. "You have a beautiful home," she told him.

He nodded in acknowledgment of her compliment, but Amelia could tell the jovial persona was gone. In its place was a cold, perceptive man who surveyed his employees and guests with eyes that missed nothing. His all too perceptive gaze shifted to one of the waiters milling around, who approached to fill Leo and Amelia's glasses with ruby-red wine.

When the waiter stepped back, Fred leaned against the back of his chair. "Leo never told me how the two of you met."

His question was a blatant lie, and Amelia knew it. Leo told her everything he'd said to his boss, and it included their imaginary first meeting. Nerves seized Amelia from head to toe, but she fought to keep her body relaxed. Turning to Leo, she forced her lips into a calm smile. "It was in an airplane," she said, remembering the story Leo had shared with her on Tuesday night. "I was on the last leg of a tour, and he was on the way home from an event. We argued over the overhead compartment."

"Amelia had taken more than her fair share of space," Leo added.

"That is *not true*, and you know it," Amelia exclaimed, affronted on behalf of Fake Amelia in The Airplane That Didn't Exist.

Leo just laughed.

Fred made a noncommittal noise, and Amelia took the opportunity to down a big gulp of wine. She glanced at Leo, whose eyes had grown serious, though his body was relaxed.

"We're here!" A gigantic man spread his arms as he entered the room. "The party can start!"

"Mark," Vanessa chided. "Not that kind of party."

"Not yet," Mark replied, winking.

Ari snorted, stepping into the room behind the couple. He'd changed from his matte black shirt to a shiny black version, and he looked very sleek and elegant, apart from his beady eyes.

The brothers, George and Gregory, were already seated across from Amelia and Leo, and Robert Lafontaine, the fixer, was diagonally across from Amelia, on Fred's left.

Ari took the empty seat on Fred's right, and Vanessa and her beau settled beside Leo.

Someone in this room had taken Nadia's twelve-million-dollar ring. Amelia scanned the faces, their expressions ranging from bored to shrewd to cheery, and she had no idea who the culprit could be.

"This color really brings out your eyes," Vanessa said to Leo, touching the fabric of his forest-green shirt. In light of their latest lesson on flirting, Amelia side-eyed the touch and the compliment. The other woman was laying it on pretty thick, especially considering her date was sitting just the other side of her, and Leo's supposed fiancée was on just the other side of him. That made her a person of questionable morals—but it didn't make her a thief.

Ari leaned toward Fred. "How's Nadia doing? Did she find her ring?"

Amelia tried not to make it obvious she was listening. Was Ari ingratiating himself with Fred to avoid suspicion because he'd stolen the ring, or was he just being polite?

"Nadia is taking the evening off," Fred said, not answering the question about the ring. So he was keeping his cards close to his chest.

"Big rock," Cora noted, eyes on her glass of wine.

Fred just grunted.

Amelia glanced down the table and found Robert Lafontaine watching her. The older man lifted his glass toward her, then bent his head toward his wife, seated to his left, to murmur quiet words to her. He was Goodhew's fixer. What did that mean, exactly? Did he do anything illegal for the company? Could he be tempted by twelve million dollars' worth of vivid pink diamond?

Mark guffawed a couple of seats over, startling Amelia out of her thoughts. Vanessa's date called a waiter over to refill his wine, clearly comfortable making the most of the free booze. Amelia, on the other hand, couldn't relax. Paranoia rose in her with every interaction and every glance. This stupid retreat was terrible for her health. She made it through the four-course dinner, chatting and laughing, pretending that everything was okay. Every time Fred's eyes landed on her, she tried not to freeze up. He watched everyone at the table as the meal progressed, and Amelia knew he was sniffing out lies.

She just hoped he wouldn't sniff out hers and Leo's. If suspicion fell on the two of them because of their false engagement, would it snowball into accusations of theft?

Best not to find out.

"So, Amelia," Vanessa said, scooping a tiny bit of semifreddo onto her spoon. "Tell me about your band." She stuck the spoon into her mouth in a sensual, slow movement. Everything the woman did was sensual. Her clothing was fitted but not too tight, with just enough cleavage to be enticing but not vulgar.

It was impressive.

If she wasn't hanging onto Leo's arm and using every excuse to brush her breasts against him, Amelia thought she might be better off asking Vanessa for flirting advice instead of Leo.

Instead, she smiled. "We're The Nymphomaniacs," she said, and she was able to keep a straight face because she'd practiced in the mirror for an hour yesterday. "We play soft pop-rock-punk." That was the description Leo had given everyone, which was as nonsensical as it was ridiculous.

The man seriously needed to come up with better cover

stories in the future. She could have been talking about airplane service and safety measures right now if he'd just told them he was engaged to a flight attendant like a normal person.

"How fascinating," Vanessa said. "And you're able to support yourself with your music?"

Odd question. Amelia took a second to study the other woman. She'd spoken loudly enough that Fred's attention swung to them. Was Vanessa purposefully planting seeds in her boss's mind? Had she stolen the ring and was now deflecting suspicion?

"Amelia's band is really successful," Leo said, stretching his arm behind her chair. "They just got signed to a major record label."

What. The. Heck.

Leo's announcement was met with an avalanche of congratulations and follow-up questions, which meant Amelia needed to lie on the fly, which also meant she wanted to take her bowl of semifreddo and smash it over Leo's perfect, expensive haircut.

By the time dinner was over, Amelia was dead on her feet. When the door closed on their suite, she was no closer to figuring out who'd taken Nadia's ring, having eliminated no one and convinced herself that any one of the people at the table could have taken it.

"You really dumped me in the shit with that record label announcement," she grumbled at Leo.

He was busy grabbing pillows from the bed to make up the sofa where he'd spend the night. He fluffed them against the arm of the couch before glancing at Amelia. "You did well."

"No thanks to you."

The undercurrent of tension and suspicion she'd felt through the whole dinner had worn Amelia's nerves down. She wasn't used to interacting with so many people, especially not when she was meant to keep up a façade. She was in way over her head, and she was beginning to realize that she'd gotten the raw end of the deal.

So, in short, Amelia was upset.

Her upset morphed into anger as Leo carried on making his bed, because he obviously didn't understand just how upset and worried she was. So it wasn't a total surprise that her mouth totally ran away with her, and what came out next was, "What's up with you and Vanessa? Did you sleep with her?"

Leo had been stretching a blanket over the couch. At her question, he straightened and turned, his eyes narrowing. His shirt really did bring out the color of them, which was annoying. *He* was annoying. This whole situation was annoying!

And she couldn't leave, because Fred would think she'd stolen twelve freaking million dollars from his fiancée! How could she prove her innocence? She couldn't prove the absence of the ring unless they found whoever had stolen it. She was stuck, and annoyed, and angry, and tired, and Leo was walking toward her with a strange expression on his face, which was *extra* annoying. *Ugh!*

"Amelia," he said, a smile twitching at the corners of his lips, "are you jealous?"

"What?" she screeched. "No!"

"You're totally jealous," he said, closing in on her.

She had her back against the door, and she crossed her arms to protect herself from him. "I am not."

His palms landed on the door above her head, caging her against it. "You're seething right now. So angry, and all because another woman was all over me."

"Wow. Arrogant much?"

"Look at how red your cheeks are." His eyes had gone lazy, lips curling into nearly a full smile.

"Go away," she said, but she didn't duck under his arms to get away herself. Her heart had started to thump very, very hard. How did he smell so good? It was unnatural. And very nice.

No! Not nice. Totally unnatural and annoying. Like him and his stupid flirty ways.

"I think we should revisit what we went over yesterday," Leo said, his voice dropping low. His body inched closer, so big and broad it was all Amelia could see. "I don't think you really got what I was trying to tell you."

She sipped in little breaths, scowling at him. "What are you talking about?"

"This."

He kissed her. This time, he didn't start soft. He dug his hand into her hair and crushed his lips to hers, hot and hard and *hot*. Double hot. Amelia whimpered, hands clinging to his shoulders, and Leo pressed the whole length of his body against hers to pin her to the door.

She wrapped her arms around his neck and lost herself in the kiss. All the tension of the evening drained out of her as Leo swept his tongue against hers, deepening the kiss with a low groan.

His hands dropped to her waist. She'd changed into a black slip dress for dinner, and the silky fabric bunched as his fingers curled against her. He slid one hand up to cup her breast, plumping it up. He then dropped his head to kiss her through the fabric of her slip and her thin bra, sucking the peaked tip of her breast into his mouth through her dress.

Amelia's head dropped back against the door as she let out a rough moan, her fingers digging into Leo's hair to hold him there.

Panting hard, Leo straightened. His hips pinned Amelia's to the door, and he watched her with nearly black eyes. Broad hands spanned her waist, thumbs making small circles on her stomach. He was hard; she could feel it pressed against her lower belly.

"Do you get it now?" he growled.

She did not. She didn't understand a single thing right now, including how to spell her own name. But she nodded and said, "Yeah. I see. I just need to get my tablet and make some notes."

Leo watched her for a beat, his eyes narrowing slightly. Then his shoulders dropped the tiniest amount, and he pulled away like it pained him to stop touching her. Amelia had the sneaking suspicion that she'd said the entirely wrong thing. Her stomach sank.

"We should get some sleep," he told her after a heavy, stilted pause. "I'll use the bathroom first."

ELEVEN

ON THURSDAY MORNING, Leo made sure he was up and dressed before Amelia emerged. He'd messed up the night before. The thought of her being jealous of another woman—of feeling possessive over him—had turned him on so much he'd pinned her to the wall before he could think about what he was doing.

Kissing her was an addiction—one he'd have to cure. It was clear that Amelia was keeping their arrangement exactly where she wanted it. He was her seduction coach, and nothing more.

And, really, that was all he deserved.

By the time they headed downstairs and partook in the delicious breakfast Fred's staff had on offer, it was time for the first event of the retreat.

The scavenger hunt.

"I've heard about this," Leo told Robert, who had wandered

over to stand beside him where they'd gathered in the backyard. "Annual tradition, right?"

Amelia peered curiously over from his other side as Robert nodded. "Spans the whole property. One year it went into Stirling proper as well, but we'll see about this year. You have to take pictures at every location on the list and post them on the company's social media. When the time runs out, the team with the most pictures up wins."

"A prize?" Amelia's eyes brightened.

Leo couldn't resist the urge to curl his arm around her shoulders. She was so cute when her face lit up like that. Mischievous and tempting. It was almost as good as her scowling irritation.

A whistle sounded, and all the guests gathered on the back patio overlooking the pool. A vast lawn stretched out as far as half a football field, surrounded by old forest. Garden beds lined the house, with a well-maintained flower garden to the right of the patio taking up a big chunk of the lawn space.

Percival appeared near the French doors leading inside, followed by Fred and Nadia. Two more staff members trailed, carrying trays full of envelopes.

"Welcome to the Goodhew Scavenger Hunt," Fred proclaimed, all traces of his suspicion from last night gone. Leo craned his head to try to catch a glimpse of Nadia's finger and saw she wasn't wearing her ring. It was still gone. Or maybe they'd found it and she decided not to wear it? His gaze lifted to Nadia's face; the woman's nose was red, and it looked like she'd been crying. Her dog came trotting out, and she leaned over to pick him up one-handed, nuzzling into his fur, looking for comfort.

No ring. He was sure of it.

"This morning's event is designed to show you the best of the Goodhew Estate," Fred said. "You'll work in pairs to check all the items on the list. When the siren sounds, the team who has uploaded the most pictures to their social media profile and tagged Goodhew will win the hunt's prize. You'll find a list of locations in your envelope."

Amelia vibrated beside him. So she liked prizes and had a competitive spirit. Good to know.

The envelopes were handed out. Most people were paired up with their partners, with Ari ending up with another single guy, and Cora pairing up with a young woman out of the Midwest office. When everyone was ready, Fred gave the signal to tear open the envelopes. Teams immediately started sprinting in all directions.

Breathless, Amelia laughed and hopped beside him. "Hurry! Why are you opening it so slowly?"

He finally pulled out a thick sheet of paper, on which a long list of locations and items was written.

"That vase is in the Blue Room," Amelia whispered, pointing. "And that painting is in the powder room near the foyer."

"It's as good a place to start as any," Leo said, taking her hand to lead her inside. They hurried down the hallways, nodding to passing staff members and glancing around for other teams. About two-thirds of the people had started with items on the grounds outside the house, so the mansion was mostly empty.

Down a hallway and around a corner they found the Blue Room. Ducking inside, Leo closed the door.

"There." Amelia pointed, and sure enough, a large vase, striped blue-and-white, was bursting with pink roses, just as indicated on the list.

Caught up in the moment, Leo pulled out his phone, put his arm around Amelia, and snapped a picture. He uploaded it to his Picstagram profile while Amelia crossed the item off with a swipe of her pen. Then Leo's gaze drifted to the little dais at the end of the room.

"This is where it happened," he said. "Nadia's ring went missing somewhere in here."

Amelia looked up from her paper and bit her lip. Her eyes narrowed as she scanned the space. "Do you really think someone took it?"

"Doesn't matter what I think. Fred and Nadia obviously believe it."

"How could you steal a ring right off someone's finger? It doesn't make sense."

Leo wandered over to the dais and poked around the bookcase behind it, not really thinking he'd find anything but feeling compelled to look. Then he glanced over his shoulder and said, "No one is in their room right now."

Amelia froze. "You want to go snoop?"

Leo shrugged. "The longer this goes on, the more chance there is of someone figuring us out."

Amelia's eyes darted back and forth, and she finally nodded. "Okay. Who do you think did it?"

Leo hummed. "I remember seeing Ari move toward the door when the screaming started. But I also think he's a raging asshole on a good day, so I might be biased."

"He and Vanessa exchanged a weird look," Amelia said, nodding. "Let's start there. What room is Ari in?"

"Two doors down from us. I saw him leave his room this morning."

"This is such a bad idea," Amelia said, but she was grinning. Then it faded into worry. "Fred kept looking at me weird anytime someone asked a question about my band or our history."

"He knows something's up." Leo moved toward her and put his hands on her shoulders. "I'm going to go up there, but you don't have to come if you aren't comfortable. I know this isn't what you signed up for."

Amelia rolled her shoulders and gave him a sharp nod. "I'm not letting you snoop on your own. We're in this together, Leo. Let's go."

AMELIA WAS ALMOST certain they wouldn't win the scavenger hunt prize, which was a shame, but she knew she needed to prioritize. If they could find Nadia's ring today, it would stop suspicion from falling on them. Not only was that more convenient for her, but she felt that it was important for Leo. He seemed to stand up straighter when he spoke to Fred. She hadn't seen him do that silly, flirty smile he sometimes affected when he was surrounded by his coworkers. This job was important to him. Important enough to lie about having a fiancée to try to fix his image as the guy who started a chlamydia outbreak in college. Important enough to go snooping in a coworker's room.

The way he'd kissed her last night had made her feel like there was more to Leo than met the eye. And, for better or worse, Amelia wanted to help him.

So that's how they ended up creeping back into the hallway on the third floor of the guest wing, testing the doorknob to Ari's room. Locked. A *Do Not Disturb* sign hung from his doorknob.

"He doesn't want the staff snooping around his room," Amelia noted, touching the edge of the dangling sign.

Leo's eyes narrowed. He said, "We can't jump to conclusions. Lots of people don't want staff in their rooms."

"Lots of people don't steal a twelve-million-dollar ring and then run for the exit when the loss is noticed."

"We don't know he did it. If we convince ourselves he's guilty, we might miss an important clue."

Amelia tilted her head to the side, relenting. Leo was right.

"You got a couple of bobby pins?" he asked, glancing up and down the hallway again.

She pulled two out of her hair, and a hank fell down across her face. Tucking her hair behind her ears, she kept one eye on the hallway and the other on Leo's hands. He bent the bobby pins open and knelt in front of the door.

"You know how to pick a lock?" Amelia hissed, half impressed, half horrified.

"My brother taught me," Leo said, and a second later, the latch clicked. His smile was brilliant, and it sent a little lightning bolt burning through her middle.

"We have to be fast. If we only put one picture up on Picstagram, people will get suspicious."

They entered the room and paused. It looked like a bomb

went off. A suitcase had disgorged its contents onto the armchair and floor around it. The coffee bar was a mess of sugar and creamer pots. The bed wasn't made, and the desk was covered in various papers and electronics. The bathroom was equally untidy, with a toiletry bag open, its items spread all over the vanity.

"Crap," Amelia said. "We'll never be able to put everything back the way it was if we move anything."

Leo moved to the suitcase and unzipped one of the front pockets, running his hand inside. "It could be anywhere," he said.

"We shouldn't be here."

They'd made a mistake. Snooping had sounded great in theory, but she'd let herself get carried away by the desire to help Leo and the burning curiosity about the missing ring. She hadn't liked the suspicious gleam in Fred's eyes last night. She was, at her core, an honest person. That's why she liked numbers, and that's what made this whole scheme so uncomfortable.

She could convince herself that pretending to be Leo's fiancée was reasonable, but she couldn't stand the thought of being accused of being a thief. If they could find the ring right now, it would solve a lot of problems. She went to the bathroom and looked through the bag of toiletries, unzipping every little pocket to check if a large pink diamond ring had been stashed there. Then she checked the vanity drawers, and even the toilet's tank. Nothing.

"Needle in a haystack comes to mind," she said when she reentered the main space.

Leo was at the bed, lifting one corner of it to check under the mattress. "Yeah. Let's get out of here and post another picture. It's taking too long."

Amelia nodded and headed for the door. She turned to wait for Leo, who frowned on his way past the desk. He pushed aside the laptop and grabbed a stack of crinkled papers.

"What is it?" Amelia asked, heart thumping. They needed to get out of there.

"Names, contact details, and dollar amounts."

"Well, put it back. We need to leave."

Leo shook his head. "This is weird."

Amelia wanted to scream. "Leo, we need to go."

Nodding, Leo folded the papers and stuffed them in his back pocket. He followed her out of the room, his hand on her lower back. But before they had time to disappear, they heard voices down the hall. One male, one female.

"Shit!" Amelia hissed, eyes wide. She glanced down the hall, then at Leo, who was fumbling with the lock on the door-knob. "Shit, shit, shit!"

There was no time to hide. No time to do anything. She hauled Leo to his feet, slammed Ari's door, and ran for their room. If they could just unlock it and slip inside—

"You are such an idiot, Ari," Vanessa's voice spat, coming around the corner. "I'm not getting involved with this. I like my job, and I'm not messing it up for you." Her heels clacked on the wooden floors, and Amelia knew they were caught. They had mere seconds.

Ari's voice was a low rumble, and she could barely make out

the words. "There's no risk, Vanessa. I've got the clients all lined up already."

What?

The tip of his glossy black shoe appeared from around the corner. Amelia shoved Leo against the wall next to their door, wrapped an arm around his neck, and pulled him down for a kiss. He froze in shock for a long, long moment, and Amelia wanted to scream at him to put his arms around her. She couldn't scream, because her mouth was otherwise occupied, so she thought very hard in his direction.

At the very last second, when two bodies appeared in her peripheral vision, Leo wrapped his arms around Amelia, slid them down to her bum, and hauled her up against his chest. Then he spun around and slammed her against the wall, shoving his groin into the cradle of her hips.

At the contact of his body against hers, the noise that came out of her was totally unplanned, and she didn't know if it was due to the physical impact or the sheer eroticism of Leo's movements. Having no other choice, she wrapped her arms and legs around Leo's body, which brought her crotch into direct contact with his. She wore a fluttery, calf-length skirt that trapped her legs tight to his body, and also meant that the only thing between Leo's jeans and Amelia's core was the thin scrap of her underwear.

Apparently, thinking very hard at someone worked really, really well.

A wolf whistle split the air. Leo tore his lips away from hers, breathing heavily, and shot a glare down the hall. Slightly dazed, Amelia blinked and followed his gaze.

Ari and Vanessa were at the mouth of the hallway, watching them.

"Couldn't even make it to the room, huh," Ari called out, a grin painted on his lips. "Didn't take you for an exhibitionist, St. James."

Vanessa's expression was pinched. She said nothing.

"Do you mind?" Leo asked, like he had every right to be making out with Amelia in the hallway, in the open, where anyone could (and did) walk by.

Ari laughed, but there was something odd about his expression. It seemed a bit forced. "Come on, Neale," he said to Vanessa. "Let's leave the lovebirds to it."

They turned away and headed back the way they came. Leo let Amelia slide down the wall until she was on her feet before creeping to Ari's room to re-lock the door. He opened it, turned the lock on the knob, then closed it again, eyes on the far end of the hallway. Then he met Amelia's gaze and tilted his head to indicate they should leave.

On shaking legs, Amelia joined him. Somewhere along the way, she'd gotten incredibly turned on. That hadn't been part of the plan.

"Are you okay?" Leo said in a low voice that made Amelia's nipples tingle.

She nodded vigorously. "Uh-huh."

"Did I hurt you?"

"No," she said. It wasn't pain she had felt when he'd pinned her against the wall. It was something else entirely.

He seemed to relax then. "Good."

There was a pause. All the stress and adrenaline of the last hour crashed into them as they stared into each other's eyes until Amelia's lips began to twitch. She covered them with a hand, but it wasn't enough. A little giggle slipped through, and when she lifted her gaze to his, she caught Leo's shoulder's shaking.

Then, like a dam breaking, they burst out laughing, stumbling to their own room. Leo opened the door, and they crashed inside, leaning on walls and furniture as they cackled.

"Worst sleuths ever," Amelia said, wiping her eyes. "What did you even take?"

Leo pulled the papers out of his pocket and took a look. "A list of clients. I don't recognize any names."

"So, basically, we're no closer to finding the ring or even knowing if it's actually been stolen."

Leo met her gaze, a wry grin teasing his lips. "Yep." He stuffed the papers under a couch cushion and spun around to look at Amelia. "We'll look at those later. We need to start participating in the scavenger hunt or people will ask questions."

Taking her hand, Leo led her back down the stairs and into the foyer. They took a picture in front of the correct painting in the powder room, and Amelia hoped she didn't look as dazed as she felt.

They took two more pictures inside and moved outside, the cool air a balm on Amelia's skin. She took a deep breath, and finally, her brain came back online. "What do you think they were doing up there? It sounded like they were arguing about something. Ari said something about clients being lined up?"

Leo was still holding her hand. She wondered if he liked

doing it, but she wasn't going to ask in case he stopped. Glancing down at her, Leo shrugged. "Not sure."

"Vanessa called Ari an idiot. You think he took the ring, and she was calling him an idiot for doing it? And the clients were buyers?"

"Maybe," Leo said, following another team into the trees. They found a treehouse, took a picture, and crossed it off the list, painting bright smiles on their faces when they came upon the other team there.

"Heard you two took a detour," the middle-aged woman said, eyes glimmering. Amelia's cheeks smarted, which made the couple laugh. "I remember when we got engaged," the other woman said, glancing at her husband. "He was insatiable."

"It wasn't all me, darling," the man replied, and the couple took off toward the next item on their list.

When they were out of earshot, Leo met Amelia's gaze. "At least our cover story is still working."

A little too well, Amelia thought. At least on her end.

If she was going to survive all the way to Sunday, she'd have to remember that Leo didn't actually have feelings for her. I was just the deal they'd struck. Once the retreat was over—and they made sure their names were never sullied by accusations of theft—they'd go their separate ways.

TWELVE

THE PRIZE WAS AN ALL-EXPENSES paid trip to Vienna. When Amelia heard that, she regretted her brief (failed) foray as an amateur detective, even if it had ended with her in a position she'd remember for the rest of her life. She gaped at Fred as he shook Robert Lafontaine's hand, then whirled to face Leo. "I thought the prize was going to be a slow cooker or a twenty-dollar gift card to Starbucks," she hissed. "The prize is a *two-week vacation?* What the hell!"

Leo winced. "Yeah. Sorry. The prizes are always pretty good."

She blew out a breath. That was an understatement.

Amelia picked up the discarded golden envelope that had held Robert's and his wife Trudy's prize. It was beautiful stationery, embossed with gold lettering.

"There'll be more games," Leo promised. "It's a whole thing with this retreat. It's why people love being invited."

"No kidding," Amelia grumbled. She gave the envelope to a passing staff member, scowling. They'd gone snooping for nothing.

The whole group was herded to lunch, where a generous buffet of sandwiches and a few hot dishes were laid out. Everyone exchanged notes about the scavenger hunt and checked out each other's pictures. As she munched on an absolutely delicious falafel wrap, Amelia realized she was enjoying herself.

Leo's arm brushed hers as he angled his phone toward Cora.

"Look at your face!" Cora laughed as she looked at the picture of Amelia under the powder room painting. "You look like you've just done the hundred-meter dash."

"Something like that," Amelia mumbled, then took another bite of her food.

Leo laughed beside her, which made Amelia scowl at him, which made Leo laugh harder. She elbowed him in the ribs.

Cora's brown eyes twinkled. "Young love," she mused. "Are you enjoying yourself, dear?"

Amelia chewed while she thought of her answer. "Yes," she finally answered. "I am."

As far as team-building went, this retreat was actually really effective. That nagging feeling of loneliness had almost totally fled, and Amelia found herself wrapped up in the easy companionship of Leo and his coworkers and their families.

She loved her friends and her family, but for the past couple of years, Amelia had felt space growing between them. Here, in the presence of relative strangers and with Leo by her side, it was like her soul let out a deep sigh, and she could relax.

There were no expectations. People didn't ask her when she'd start dating again ("Hasn't it been over six years since Josh broke up with you?"), or wince at her tales of romantic woe ("You'll find someone. You just have to keep trying!"). She wasn't some loveless freak; she was Leo's fiancée. It was accepted without question that she belonged by his side.

Amelia glanced at the man beside her, whose eyes crinkled. He winked, then slung an arm across her shoulders and pulled her closer. These were easy looks and touches, like they'd done it a thousand times.

Maybe if Amelia got out of her own way, she could have this for real. The problem was, whenever she thought about a man slinging his arm around her shoulders or squeezing her hand, she couldn't picture anyone but Leo. And that was a problem, because she barely knew the man, and also because this was all supposed to be fake.

"Don't sound so surprised," Fred chided, coming up to Amelia, Cora, and Leo. "Leo did tell you this retreat would be fun, didn't he?"

"Of course!" Amelia smiled. "It's just that—" She stopped herself right before she said, *It's just that my idea of fun is figuring out a thorny problem with various sets of data. It's just that this was all some silly deal we worked out, and I didn't expect to actually enjoy it.*

"It's just that...?" Fred prompted.

Horrified that she'd almost just outed herself as a fraud and a liar, Amelia's face went hot. "It's just that I don't associate 'company retreat' and 'team building' with fun. But that's more a reflection on me than you, Fred."

His eyes were sharp as he nodded. The older man studied her for a beat, his lips flattening ever so slightly.

He knew she was lying. A man like Fred, who'd built a huge company and steered it to success year after year after year was good at reading people. That was a given. His eyes were too shrewd.

"Amelia isn't exactly a paragon of Corporate America," Leo inserted smoothly. He grinned at her, but his eyes were a bit desperate, and Amelia thought he was trying to communicate something along the lines of, *Get it the hell together, girl.*

"No," Fred replied, still watching her, probably noting the redness sweeping across her cheeks. "I suppose touring with a band doesn't involve company retreats and scavenger hunts."

Seized with the fear that they were about to be discovered, accused, and locked up, Amelia could only manage an awkward laugh.

They needed to find that ring—and fast.

BEFORE THEY COULD GO UP to their room and study Ari's papers, Leo was disappointed to discover they had to play giant Jenga with the rest of the guests. The huge pieces were stacked on the back patio. There were ten sets, which meant the game was to be played in teams of four.

Leo and Amelia were paired with Robert and his wife. Ari, the guy he'd done the scavenger hunt with, Vanessa, and her boyfriend Mark were working on the set to their left.

While Leo set up the pieces, Amelia glanced at the other team, then schooled her features and smiled at Robert. "Are you sure you want to play? Maybe you should leave some of the prizes for the rest of us."

Robert winked. "Maybe I want a clean sweep this year."

"Have you been to Vienna before?"

"No," he admitted and glanced at his wife, "but Trudy already has our itinerary planned out."

"Schönbrunn Palace on Day One." Trudy ticked off on one of her fingers. "Then we'll hit up a couple of Mozart concerts, maybe tour some churches..."

Robert pretended to grumble, but Leo could tell he loved his wife and looked forward to the trip. Amelia smiled at the two of them, then glanced at Leo. He couldn't read her gaze.

For a brief moment—a mere handful of seconds—Leo allowed himself to imagine taking Amelia on a trip like that. He wanted to see her face brighten. He wanted to watch her lean over to read placards in museums. He wanted to slip his hand into hers and tug her toward an ice cream shop at ten in the morning, just to see the bliss take over her features when the sweet treat touched her tongue.

He wanted all that and a whole lot more.

But she didn't want him. Even though she'd kissed him today, it was only to save them from uncomfortable explanations.

A sour taste coated his tongue as the thought settled into his mind.

Reeling himself back in, Leo turned his attention to the Jenga blocks. "What's the strategy here?"

"Well, we have fifteen minutes to make the tallest possible tower. If it falls over, we're disqualified." Amelia's brows tugged together as she considered the problem. He could almost see the calculations going on behind her eyes, and he discovered that he loved this expression on her face almost as much as all the others.

Amelia nodded, like she was a human computer that had just completed a complicated computation. She glanced at Leo, Trudy, then Robert. "We should play it safe for the bottom half, only taking out the middle blocks. Then when we get closer to the top, we can start taking out edge pieces. That way we have a good balance between stability and height."

Trudy whistled. "Not only can she sing, but she can also Jenga. You'd better hold onto her, Leo."

If only. Leo smiled at Trudy, just in time to hear Fred's voice count down the start of the competition. As soon as the buzzer went off, every team started working to build their towers.

With no chance to slip away to do more snooping, Leo was stuck here. He might as well mine the company fixer for information.

"What do you think about Nadia's ring going missing?" Leo asked quietly, leaning toward Robert to make sure they couldn't be overheard.

The surprise on Robert's face looked genuine. "They haven't found it yet?"

Leo shook his head. "I heard they think someone took it."

A frown tugged the other man's brows. "Off her finger? How?"

"I don't know."

"You know if anyone here is in trouble financially?" Leo asked, even more quietly.

Robert grunted, but it was his turn to take a block out of the tower and place it on top. Then it was Leo's turn. By the time he stood next to the other man again, Robert's expression looked troubled. He glanced at the team next to them, and Leo held his breath.

"Since Vanessa broke up with her boyfriend last year, she's asked for an advance on her paycheck three times. I only know because Cora said it to me yesterday when we were discussing the MacMillan party I had to clean up."

The MacMillan party was a sweet sixteen thrown for a very wealthy family in California. A two-hundred-thousand-dollar car ended up smashed into the MacMillans' living room, and they tried to blame Goodhew. Robert had to spend two months dealing with the fallout. Vanessa had been the event director for that party, and she'd forgotten to get the clients' signatures on the release forms. It was a crazy oversight; no one would forget to get the client to sign the most important piece of paper in the contract.

Leo glanced at the team next to them. Ari and Vanessa were watching Mark pull out a block of wood from their growing tower before placing it on top. They were speaking urgently to each other, and neither of them looked happy.

Amelia followed his gaze, then glanced back at Leo. She frowned.

Something was going on between Ari and Vanessa—but would he have stolen the ring to help her financial issues? What was the list of names he'd found under Ari's laptop? Buyers for the ring and other stolen goods, maybe?

By the time the Jenga game was over, Leo's mind was spinning. The four winners—George, Gregory, and a couple who worked in the company's finance department—each won a top-of-the-line smartwatch.

Amelia let out a dramatic sigh as she clapped for the winners, and Leo wanted to wrap her in his arms and kiss her stupid. Instead, he just led her up to their room when the group broke up.

"We have two hours until dinner," Amelia said as she locked the door behind them and spun around to look over their suite. "Should we check out those papers?"

Leo nodded and grabbed the stack of papers from under the couch cushion. He grabbed a couple of waters before sitting down, then shifted over to give Amelia enough space to slump down beside him. She picked up her tablet and pulled open the browser, fingers hovering over the keyboard as her eyes scanned the paper.

She googled the first name on the list, and a number of listings from various social media sites came up. "You recognize any of these people?"

Leo looked over the list, trying to ignore the heat of her arm against his. He shook his head. "No."

They scanned the list and looked up a few names, but it wasn't until the third page that Leo saw something he recognized. "Paul Walters," he said. "He's a multi-millionaire who made his money from a gaming app. He threw a huge party for his thirtieth birthday last year." Then another name jumped out

at him. "Barbara Hulme. She and her husband had an engagement party in Barbados." He flicked through the pages. "These
must be clients of Goodhew."

Amelia leaned back, hands around her tablet. She stared off
into space, frowning. "Are they all clients that Ari worked
with?"

Leo shrugged. "I'm not sure, but it's a reasonable
assumption."

"Well, there goes our theory that they're buyers for the ring.
If they're already wealthy, they probably don't need to buy
stolen goods."

"Unless they're criminals. But it's a pretty long list, and I
doubt all of our clients engage in illegal activity."

"The money must be the budget they spent on the parties
Ari planned," Amelia said, then glanced at Leo. "Don't you
think?"

"Maybe," he conceded. Sighing, he tossed the papers away.
Why would Ari have a list of old clients at the retreat? "He's
got some sort of shorthand notes in front of some of the
names."

"And some of them are crossed out," Amelia added, peeking
at the fourth page. "Is it just record-keeping? Does he just keep
track of his projects this way? If so, I'd like to introduce him to a
computer sometime."

Leo shook his head. "There are proprietary systems in the
company for that. Besides, the accounts department does the
reckoning for the final budget and all the payments. Once the
contract is signed, the event directors no longer handle the
finances directly. We only get roped in if clients are refusing to

pay and the finance department isn't getting anywhere with follow-ups."

"So you don't usually have this information?"

Leo frowned. "I'd be able to access it on the system, but I'd have to go looking."

"Why would Ari collect it like this? And why would he bring it here?"

Leo shook his head. He was at a loss. It didn't make any sense.

"Vanessa seemed angry when she showed up in the hallway with Ari. She said something like, 'I'm not getting involved with this. I'm not messing my job up for you.'" Amelia glanced at him. "Remember?"

Leo hummed. He slumped down on the sofa beside Amelia, which brought his whole side in contact with hers. She didn't shift away.

Instead, Amelia turned her head to face him. They were both leaning their heads on the back of the sofa, and the pose was oddly intimate. "What if Ari is selling the contact information for all these rich people? I bet their phone numbers aren't public knowledge."

Her white-blond hair was in delicious disarray, and her silver eyes looked darker in the dim light of their room. Leo wanted to kiss her. "Who would he sell their phone numbers to? And why? And what does that have to do with the ring?"

Amelia bunched her lips to the side, and that made Leo want to kiss them more, just to feel her mouth relax against his. She sighed. "Well...maybe he's in financial trouble. Both he and Vanessa," she amended, because they'd discussed what Leo had found out from Robert earlier. Her eyes brightened, and she put her hand on Leo's thigh. "He's scrambling to make money. Maybe he's selling this information to a competitor?"

She was so beautiful and clever and magnetic. Leo stared into her eyes and felt an uncomfortable tightness in his chest. In this moment, despite the conversation they were having, he couldn't give two shakes about a missing ring. He wanted to haul Amelia over his lap and kiss her until she made those delicious little moans again, and then he wanted to do it again a hundred times over.

"That's a good theory," he grated, trying to keep a handle on what she'd said.

"Because Vanessa would be angry that he's compromising her," Amelia said, excited. "She's already in some kind of financial trouble, and now he's risking her job, so she's mad."

"Doesn't mean they took the ring."

Amelia slumped. She bit her lip. "Right. Selling contact information isn't exactly the same as stealing a crazy-expensive piece of jewelry."

Needing to shake off the tightness in his chest and the odd heaviness of his emotions, Leo shifted his gaze to Amelia's tablet. "What's next on your spreadsheet?" He cleared his throat and forced himself to say, "We have to get you a date by the end of the week."

She looked down at her lap and swiped the tablet to unlock it. Deft fingers tapped on the screen, and Leo shifted to grab a bottle of water he'd left on the coffee table. He needed to cool himself down. Being this close to Amelia was rattling him in a way he wasn't accustomed to.

But she didn't want him, not the way he wanted her. She only wanted him for his expertise in sex and seduction, which was all he was good for in the first place. The only reason she was enjoying herself right now was because she was curious about the ring. Amelia liked problem-solving, and he'd brought her here and handed her a thorny one.

She didn't actually like *him*, and why should she? Besides his job at Goodhew, seduction was the only thing he'd really applied himself to mastering in the past decade. He wasn't good at anything else.

Cool water ran down Leo's throat as he took a long drink. Meanwhile, Amelia tip-tapped on her screen. Half his water was gone by the time she spoke again.

"Next," Amelia proclaimed, "is blowjobs."

THIRTEEN

WATER SPEWED out of Leo's mouth in a fine spray, speckling the table, their legs, and Amelia's tablet. Beside her, Leo began to cough and splutter, his body racked with violent spasms. She tossed her tablet aside and smacked his back in a panicked attempt to help.

"Are you okay?" she half-screeched, whacking his broad back once more. Jumping off the couch, she rushed to the bathroom and grabbed a towel. She tossed the towel at Leo and watched him wipe his face, then his chest, then the table, then her tablet.

Finally, Leo lifted his gaze to meet hers and growled, "What did you say?"

"I said, 'Are you okay?'"

"Before that."

"Oh," Amelia whispered, her skin suddenly hot all over. "That."

"Yes," Leo rumbled, tossing the towel at the armchair. It landed on the arm, then slid to the ground. Neither of them moved to pick it up. His eyes were dark and hot and dangerous, and Amelia couldn't move from where she stood on the other side of the coffee table.

She wrung her hands. "Well," she started, when the silence stretched too long. "You see... I don't..." She huffed. Didn't they have a deal? Wasn't this a once-in-a-lifetime opportunity to talk to an expert? This was no time to get embarrassed! They had a simple exchange, and yes, things had gotten more complicated, but a deal was a deal. She squared her shoulders. "I want to learn about blowjobs."

A small, wheezing sound escaped Leo's lips. After a beat, he forced out, "Blowjobs."

"Yes. Oral sex."

"I know what blowjobs are, Amelia."

"Right," she whispered. "Well, I'm not very good at them, and I hear from my friends that it's really not that complicated, but in the past, I've been told by partners that—"

"*Who?*"

Amelia jumped at the vehemence of the word as it exploded from Leo's mouth. She smoothed her hands over her stomach to wipe away the dampness that had started to coat her palms and took a small step back. "What?"

"Who said that to you?" Then, oddly, something shifted in Leo. He went from looking angry and intense to slowly, purposefully relaxing back into the sofa. He unclenched his hands, which had been gripping his knees, and spread his arms across the top of the couch cushions. He nodded to the seat she'd vacated a moment ago. "Sit down."

"You know, I really don't appreciate being ordered around like that," she mumbled, but somehow her feet didn't get her strong-independent-woman memo, because they were already carrying her toward the sofa. She sat down as far from Leo as she could.

He turned to face her, and although his movements were smooth and relaxed, there was an intensity to his eyes that made no sense to Amelia. "Tell me who said these things to you, Amelia."

"I don't see how that's relevant."

"It's relevant because he lied."

"And how could you possibly know that? It's not like I've ever given you a blowjob."

The intensity of his eyes faded slightly, and a dangerous grin tugged at his lips. They were entering perilous territory. Amelia had *not* thought this through. She just wanted to know what he liked, so she could replicate it on future sexual partners.

Future sexual partners—not him. Definitely not him. Some nebulous future man whose penis she couldn't quite picture right now, but she imagined she'd be enthusiastic about the idea when the time came. That was all.

But now, locked in a room with a sexy, red-blooded man, talking about blowjobs didn't seem like such a wise course of action, especially because he was asking her questions that had to do with her past sexual experiences, and that was a whole pot of boiling acid she had no desire to dunk her head into.

"Okay, so, I think we might have taken a wrong turn in this conversation," Amelia said, putting her hands up. "Let's restart."

"No."

She reared back. "No?"

Leo shook his head. "Nope. You're going to tell me what sniveling asshole told you all these lies about yourself, then we'll talk about why the hell you believed him, and we'll go from there."

She blinked. The thought of sharing her past with anyone— let alone a man as attractive and out of her league as Leo—made her want to vomit. "I don't see how that's relevant, Leo."

"It's relevant because no matter what I tell you about sex and dating, you're not going to believe any of it."

Well, that was just a bunch of bullshit. Amelia crossed her arms. "Excuse me?"

"You won't believe me, because you still think what that dickwad said to you is true. So we're going to hash it out. Right now."

Her heart began to thump. Fear clawed up her throat, and Amelia's gaze slid away from Leo's. "Maybe we can go back to talking about blowjobs."

A low, pained groan sounded, and Leo reached over to grab Amelia's arm. Then his hand went around her waist, and he hauled her over his lap, just like he did when they first kissed. When she was firmly planted sideways across his legs, with his arms loosely circled around her upper back, his fingers dangerously close to the side of her breast, he spoke again. "You have no idea how much it grieves me to say this, but I don't want to talk about blowjobs with you right now. I want you to tell me why you struck this deal with me in the first place. Why do you think you need any of this advice, Amelia?"

She considered wriggling out from his hold, but the truth was, it felt good to be in his arms. So, Amelia let her head fall on his shoulder as a sigh slipped through her lips. Leo's fingers began to sweep slowly up and down her arm, soothing her pulse down to a manageable level.

"It started with my ex-boyfriend, Josh," she admitted. "We met in college. I was studying statistics, and he was in mechanical engineering. He was the first guy to ever pay attention to me."

The soothing strokes didn't stop, and Leo remained silent, but Amelia could tell he was listening.

"You have to understand, growing up, I was never Amelia Darcy. I was Maggie Darcy's little sister. And I don't resent her for that; it's impossible to resent Maggie. She's so beautiful and smart and so, *so* kind, and I'm just awkward. I was really gangly in high school. I had braces and acne and was one of those weirdos who actually enjoyed my classes, especially math, and I just was not at all on Maggie's level. So when I met Josh and he actually made me feel pretty, it was really special to me."

"Fucking Josh," Leo mumbled.

Amelia let out a snort, nuzzling deeper into Leo's chest. He was warm and solid, and his strokes were so gentle they sent delicious, calming shivers coursing through her body. She never would have guessed he was capable of being this tender.

"Anyway, we started dating. And I was young, and he was my first boyfriend—first everything—so I probably didn't have the experience to see any red flags. We moved in together to save on rent, and that's when he started criticizing me."

Her throat grew tight, and Amelia stopped speaking. Leo kept stroking her arm, kept encasing her in his safe warmth. His chin tilted as he pressed his cheek to her forehead, a wordless touch that made comfort swell in Amelia's breast.

"It started with innocuous things, like how I did the dishes or how I cooked. Or maybe telling me to change my outfit because it made me look fat or flat-chested or the color was all wrong. Then he started talking about our sex life, and I think he could sense that I was insecure about sexual stuff, so that's what he started to really focus his critiques on."

Leo turned solid beneath her. His movements stopped for a moment, and then Amelia felt a long sigh ruffle the hair at her temple. His hand began to stroke her arm again. "He knew your weakness," he rumbled.

Amelia nodded, her nose just brushing the soft skin at the side of Leo's neck. Her hand slid up to hook over his opposite shoulder, and she let her eyes close. It felt so good to be in his arms, and surprisingly, it felt even better to unburden herself of these truths.

She'd told her friends, of course, and been met with outrage and denials. But there was something nice about telling Leo. He just let her speak, let her explain.

Amelia swallowed. "So, that's how it started. He said I was bad at kissing. He'd tell me that he didn't like the taste of me, you know, down *there*, so he stopped going down on me. He said I was too wet, but then if he touched me when I wasn't turned on, he'd complain that I was too dry. He nitpicked my body. He'd ask me for blowjobs and then complain that I wasn't as good as his ex. He'd want to get really rough, but I didn't like it, and he'd complain about that too. He said a lot of stuff, and I guess they grew roots inside me and now it's hard not to think they're true, especially considering how disastrous my dating life has been since we broke up." Memories swarmed her, and Amelia kept her eyes closed. "In my head, I know he was an abusive asshole. I went to a counselor and that helped a bit, but I still just feel so awkward around guys. And I think it's a self-fulfilling prophecy now. I think I'm bad at sex therefore I become bad at sex. I'm so ashamed of it, and I'm ashamed that my stupid ex-boyfriend still has this much control over me. We broke up six years ago, Leo. I should be over it by now."

It was a long speech, a confession of all her deepest, darkest secrets. So, it wasn't until she stopped speaking that she realized Leo was trembling. His arms had tightened around her, and when she opened her eyes, his jaw was stone hard.

Pushing off his chest, she tilted her head to look up at his face. A muscle jumped in Leo's cheek as his nostrils flared. Finally, he lowered his gaze and met Amelia's. "I'm having homicidal fantasies," he admitted quietly at her worried glance.

Warmth and light flooded through Amelia's chest, and she couldn't help the smile that bloomed over her lips.

Leo scowled at her mouth, then met her gaze. "It's not funny."

"No," she agreed. "It just makes me feel good to hear you say that. Does that make me a bad person?"

He shook his head. "No." His hand moved to stroke her

cheek, the backs of his fingers sliding down her face. "What made you finally break up with him?"

"I found out he was cheating on me, and he tried to make me feel like it was my fault. He said if I hadn't studied so hard and made time for him, he wouldn't have done it. I guess after everything, that was just one thing too far. I realized I needed to leave him."

"Strong woman," he said, brushing his lips over Amelia's forehead.

That made a bitter laugh fall from her lips. "I wouldn't go that far."

The couch groaned as Leo shifted slightly, then he brought his hand back to her cheek. He cupped her jaw and tilted her face so they stared at each other. His green eyes glittered, the rigid planes of his face carved in light and shadow. But his touch was tender, and his voice was soft.

"You are strong, Amelia. You survived what he did to you, and you had the courage to ask for help. You know what you want and you're not afraid to go for it. That's strength. It's resilience. It's courage."

"You're just saying that," she whispered, even as butterflies took off in her chest.

Green eyes stared into hers, and something shifted within them. His hand slipped down to her neck, curling around to her nape. Leo's head lowered so his breath coasted over her lips, sending tiny shivers darting through her veins. "I want to make you feel good," he told her, his gaze sliding down the length of her body before returning to her face.

A breath gusted out of her mouth. "Oh," she managed to say.

"Can I do that? Can I make you feel good?" He shifted so her head was supported on his bicep, and his other hand slid from her nape around to her shoulder, then her chest, barely brushing her breast on its journey down to her waist.

Amelia shivered. "I don't..."

His hand paused.

She gulped. It would be so easy to push him away, but need clawed inside her. She *wanted* to feel good. She wanted to revel in the safety of Leo's arms. She wanted to feel sexy, damn it.

But—

She reached up to touch Leo's jaw. "If I don't come, please don't take it personally. It's...hard for me. To get all the way there."

The expression on his face grew harsh as her words sank in. His hand tightened on her waist as he leaned down and brushed his lips over her forehead, down to the tip of her nose, and finally brushed her lips oh-so-softly. "We'll just see what happens, okay?"

She nodded once, jerkily. "Okay," she whispered.

Then he kissed her. It was as mind-bending and life-altering as before, except this time, Leo's hand slid under her top and came to rest on her bare stomach. For a moment, Amelia worried that her belly was too soft, that he'd feel her imperfections, that he'd pull away—

"Your skin is so soft," he said reverently against her lips, fingers spreading to span from hip to ribs. He squeezed and stroked her body until she settled, then slid his hand up to peel the shirt off her body. She lifted her arms as he took the garment off, then settled back down, biting her lip as she looked at Leo to gauge his reaction.

What greeted her gaze was a look of pure, barely leashed hunger. His hand slid from her collarbone to her breast, touching the lacy fabric of her bralette as his eyes devoured her. "Pretty," he said, almost to himself, his fingers tracing the scalloped edge of her undergarments.

His fingers trailed down to her navel, then over the waistline of her skirt. He skimmed his hand down the outside of her thigh, down to her knee while his head dipped down to kiss her once more. Despite herself, Amelia felt her body relax. She wrapped her arms around Leo's neck and tugged him closer, wanting to explore his body as he was exploring hers.

A rough grunt tore through Leo's throat, and he pulled away. Then, with jagged movements, he lifted Amelia up and spun her around so she sat directly on his lap, her back to his chest. Her legs dangled over his knees. When he spread his legs, he pulled her knees wide. Her skirt dipped down in the gap made by their spread legs, and Leo's hands came around Amelia's waist.

"Look at yourself," he commanded, his lips near her ear. He nudged her so she looked at the mirror above the mantel. It was angled in such a way that she could see herself atop him. "See how beautiful you are." His hands slid up from her waist to cup her breasts. He shaped her, groaning at the feel of her flesh in his palms.

She watched the reflection and felt cool air on her spread inner thighs.

This was *not* in her spreadsheet.

Leo dipped down to kiss her neck, his teeth grazing down to her shoulder. His hands worked her breasts, fingers tweaking and teasing her nipples until they were hard points, clearly visible through the lace of her bralette. Melting against the man at her back, Amelia let her head fall against his shoulder with a sigh.

"Does that feel good?" he said, voice low and rough as he pinched her nipples again.

"Yes," Amelia panted.

A rough tug, and her breasts were freed. She jerked at the feel of Leo's calloused palms against her oversensitive skin. A whimper escaped her and was met with a low, rumbling chuckle. "My girl likes her tits played with, doesn't she?"

"Yes," Amelia breathed. She also liked being called his girl, but she was too far gone to acknowledge it.

Sliding one hand up to her jaw, Leo tilted her face forward again. "I want you to see what I see, Amelia," he said, low and commanding and hot. "Open your eyes and look." One hand on her jaw, he moved the other hand to plump her breast. "A beautiful body with rosy nipples that got so nice and hard when I touched them." His thumb brushed the tips of her breasts for emphasis and Amelia shivered. Then his hand slid down to her waist. "All this soft skin," he whispered, lips brushing the shell of her ear.

Then his hand slid lower. "And this," he said on an exhale. "I can feel how hot and wet you are even through your skirt." He squeezed her, and a spasm gripped Amelia. The spasm was delicious. The way he said the words made it obvious he thought it was a good thing she was wet already. A very good thing.

This was further emphasized when he clawed at the fabric of her skirt, spread his knees wider to pull her legs apart, and slid his hand over her underwear. He groaned, his head dropping until his lips brushed her shoulder again. He liked the feel of her so much, Amelia could feel him getting hard beneath her. His bulge was growing under her butt, and the feel of all that hot, hard, male flesh made Amelia want to tear all their clothes off, lock the door, and forget about everything except their bodies and their pleasure.

But Leo had other ideas. He slid his fingers up the gusset of her underwear and circled her where she was most sensitive. Even with a layer of fabric between them, she jerked at the touch, a moan slipping through her lips. Then he slid his fingers higher, and Amelia let out a whimper of disappointment until Leo moved beneath her underwear to slide his fingers over her aching core. Then her whimper turned to a moan.

A harsh breath swept over her shoulder as Leo exhaled. "Let me tell you something, Amelia," he said, voice low. His fingers slipped down to tease her opening then back up to that maddening bundle of nerves. "I love feeling you this wet. I'm dying at the thought of how good you'll feel when my cock is inside you. So hot and wet and tight."

Leo's fingers found the sensitive left side of her clit, and he was so in tune to her every twitch that he understood exactly what she liked. He rubbed her softly, then harder, and soft again, until Amelia was sure she'd lost her mind.

"Leo," she panted, then stopped.

"What is it?" His fingers kept performing magic between her legs, and Amelia didn't know what she so badly wanted to say to him. "You like the way I touch you?" She nodded and he said, "Not as much as I like doing it."

His big hand slipped down, and he plunged his fingers inside her. Gasping, she watched herself in the reflection, feeling his touch, his body beneath hers, and she felt the truth of his statement. Pinning her skirt to her stomach with his forearm, he wrenched her panties to the side so she could see what he was doing in the mirror. Fingers plunging into her, Leo ground his palm against her clit, and she came.

Her orgasm hit without warning, locking all her muscles. A cry sounded, and Amelia realized it had come from her. Pleasure washed over her, exploding out from the juncture of her thighs, sending heat and honey spreading through her veins. Leo held her through it, urging her on with whispered words, his arms wrapped around her body as he guided her through every wave and aftershock. It wasn't until she jerked at the lightest touch that he pulled his hand away and gently replaced her underwear.

Her body was utterly limp on top of his. Her bralette remained tangled and bunched beneath her breasts, her skirt in disarray. But it took so much effort to even blink that Amelia doubted she had the strength to put herself to rights. Leo lifted her and spun her around so she was sitting across his lap again, then he dipped his head to hers. He kissed her with long, languorous touches until she let out a satisfied sigh.

Then Leo pulled away and readjusted her bralette. He twitched her skirt so it fell over her legs. He swept his hand over her side, up her ribs to her shoulder, then down her arm. Then he tangled his fingers with hers and brought her knuckles up to his mouth. His touch was gentle, a soft touch of his lips to her skin.

"What about you?" Amelia whispered.

"This isn't about me."

That was a nice thought, but it didn't sit right with Amelia. Something about the way Leo said it, the pain he tried to hide in his eyes... There was more to Leo than the playboy. He used his reputation as a mask, but she could see through it.

Sitting up, Amelia turned so she was straddling him, her hands resting on Leo's shoulders. He tilted his head back, those lazy catlike eyes falling to half-mast as his hands slid to her hips. They watched each other for a beat.

"That was nice," Amelia finally whispered, a bit stupidly.

Leo grinned. "I know."

"I want you to feel good too."

His grin softened around the edges, and his thumbs started making slow sweeps over the skin at her waist. "I told you, Amelia. That wasn't about me."

Pleasure still buzzed in her veins. The image of her body draped over Leo's was burned into Amelia's memory, and for the first time in a long, long time—maybe ever—she felt sexy in a way that was innate. It wasn't like she was trying on an ill-fitting piece of clothing and thinking she could get used to it if she only wore it more often. No, for the first time in her life, Amelia understood that she was a sensual creature when she felt safe enough to embrace that part of herself. With Leo, she was safe.

And it was a very, *very* good feeling. She tilted her hips and settled on Leo's body a little more firmly, eliciting a groan from him. Then she whispered, "You were supposed to teach me how to give the perfect blowjob."

A pulse occurred in his crotch, like her words had a direct line to his dick. It twitched against her still-damp panties, causing her own body to spasm in about fourteen different places.

Leo blinked slowly and finally chuckled as he shook his head. "Nope."

"No? You're rejecting me?"

"I'm sticking to my principles. This was about making you feel good. If you start trying to please me, it'll ruin all my efforts."

But Amelia wasn't ready to let go of this nascent feeling. She wanted to wrap it around herself like a blanket. She wanted to feel sexy for a little bit longer. And beyond that, she felt that Leo needed to be drawn out of the armor he'd built around himself. She'd seen past his mask, and she wanted him to know it. She wanted him to feel as seen, as appreciated, as she did in his arms.

Letting her hands drift to the back of his neck, she played with the ends of his hair and asked, "How do you know I wouldn't enjoy sucking your cock? What if it felt good for me?"

Another pulse from his crotch, this one much, *much* stronger. He groaned and tightened his hands around her waist. His eyes were closed. "I'm trying to be a gentleman, Amelia."

"That wasn't in our agreement."

"A lot of what we've done wasn't in our agreement."

Hmm. That was true.

Leo laughed and brushed his thumb between her brows. "Stop frowning. Even though you're cute when you're not getting your way."

"I never thought I'd have to beg to give a guy a blowjob."

The smile Leo gave her in response was nothing short of villainous. "You're nowhere near begging, Amelia. But we can do that too, if you like."

Now it was her body's turn to spasm. She thought of getting on her knees, begging, seeing his face turn predatory when he refused her...

Lust swept through her, warming her cheeks, making her hips jerk against his.

But... How was it possible to be turned on by something like that when her entire sexual history had been one long line of awkward and downright terrible experiences? Was there something wrong with her? Maybe all her bad experiences had warped something inside her, and now the thought of being humiliated by Leo in that way actually turned her on.

"Hey." His voice had gentled again. "Come back to me."

She lifted her gaze to his and gave him a half-smile. "Sorry."

With slight pressure on her back, he urged her to lie against his chest. She did, and was immediately engulfed in the warmth of his embrace. It felt amazing. Leo tucked her head under his chin and held her until it was time to get ready for dinner.

That night, when she closed the pocket doors after saying goodnight, Amelia wished she had the courage to ask Leo to join her in the big king-sized bed.

But there was a reason he hadn't wanted to take things further earlier. He was putting up a boundary between them, and Amelia had to respect that. Leo didn't do relationships; he certainly hadn't given her any indication he wanted more than a fake fiancée for a few days. Sure, they'd muddied their agreement already with kisses and touches, but that didn't mean Leo wanted it to last beyond the retreat.

Amelia would be a pretty terrible person if she pushed him to do things he didn't want to do. She had the feeling Leo was used to being used for sex, and she didn't want to be one of the women who did that to him. She didn't want to cheapen what was happening between them, even if it only lasted a few days.

So she closed the doors and got into the big bed—alone.

FOURTEEN

LEO HARDLY SLEPT THAT NIGHT. The couch was a bit too short, the cushions were a bit too hard, and he was a bit too horny.

He shouldn't have given in to temptation. The more time he spent with Amelia, the more he admired her. She was intelligent, beautiful, driven, and so charmingly funny—especially when she didn't intend to be. He'd remember the outrage on her face when she found out about the scavenger hunt prize for the rest of his days. Then after Jenga, when the other team won smartwatches, she looked as grumpy as she had when she fixed his bow tie at Maggie's wedding. She was irresistible, even when she was annoyed.

But Leo wasn't stupid: He knew why she was spending time with him.

She hadn't asked for orgasms. She hadn't asked for an easy

hookup. She hadn't asked for Pestilence to fire his arrows across Stirling and to spread disease in her life.

Amelia wanted to find a partner worthy of her. That person sure as hell wasn't Leo.

Dull, gray light filtered through the thin curtains as dawn slowly won its war against night. Leo watched its arrival through slitted eyes, his body sore, his spirit aching.

That's when a realization swept through him, growing as slowly as the light of day: He was falling in love with Amelia Darcy.

The kicker was, he couldn't have her. Not for real—not after this retreat was over.

Sitting up, he rubbed the heels of his hands into his eye sockets and stretched his back, scowling at the sofa. Stupid thing. He'd be sore for weeks after this damn retreat. Dragging his bones over to the breakfast bar, he started the coffee machine and watched it brew. Then, sipping a fresh mug, he leaned against the window frame and cast his eyes over the forest. Birds called to each other as the day arrived, a breeze floating through the open window. It smelled fresh and earthy, a smell that was distinctly Stirling. For the first time in decades, he thought it smelled good.

It had been a long, long time since he appreciated this place. He'd moved away at eighteen and vowed to never look back to the town where he'd spent his childhood. Those years of pain had hardened him to life, and he wondered, looking out at the trees, if the damage was irreparable.

"Is there enough coffee for me?"

Leo turned to see Amelia sliding open the pocket doors that

led to the bedroom. She wore tiny sleep shorts that exposed most of her shapely legs. On top, she had a matching button-down pajama shirt, navy blue piped in white. Her nipples were visible through the thin fabric.

Leo cleared his throat and tore his gaze away. "Morning," he said. "There's enough for a couple more cups."

"You're my hero," Amelia breathed. She stumbled across to the breakfast bar and fixed herself a mug (two creams and four sugars, to Leo's combined disgust and amazement). Amelia stirred her coffee and joined him at the window. "What are you looking at? Anyone skulking around out there?"

He grinned. They'd spent dinner studying everyone around the table but had come no closer to finding any clues about the missing ring. Truthfully, Leo's thoughts had been dominated by the memory of Amelia's body splayed over his. It had been hard to care about his billionaire boss's eye-wateringly expensive engagement ring when the woman of his dreams was seated just beside him. They hadn't stolen it; why did they care who had?

"I was just thinking how little I appreciated this town growing up," Leo admitted.

"When did you leave?"

"As soon as I graduated high school. Went to college in Boston and never looked back."

"I only moved here for work when I was in my early twen-ties," Amelia told him. "Maggie and my parents came later, when I kept telling them how great Stirling was. What was it like growing up here?"

Leo couldn't hide his grimace. "It's a nice place for a kid," he said noncommittally.

Amelia could read him like a book. "But...?" she prompted.

He slurped his coffee to buy himself time. "But my parents weren't exactly loving."

"Oh. I'm sorry."

"Don't be. I survived." He gave her his best, brightest smile —the one that usually turned aggressively flirtatious and had landed him in bed with whoever he aimed it at—but Amelia only frowned at him.

Leo sighed. Of course that look didn't work on Amelia. It never had. To his surprise, he heard himself say, "I mostly lived with my grandparents. Dad was out of the picture. Mom was off getting high and finding new boyfriends every couple of weeks. She died when I was eleven, and we moved in with my grand-parents full-time. They died within six months of each other when I was sixteen, and Marlon and I were on our own. He ended up buying me out of my half of the house they left us so I could afford to go to college."

His voice sounded oddly flat, like he was describing what he'd eaten for breakfast. He took another sip of coffee and let his eyes drift to the distant mist curling around the treetops that would soon be burned away by the sun.

Amelia nodded but stayed silent.

Maybe it was her silence—comforting, steady—that prompted him to go on. "I was nervous about coming back here for the wedding and the retreat."

"Is it the first time you've been back in Stirling since you left?"

Leo nodded. "Marlon never left, and Archer and Cormac came straight back after college. But I stayed away. We'd meet up in Boston every couple of months, and they always came down. I told Fred I'd grown up here in my interview with the company years ago, and I think it helped me get the job. Home court advantage. But I hadn't been back since I left at eighteen."

After a pause, Amelia asked, "What do you think about the town now?"

The town, he could take or leave. He didn't care. The woman leaning on the opposite side of the window was another story. "It's been good," he finally replied, and he was surprised to realize it was the truth.

Amelia beamed at him, and a thunderbolt pierced his chest. She was charming when she frowned, but she was utterly breathtaking when she smiled.

"I'm going to shower first," she told him, gulping down the rest of her coffee. "We have to go over what we've found out about the ring and figure out what we're going to do. Fred keeps looking at me and asking pointed questions about my band. It's getting uncomfortable."

"He knows you didn't steal the ring, Amelia."

She tilted her head from side to side. "I don't know. He's suspicious about something. Last night, when you went to the bathroom after dinner, he asked me about my last tour and the way he worded the questions sounded like he was trying to catch me in a lie."

Guilt squirmed in Leo's stomach. "I'm sorry."

She pursed her lips, flicking her gaze up to his. "It's worth it."

As she walked away, Leo wondered what, exactly, was

worth it. Did she mean Fred's suspicion was worth it because she got to spend time with Leo?

But that was just wishful thinking. She was probably grateful that she was one step closer to finding a partner who was worthy of her. If such a man existed.

By the time he'd drained his second cup of coffee, Leo felt halfway human. The shower had stopped, so he was readying his clothes to take his turn in the bathroom—when there was a knock on the door.

"Ari," he said, surprised, when he pulled the door open.

The other man scowled, dark brows pulled low over his eyes. "Hey." He glanced over his shoulder, as if to check he was alone in the hallway. "I have a question for you."

Leo nodded, trying not to betray his nerves. Had Ari noticed his papers were missing? Did he suspect Leo and Amelia of taking them?

"Was anyone else in the hallway yesterday morning when you and Amelia were here?"

"Yesterday?" Leo asked to hide his surprise.

"Yeah. During the scavenger hunt."

"Not that I saw. Why?"

Ari let out a breath and combed his fingers through his hair. "I think someone was in my room."

"What?" Leo's voice rose, and he hoped it sounded like surprise and not guilt. His hand tightened on the door so hard his fingers ached.

Ari pursed his lips and let his gaze slide to the side. "I know it sounds crazy, but things were shifted around."

"Oh, man..." Leo said with exaggerated concern. "That's... wow."

"Yeah. And my Patek Philippe was missing."

"What's a patate flip? Something to do with potatoes?" Amelia's voice was so close, it made Leo jump. He glanced over his shoulder and did a double take. Then he slammed the door in Ari's face.

Amelia gave him a look like she thought he was crazy.

"What are you wearing?" Leo demanded.

She glanced down at herself. "A towel." She said it like he was an idiot for asking.

His breath was coming in fast. The towel barely skimmed the tops of her thighs, and her breasts were pushed together at the top. It was *not* big enough to cover Amelia's body. Not by a long shot. When she moved, the fabric opened in a slit at her hip. "You can't walk around like that when the door's open, Amelia."

She reared back. "Excuse me? And who opened the door? Am I supposed to stay hidden like a little mouse? Please."

"I don't want Ari or any other man seeing you like that," he growled.

Amelia planted her hands on her hips. Leo could almost feel the anger rising in her, like the first puff of ash on a volcano about to erupt. He knew she was right; he couldn't tell her how to dress. But...but...

"I'm wearing undies," she said, flipping the front of the towel up. "See? It's not like I'm going to flash anyone."

Leo groaned. Blood rushed away from his brain so fast, he

wobbled on his feet. Amelia was, in fact, wearing underwear. It was red, lacy, and it curved attractively up over her hips.

"Plus," she went on, "you have no right to tell me how I can walk around my own room."

"I am your fiancé," he growled, which was a ridiculous thing to say seeing as Leo wasn't, in fact, Amelia's fiancé. But she was nearly naked. "And I don't want some asshole drooling over you."

Amelia's eyes narrowed. "No one is drooling over me, Leo."

"I beg to differ." So did the tent in his pants, but he wasn't about to point it out to her.

Her chest had flushed a pretty shade of pink. One sharp tug, and her towel would be on the floor. Leo's hands itched. But Amelia just rolled her eyes, grabbed something out of her suitcase, which was just outside the bedroom door, and headed through the pocket doors. At the last moment, she spun around and stuck out her tongue.

He bit back a laugh. The pressure on his chest increased as he watched her disappear into the bedroom.

Turning back to the front door, he opened it with a yank. Ari was still waiting on the other side, an eyebrow popped. "Trouble in paradise?"

"Your watch is missing?" Leo prompted.

Ari nodded. "Yeah. And...yeah, the watch."

"We didn't see anyone."

The other man sighed, his gaze meeting Leo's. Leo met it head-on, knowing it was only a matter of time before Ari began to suspect them. If they were the only ones alone in the hallway, it was only logical.

"What about you?" Ari asked, jerking his chin over Leo's shoulder.

Amelia had slipped into a white sundress with a red-and-pink floral print. The straps were thin, holding up a crisscrossed bodice and a flouncy skirt. Leo wanted her to slip right out of it again, preferably somewhere he could watch.

Scrunching a towel into her wet hair, Amelia shook her head. "Didn't see anyone. What did you say they took?"

"My watch." Ari narrowed his gaze at her, then shifted to look at Leo. "Strange that Amelia wouldn't know what a Patek Philippe is, though. Surely she would have heard of the brand before now. Isn't your watch collection worth a couple hundred k?"

A strangled noise came from Amelia, and she covered it up by coughing.

"She was just trying to be funny," Leo lied.

"Uh-huh!" Amelia said, voice muffled by the towel she'd shoved over her face.

Ari, looking troubled, said goodbye to the couple and walked toward his room. Leo closed the door and turned the lock. He met Amelia's wide-eyed gaze.

"You think he was telling the truth? His watch is really missing?"

Leo let out a sigh. "Either that, or he was trying to cover for the missing papers."

Amelia bit her lip. "We should go down to breakfast soon. Maybe we can corner Vanessa and ask her why she was up here with Ari instead of with her boyfriend doing the scavenger hunt."

Leo nodded. "Good plan. I'll shower, and we'll head down."

But when Leo emerged from the steamy bathroom, he saw Amelia sitting on the couch, frowning at her phone. She glanced up at him, brows still drawn low over her eyes.

"What's wrong?"

"Nothing," she mumbled.

"Did something happen?" Leo approached, trying to ignore the banging of his heart. If Amelia had to leave the retreat, it'd only raise the suspicion on them. He'd have to come clean to Fred—and then what? As he came closer, his worry grew. What if something was wrong with Amelia's family? Her work? If something was truly wrong, he'd face Fred, come clean, do whatever he had to do if Amelia was in trouble. "What's going on?" Leo demanded. He needed to fix this. Immediately.

Amelia let out a sigh and shook her head. "Sorry. It's nothing. I'm just kind of shocked." She turned her phone to face him. "I got a message from Ben."

Leo's first instinct was to grab Amelia's phone and fling it into the blazing depths of an active volcano. But he wasn't a savage, so he wiped the scowl off his face and sat down beside her. "Ah. Congrats."

"Don't sound too excited," she mock-grumbled, elbowing him.

"This is what you wanted, right?" Leo asked, his voice sounding thin through the tightness of his throat.

Amelia bunched her lips to the side. "I guess."

Silence dropped between them like a lead weight. Leo forced himself to be civil. Wasn't he supposed to be helping her get a boyfriend? "What did he say?"

"He said, 'Hey.'"

Leo's eye roll proved he'd spent a past life as a fourteen-year-old girl. "What a fucking charmer."

Amelia clicked her tongue, frowning at him. "Be nice. I said 'Hey,' back, but with a smiley face added." She stared at her phone screen and cringed.

Leo revised his previous thoughts. He didn't want to fling her phone into an active volcano; he wanted to fling *Ben* into it. "The guy has the personality of a clump of dryer lint."

"You've never even spoken to him. How could you possibly know that?"

"I know his type."

"And what's that?"

This conversation was starting to annoy Leo. He crossed his arms and stared at the coffee table. "The type who stalks a woman's online photos for days and can't even think of a single interesting thing to say. What time did he send you that message?"

"What does that matter?"

"What time, Amelia?"

She gave him a sideways glance. "Three o'clock in the morning."

Leo spread his hands. "I rest my case."

"You haven't *made* a case."

"This guy isn't worth your time, Amelia. If he was, he'd have thought of something to say that was more than one word when he was lying in bed creeping on your photos."

"Unless you've forgotten to engage your brain this morning,

Leo, I'll remind you that I don't exactly have men beating down my door. This message is more than I've gotten in over a year."

A hot, achy feeling was climbing up Leo's throat. "That doesn't mean you don't deserve more. What's so special about this guy?"

"Nothing!" The word exploded out of her, and Leo was shocked to see something like anger on her face. "Nothing is special about him, just like nothing is special about me. Not everyone can be a super-sexy, super-confident hunk, all right? For us mere mortals, sometimes this is as good as it gets." She shook her phone for emphasis.

Leo hadn't known it was possible to want to kiss someone and shake them all at once. Nothing was special about her? Was she serious? "You're special, Amelia. Everything about you is special."

"Oh, spare me." She stood up, her jaw set. "Let's go get breakfast and find this stupid thief so we can get this retreat over with."

FIFTEEN

AMELIA MARCHED into the dining room and went straight for the apple Danishes. She recognized Camilla's baked goods anywhere (and she'd seen the box they came in), so she knew they'd be delicious.

She needed something delicious to ease the burn at the back of her throat. Ben's message was lame. She knew that. But Leo had seemed...angry? And his anger made *her* angry, and then she'd stormed out of the room without meeting his gaze.

But now that the flash of emotion had faded, Amelia felt silly. She was only mad because her feelings for Leo were growing with every minute they spent together, and she knew that would blow up in her face. Leo didn't deserve her ire; she should figure her shit out herself. She resolved to apologize to Leo as soon as she could swallow her pride, which would likely happen after her second or third pastry of the morning.

"Good choice," Percival said, breaking down one of the

white bakery boxes behind the table where the Danishes were displayed.

Amelia grinned. "Camilla's one of my best friends. I usually get these when they're a day old and unsellable, but I *know* this one is going to be incredible."

The man inclined his head, then cast an eye across the table. As soon as he saw that the scrambled eggs were quickly running low, he nodded to Amelia and took his leave. The man was observant and *very* good at his job. Amelia thought that if anyone found out who had stolen the ring, it would be Percival. Unless she and Leo did it first.

The thought made her square her shoulders. She couldn't get distracted by lame one-word messages from a guy she no longer had a crush on. Ben could wait; the ring thief couldn't.

While she was loading up her plate with an altogether unhealthy breakfast, Amelia sidled up beside Cora. If there was one thing Amelia had learned in her stint working in an office, it was that the administrators were all-seeing and all-knowing. They had the power to make your life a dream—or a living hell.

She suspected that Cora, having worked at Goodhew since its inception decades ago, was no different.

"Morning," she greeted the older woman brightly.

"Hello, dear," Cora said with a smile, brown eyes crinkling. She had half a grapefruit on her plate and was waiting for toast to brown in the toaster.

"How did you sleep?"

"Like a baby. You? Did that man keep you up all night?" Cora angled her head toward Leo, who was watching them from across the room.

He'd been watching her like that all morning. It was as thrilling as it was unsettling. She wasn't used to having men—especially attractive men—pay that much attention to her. Was he still angry about this morning? She couldn't keep up with how she was supposed to feel or act around him.

Amelia turned back to Cora. "Oh, you know how they are," she deflected, trying not to squirm.

"I certainly do."

"Go Cora," Amelia said with a laugh. "Are you saying you were a man-eater?"

"There's no past tense about it, girl," Cora replied with a wink.

Laughing, Amelia perused the fresh fruit on offer. She had to turn this conversation to something more productive. She placed a couple of strawberries on her plate and asked as casually as she could, "Did you hear that they think Nadia's ring was stolen?"

Cora's fingers paused above the toaster. "I did," she finally admitted. "Fred's been on edge since it went missing. Haven't seen him this bad since '92, when he almost went bankrupt planning children's parties here in Stirling." The old lady glanced over her shoulder, then leaned toward Amelia. "You ask me, I think buying a ring worth twelve million is just asking for trouble."

"I don't know that I'd go that far. Stealing is wrong, and it isn't the victim's fault."

"I wouldn't be flaunting it all around, that's for sure," the old lady said. She hiked her purse up on her shoulder and shook her head. "But Fred doesn't deserve that. This retreat is one of the only times I see him truly enjoy himself."

"Maybe they'll find it in a heating vent," Amelia offered.

"One can only hope," Cora said, then nodded to Robert Lafontaine, who had just entered the room. "If anyone took it, it was that man. Started his career with the Mob, you know. An outfit out of New York City. You can take the man out of Little Italy, but, well, you know how the saying goes."

Amelia's eyes widened. She glanced at Robert, who gave her a sunny smile and a wave from his side of the room. He didn't look like a mobster. He and Trudy looked like they were looking forward to a sunny retirement in Florida.

"Lafontaine isn't an Italian name."

"Either him or Vanessa," Cora continued, ignoring Amelia's comment. "She's been stuck for cash since her sugar daddy left her, and she has the integrity of a wet noodle." She grabbed a little packet of butter and placed it on top of her toast before turning to face the room. "Well. Enjoy your breakfast!"

Hurrying to Leo's side, Amelia slumped into a chair. She leaned over and said, "Cora thinks it was Robert or Vanessa."

Leo reared back. "Really?"

"Apparently Robert was part of the Mob, and it's like you heard yesterday, Vanessa's got money troubles."

"Doesn't explain Ari's list."

Amelia bit into a strawberry and shook her head. "No," she said after she'd swallowed. "It doesn't. And if his watch went missing, he'd hardly have stolen it from himself. Unless he's trying to deflect suspicion?"

Leo's hand lifted, and his thumb swiped at something on her

lip. It came away pink with the strawberry's juices. "Messy," he said, eyes still on Amelia's lips.

Heat wound through her stomach, settling down between her thighs. She shifted on her seat and turned her eyes to her plate. The Danish was, indeed, as delicious as she'd anticipated. Camilla was a maestro.

Amelia was just staring down the third pastry on her plate, wondering if it was a bad idea to go for it, when she realized Leo was staring at her. She picked up a napkin and daintily patted her lips. Maybe two Danishes was enough. She frowned at him. "What?"

"Nothing," he said.

Her frown deepened. "Tell me."

"Never mind, Amelia." He curled his hand onto her shoulder, like he couldn't help but touch her, and she smelled the fresh scent of his skin. It rivaled Camilla's Danish for deliciousness. Her head spun, doubly so when Leo leaned over and pressed a soft kiss to her temple.

It was part of their loving couple act, of course, but it still made her vision go fuzzy around the edges. No midnight message from Ben could rival one touch from Leo.

In an attempt to distract herself—and maybe, in an attempt to ignore the truth beginning to reveal itself right in front of her eyes—she glanced around and saw Vanessa slinking out of the room. The other woman gripped her phone in one hand. The look on Vanessa's face was nothing short of thunderous.

"Come on," Amelia urged. "Let's see what that's about."

It was only when they'd stepped out of the breakfast room

that Amelia realized Leo had kissed her temple when no one was watching them at all.

LEO FOLLOWED Amelia out of the breakfast room and down the hall. They passed the Blue Room and a small dining room and saw Vanessa disappear into a network of interconnected spaces. Creeping through lushly decorated rooms, they followed through big double doors into a salon, through a dressing room filled with empty shelves and a velvet-upholstered seat, stopping when Vanessa crossed into a guest bedroom and slumped down onto a window seat.

She tapped on her phone, frowning.

With their heads poking around the doorway, Leo knew that Vanessa only had to look up to discover them. He put a hand on Amelia's hip to urge her to lean back. They needed to find somewhere to hide, and fast. That's when he heard the click of Vanessa's heels on the bedroom's parquet flooring.

"Nice of you to pick up the phone," she barked, her footsteps approaching.

There was nowhere to hide. If they ran for the salon, she'd have a clear line of sight. If they stayed in the dressing room, she'd come in and find them as soon as she stepped through.

Clearly, they were terrible at detective work.

Leo opened a door beside them and found a tall, narrow closet with angled shelves on both sides obviously designed to hold dozens of pairs of shoes. He shoved Amelia inside and followed, closing the door just in time to see Vanessa's head pop into the dressing room.

She paced the length of the carpeted space. "Yes, I'm still at the retreat. No, I can't leave. His stupid fiancée lost her ring, and she's got it in her head that it was taken. If I leave now, it'll look like I'm guilty and it'll be a nightmare to straighten out."

The closet door was made of angled slats, so Leo could see Vanessa as she paced. Then he felt a tap on his shoulder and turned, horrified to see Amelia smooshed against the shoe shelves. He eased back to give her more space, but then he was pressing against the door.

Finally, he turned around to face Amelia, putting his arms around her so they'd have more space. Her eyes were wide, and the pulse jumped in her neck. She smelled like strawberries.

"I don't know!" Vanessa huffed. "Look, I'll send you some money next week, Dad. Yes, I'm sure. Can you last that long?"

Amelia tilted her head, frowning. Her body was so soft against Leo's. He wished he had the right to press himself up against her like this all the time, without the pretense of their fake relationship.

There was a long sigh. "Fine. Me too. Bye." Vanessa's voice was tight, and Leo strained his ears to listen. He looked over his shoulder and saw her cross the slatted door once more, then her steps receded back the way they came.

"What was that about?" Amelia whispered. "It didn't sound like she took the ring. Her money problems might be a family issue?"

Turning his head to face her again, Leo was surprised to discover he'd wrapped his arms around her waist, and she was clinging to his shoulders. Her eyes were shadowed in the low light of the closet, her sweet, fluttery dress soft beneath his touch.

Leo didn't give a damn about the ring, or Vanessa, or anything other than the beautiful woman in his arms. The thought of her lacy red underwear covered with only the fluttery, floral skirt dancing around her thighs was driving him wild. "Not sure," he grated.

She bit her lip, then seemed to steel herself to say something. "Leo," she whispered.

"Yeah?"

"I'm sorry about this morning. About Ben. It was a lame message for him to send, and I feel kind of pathetic for being flattered by it. I...I just want you to know I appreciate you making me question these things. You make me feel more confident than I have in a long, long time."

"You deserve more than some asshole who can't even ask you about your day," Leo grated, tightening his hold on Amelia's waist.

"Thank you," she breathed. Fingers dug into his shoulders as Amelia leaned into him. Her breaths were shallow, the sound of them filling the small space. She was temptation wrapped into a feisty blond package. She was the woman of his dreams, and he hadn't even known he had dreams of a woman like her until she'd yanked on his collar at her sister's wedding.

Leo only had a couple of days to hold Amelia in his arms. Another man was already sniffing around her, and it wouldn't be long until she realized just how much she deserved. He might as well make the most of the time they had left.

So, without giving himself time to rethink his urge, he slanted his lips against hers and kissed her.

There was no excuse this time. They weren't about to get caught. They weren't talking about her color-coded spreadsheet. Right now, the only thing on Leo's mind was tasting this woman's mouth simply because he wanted to. With a soft moan, she melted against him, her arms wrapping around his shoulders.

Groaning in response, Leo slipped both hands down and cupped her ass, then clawed at her skirt until he felt skin. His thumbs swept over the edge of her lace panties, but most of her butt was beautifully bare flesh. He squeezed, and Amelia leaped into his arms in response. He pressed her against the shelves and kissed her harder, sliding his tongue against hers, moaning as she tugged on his hair and bucked her hips like she couldn't get enough of him.

He was losing his mind for her. When she melted for him like this, it felt like they had a chance. Like this heat between them could mean something more.

"Feel how hard I am for you," Leo said, using his hands to pull her core against his aching cock. "You feel it, baby?"

"I want it inside me," she panted, eyes glazed. "So bad, Leo."

He groaned, letting his forehead drop to hers. His hands kneaded her ass as she rolled her hips against him. He couldn't fuck her in this closet. Not when they were expected outside for some stupid team-building activity within minutes. Not when she deserved a bed and rose petals and champagne.

He couldn't fuck her in a closet. He *couldn't*.

But if she kept bucking her hips like that, all he'd have to do was hook his fingers into her underwear, shove it aside, and—

"Well, well, well," Ari said behind them. "I thought I heard something strange over here."

Amelia screamed, let go of Leo's shoulders, and shoved him as hard as she could. Unfortunately, her legs were still locked around him, and his hands remained firmly clamped on her generous bottom. So, when she shoved, Leo stumbled back and took her with him. They fell in a heap on the floor while Ari watched on, looking vaguely amused.

"The puzzle challenge is starting in five. You're expected out at the gazebo, and Fred's in a hell of a mood this morning. If I were you, I'd leave the marital activities for the marital bed."

"Do me a favor and fuck off, Ari," Leo grumbled from the floor.

Amelia's face was hidden in his neck, her hands curled into his shirt so hard he'd never get the wrinkles out. When Ari walked away, she sat up, looking rumpled and disheveled atop him. He held onto her hips, not ready to leave this particular position.

"Um." She bit her lip.

It was unbearable how hot she was. She looked part innocent, part embarrassed, part flushed with arousal, and still with that harsh edge of annoyance dancing just out of reach. It was a cocktail designed to drive Leo out of his mind. Amelia's eyes widened when she felt his cock throb against her core.

Leo huffed, shaking his head. "Sorry. Can't help it when you're straddling me like that."

He didn't know if she did it on purpose, but after he spoke,

Amelia rocked her hips the tiniest—*tiniest*—bit. And he nearly came, it felt so good. A grunt rumbled in his throat as his hands tightened on her hips.

"We should go out there," she whispered.

"Uh-huh," he managed past his clenched teeth.

"You think he saw us following Vanessa?" she whispered again, even more quietly, her hands leaning against his chest.

"Don't know," he grated. "Don't care."

She huffed and stood, and that mind-blowing friction against his stiff member was taken away. Thought slowly returned to Leo's mind as he sat up, blinking, more than a little dazed. He followed Amelia out of the dressing room and through the salon. They nodded at a staff member on their way to the back of the sprawling house, finding Percival there to hold the French doors open for them. The butler gave them a shallow bow, his face utterly blank.

Then they headed for the gazebo, where the rest of the guests awaited.

SIXTEEN

TABLES HAD BEEN SET up at the foot of the gazebo, around which clustered teams of four. Amelia and Leo joined Ari and his partner in front of a table near the far end of the line.

"Today's challenge is a logic puzzle," Fred announced. He stood on the steps of the gazebo wearing a crisp white shirt, its top three buttons undone. His slacks were dark blue, tailored perfectly around his powerful frame. Amelia watched him survey his employees and their partners, noting the steel-hard look in his eyes. When Fred's gaze landed on her, she stiffened her spine. Was his gaze lingering on her for a bit longer than most? Did he look particularly suspicious?

Amelia gritted her teeth. Curling her hands into fists, she used the bite of her nails against her palms to center herself. Paranoia wouldn't help anyone. Plus, if people kept walking in on her making out with Leo, there'd be no question about the

legitimacy of their relationship. It was getting kind of embarrassing.

Yeah—that's what the lingering heat in Amelia's cheeks was
about. Embarrassment.

"In front of you, you'll see a board containing various
vehicles."

"Oh, this is *Rush Hour*," Amelia murmured, studying the
puzzle on the table. "I used to love this game when I was a kid."

The board on the table was larger than any of the versions
she'd seen before, with the vehicles making up the puzzle
carved out of timber. One car, in the bottom left corner, was
painted red.

"The goal is to get your car—the red one—to exit through
the gap at the edge of the board. You'll have to move the other
vehicles to do so, but you can't lift or dislodge them. They must
move along the slots in the game board. They cannot be
turned."

"It's a sequence puzzle," Amelia said with a nod, studying
the board. She could already see the first three moves. "We have
to slide the cars out of the way in a specific order to clear the
way for the red car."

"Work as a team. When you've freed the red car, run to the
finish line and press your buzzer. Your time...starts...now!"

Amelia elbowed the men out of the way. This kind of game
was her *thing*. Puzzles? Logic? Please. "Stand aside, boys," she
said and vaguely heard Leo let out a low chuckle.

She started at the opposite end of the board from the red
car, because she could see that the long semi-truck blocking the
entrance would be what tripped most people up. It had to be

moved at the very beginning; otherwise, they'd get stuck halfway through the puzzle.

The carved timber vehicles made satisfying thunking noises as she slid them into their slots.

"Tell me when to run," Leo said.

"Hold on—why did you move that one?" Ari leaned over her shoulder and tried to reverse her last move. "It's going to—"

"This is what I do, Ari," Amelia barked, smacking her hand away. "Logic and analysis is my full-time job."

Amelia loved to win. Her competitiveness had helped her build a successful business. She loved to succeed. Unfortunately, that hadn't been so great for her dating life, because apparently the men she'd interacted with had brittle, fragile egos, and they found her drive intimidating. She'd learned that the hard way, but it wasn't something she could just flick off like a switch.

She wasn't giving up a new smartwatch or a trip to Europe just to save Ari Ashfield's ego. Not after he'd looked so smug when he opened the closet door on them.

"Boom!" She slid the red car out, thrust it into Leo's hands, and Leo took off at a dead sprint. Past the finish line, there was another table holding a buzzer. He slammed his palm down on it, and Amelia threw her hands up with a cheer.

Ari laughed, hooking his arm around her shoulders. His partner—she hadn't caught the guy's name, as focused as she was on the puzzle—gave her a high five. As Fred and Percival came to inspect their game board to make sure the win was legal, Leo jogged back and lifted Amelia in his arms.

Setting her down on her feet, he smiled at her with soft eyes. "Smart woman."

She beamed. Unlike some of her worst dating attempts, when Leo said it, it actually sounded like a compliment.

"What did you mean when you said logic and analysis is your full-time job?" Ari asked as Percival checked the pieces on their board against the diagram printed on a piece of paper.

Fred's gaze lifted, eyes narrowing on Amelia.

"Yeah," their fourth team member said, and she should really learn his name, but now it was too awkward to ask. "I thought you were a singer in a band. The Sex Maniacs or something?"

The urge to throttle Leo was strong, but the panic that gripped Amelia's chest was stronger. "I, um." She cleared a blockage from her throat. "Well, music is mostly math, you see."

Fred tilted his head. "Is it?"

"Sure," Amelia said, brazenly talking out of her ass. "Half-notes, quarter-notes, etcetera. Harmonies, octaves." Now she was just listing all the musical nomenclature she could remember from playing the recorder in elementary school. "It's all logical sequences. That's why there's music theory." Or something. She hoped.

"That's true." The lifeline, surprisingly, came from Ari. As the rest of the group turned to him, he shrugged. "I've been learning how to play the guitar."

Fred grunted, and Percival said, "The puzzle is correct. We have a winning team!"

Pride glowed in Amelia's chest. She looked at Leo and found him smiling at her, his hand reaching out to tug her close.

His hug felt like heaven, strong arms encasing her in warmth and safety.

It was strange, to be this comfortable with a man. Leo's green eyes twinkled in the sunlight, and he leaned down to press a soft kiss to the tip of her nose. "You're incredible, Amelia."

"I think what you meant was, 'incredibly nerdy,'" she corrected in a whisper.

He chuckled. "Same thing to me."

The warm glow in her chest spread through her body.

"Now it's time for the face-off!" Fred clapped his hands. "Gather round, everyone. Ari and Hank"—*Hank!* Amelia thought—"are about to go head-to-head with Leo and Amelia."

An army of staff cleared the puzzles from the tables and set up a new one on only two tables. One for Leo and Amelia, one for their rivals.

It was a giant Sudoku, where instead of writing numbers down on a piece of paper, they had to place numbered tiles down on a board.

"Nine numbers," Fred announced. "Each row, column, and box must contain numbers one to nine. No duplicates. You know the drill."

Freaking *easy*. Amelia could already see how to place every single number three on the board.

"The twist," Fred intoned, "Is that one of you will be the eyes, and the other will be the hands."

"I'll be the eyes," Amelia said immediately.

Ari, standing at the table next to them, grinned. "Same here."

"Okay, Eyes, put your hands behind your back. Your partner will slip their arms beneath your armpits, but first we need to blindfold them."

Oh, this was going to be messy. Amelia giggled, completely forgetting that she was supposed to be keeping an eye on everyone around her to spot any suspicious behavior. Right now, she didn't care about a silly, expensive ring. She didn't care about the mysterious list Ari had been hiding. She didn't care about Vanessa's money troubles or Robert's dark past as a made man.

She just wanted to win the puzzle challenge prize.

Leo was blindfolded, then he threaded his hands under Amelia's arms. Then Fred counted down, and they were off.

"Okay, we need a number three," Amelia said. "They're stacked in the top right corner of the table—no, other right—a bit higher. Bit higher. Yeah. Okay. Now it needs to be placed on the second slot from the left, top row. A bit more. A bit more. There. Okay. Grab another three. Other side. Yep."

This went on for a long time. Leo had to do things by feel, and Amelia had to wrestle her impatience into submission as the seconds ticked by. She glanced over, and it looked like Ari and Hank were making better progress.

"Gotta speed it up, babe," she said. "Next slot to the right for that piece. Yep. Okay. We're doing number nine now."

Minutes bled together as their audience watched on, laughing and commentating. Staff members milled around with refreshments and snacks, but Amelia had eyes only for the Sudoku board. It was down to the wire. Ari and Hank had only a few more numbers to place down, so she urged Leo to move a bit faster. A bit faster. Just a little bit more—

"Yes!" Amelia cried. "Done!"

"Percival," Fred called the butler over, who looked over their board to make sure it was correct. Leo pulled off his blindfold, but immediately returned his arms to Amelia's waist. She could feel him all against her back, butt, and legs, and she leaned into him while Percival officiated the game.

It was for show, she told herself. Not because it felt good to lean against Leo. Not because his body fit against hers like two pieces of a jigsaw. They were just pretending to be an enamored couple about to be married.

Percival glanced at Fred and nodded. Leo squeezed his arms around Amelia's stomach, and she couldn't stop the smile from spreading over her lips.

"We have our winners," Fred said, and the assembled group of guests—most of whom had obviously lost interest after being knocked out of the first round—gathered closer. "Leo and Amelia have won the puzzle challenge!"

Polite applause and a few cheers rose up, and Amelia beamed. Glancing over her shoulder, she caught Leo's eye. He winked, then dislodged his arms from her waist and came to stand beside her.

"Now for your prize," Fred announced. Everyone grew quiet, anticipation rising in the crowd. Amelia could feel it against her skin like static electricity. She'd won! She'd done it. And now she'd have something to show for it.

Fred motioned to Percival, who produced a gilded envelope. Heartbeat thundering in her ears, Amelia watched as Leo accepted it, flipping it around to run his fingers over the wax seal. He met her gaze. "Would you like to do the honors?"

"She deserves to," Hank said, smiling. "Clever woman you've got there, St. James."

Leo's gaze was warm as he handed the envelope over. Amelia's stomach was full of butterflies, her smile so wide it creaked around the edges. She broke the seal, opened the golden envelope, and pulled out a sheet of paper. It was thick vellum, folded in thirds.

Would they get a trip? A piece of tech? Maybe a romantic dinner reservation at a special restaurant? A gift certificate to a luxury spa? Oh, the possibilities were endless! A man like Fred, with connections and money...this was going to be good.

Hands trembling, Amelia unfolded it—and discovered their prize.

SEVENTEEN

"'TEN PERCENT off your next order at Marco's Pizzeria,'" Amelia read, voice flat. Hoots rose up from the audience all around, Fred's booming laugh grating on her nerves. There was fine print too: "'Order value must be over $200.'"

Laughter around them redoubled. Amelia glared at Leo, who cringed. "Sorry," he said. "There's one dud prize per retreat. They're handed out randomly. It gets talked about every year."

"Lucky losers!" Ari cackled and slapped Leo on the back. "Sounds like we're having a pizza party tonight."

"Make sure to get a vegetarian one for me!" Vanessa called out, leaning on her boyfriend's arm, a mocking smile on her lips.

"All right, people," Fred called out, "Get your orders in to St. James. We'll have to warn Marco's early so they have time to prepare."

"Wait," Amelia called, "not only do we *not* get a free trip to Europe, but we actually have to use our prize to feed you all?"

"It's tradition," Robert said with a wink, and he immediately moved up to the top spot on Amelia's suspect list. He was way too gleeful right now to be a good person.

"This is just great," Amelia grumbled, rereading the luxurious paper in her hands in case the letters had magically rearranged themselves (they hadn't).

Leo's arm curled around her shoulder, and he tugged her close. "You did a good job, though. I'm proud of you."

"Don't even," Amelia said, but her lips curled. "I'm so mad right now."

"No, you aren't." His lips brushed her temple. "If you were mad, you'd get that cute little wrinkle between your eyebrows." He laughed. "There it is."

"You're the worst."

His smile was devastating. She'd never been a good liar.

Lunch was served on the lawn, a long buffet of delicious food. Teams congratulated Amelia and Leo on their win, and Amelia got the sense that the dud prize was actually coveted among the group. She got more slaps on the back and vigorous handshakes than any of the other winners, and Trudy actually seemed a little jealous.

Given the choice, Amelia would still take Vienna, though.

Leo went around taking orders from everyone so he could call the pizza place. When he leaned over to write them down on the back of the envelope that had held their prize, he stuck out his tongue ever so slightly on the left side. It was cute.

"I know you were following me," Vanessa said quietly.

It took all of Amelia's self-control not to jump. She sipped the water bottle she'd nabbed from the drinks table and popped a brow at the other woman. "Excuse me?"

"Earlier. I know you and Leo followed me to that room."

"I don't know what you're talking about."

"My father is a gambling addict," Vanessa blurted. For a brief moment, her gaze was raw. Then she straightened her spine and sneered at Amelia. "There. Happy? He just had a bad relapse, and he needs money. It's been...a tough year."

"Oh. I'm so sorry."

"Spare me." Vanessa flicked a piece of lint off her shoulder. "I don't need your pity. I've been dealing with this for years, and it's no different from any other time. I wouldn't send him a dime, except he's my father and he'd be on the street otherwise. All right?"

"You sound like a good daughter."

Vanessa snorted, beautiful lips curled into a snarl. "And I don't need you spreading my business to everyone in the company, so keep it to yourselves and stop following me around, yeah?"

Amelia nodded, chastened. "Of course. I'm sorry."

This was Amelia's chance to ask about Ari. She could find out what they were talking about the day of the scavenger hunt, what she meant by not getting involved with him.

Vanessa held Amelia's gaze. She was fearsome, beautiful, and extremely scary. Words stuck in Amelia's throat.

The other woman pursed her lips. "And tell your fiancé not to forget my vegetarian pizza."

As she walked away, Leo approached. "What was that about?"

"I don't think Vanessa took the ring," Amelia answered quietly.

"No?"

"Her father has a problem with gambling," she told him, "but it didn't sound like he'd had a big loss or anything. Sounded like an ongoing thing. Not a good enough motive."

"You still like Ari for it?" Leo asked. They were a little ways apart from everyone, and it gave them the chance to look at all the guests and staff. Nadia even made an appearance, heading for Fred's side on the other side of the gathering. She still looked sad, but she was putting on a brave face. Her cast hadn't changed color since the first day of the retreat, and she cradled her dog in her good arm.

"I don't know. The list is weird. Why would previous clients of Goodhew want to buy a ring? It makes no sense."

"Let's call one of them and find out."

Amelia's gaze widened. "What?"

"Tonight. After dinner. We'll call one of the names on the list."

"No," Amelia said, then poked Leo in the chest. "*You* will call one of them. I'll listen and deny any involvement when you get caught."

Leo grinned. "Fine." He presented her with the list of requests for tonight's pizza party. "You can make this call instead."

. . .

NOTHING OF NOTE happened for the rest of the afternoon. The hours between lunch and dinner were free of team-building games, but a large group went for a walk around the estate together, and another group lounged by the pool. It was still a bit nippy to be lying outside in a bathing suit, so Leo tugged on Amelia's hand and went wandering in the house. They crossed Cora, George, and Gregory, who'd evidently had the same idea and were enjoying the ornate interior of the mansion. Based on George's recommendations, Leo and Amelia found a gorgeous library full of old books. It filled the entire round turret Leo had spotted when they first drove up to the house, bookshelves built into the curving walls, chairs clustered around the center. There were a few display cases holding antique-looking vases, glittering bits and bobs, and various curiosities that were no doubt priceless.

They lost themselves there for a couple of hours.

Leo stole glances at Amelia whenever she wasn't looking. She read with full focus, like the rest of the world disappeared as soon as she opened a tome. He imagined that's what she looked like when she sat down to work on a data analysis problem. It was hot.

Then again, he thought everything about her was hot. The more time he spent with her, the more attractive he found her. That had never happened to him before, and it threw him. There was no denying it: Leo had it bad.

Maybe it was a passing crush. Maybe as soon as they were out of here and back in the real world, his fondness for her would fade. It wasn't really love. After all, he didn't know what love was. This was just a strange reaction to a strange situation.

That evening, the pizza party was a huge hit. Amelia even seemed to enjoy herself, spending most of the time sitting next to Cora, their heads bent close together as they talked.

"Smart woman you've got there," Fred said, nudging his shoulder to Leo's.

He was becoming increasingly uncomfortable with the lies he'd had to tell this week. He respected his boss, and he loved his job. He hated that he'd dug this hole for himself. His response, at least, was true: "She's pretty incredible."

Fred studied him for a beat. "I'm glad to have you here this week, St. James. Your management of the Montague vow renewal was excellent. You stayed cool even when the clients were difficult, and you made sure you delivered on the brief. I want you to know you deserve to be here with all the rest of the team. The work you've been putting in the past twelve to eighteen months hasn't gone unnoticed."

Throat tight, Leo dipped his chin. That was high praise from Fred. The big man had a gregarious personality, but it was rare that he was so generous with his compliments.

"This job means a lot to me," Leo told him. Another truth. "People don't always take me seriously, but I feel like I've finally found something I'm good at. I appreciate you trusting me with larger events this year."

Fred's gaze was solemn. He let out a short sigh and opened his mouth to speak, but Percival, wearing his tails and tie, as always, materialized at Fred's elbow. "Sir," the butler said quietly. "A word."

"Excuse me." Fred followed his butler a few steps away, but not far enough that Leo couldn't hear what they said.

"Some items seem to be missing," the butler said. "We've done a search of the house, and three of the rare coins in the library collection have been removed. The lock on the glass cabinet was broken."

Leo's heart thundered.

"Grandmama's cake topper and tiara?" Fred hissed.

"Still secure, but it looks like the lock on their display case was tampered with. With your approval, I'd like to move them to a more secure location."

"Do it." Fred's voice was a low rumble that promised death. "Who's been in the library? I want a list of names. Check the cameras."

Uh-oh. That was not good.

Leo willed himself not to glance at the two men and instead smiled as Trudy touched her glass to his. As she greeted him, the rest of Fred and Percival's conversation was drowned out. "You're a lucky man, Leo," she said, fondness in her gaze when she glanced at Amelia.

"I am," Leo agreed.

"Did you know, Robert and I were beginning to believe your fiancée didn't exist at all." She laughed, shaking her head. "He had this whole theory about never having met her, and her silly stage name that sounded like something a toddler would come up with when they were trying to lie." She batted at his arm, shaking her head fondly. "Hilarious."

Leo's smile was tight. "Yeah. Ha...ha. Hilarious. Kind of like the rumor that Robert was in the Mob."

Trudy's expression froze for the slightest moment. Then she chuckled a bit woodenly and shook her head. "Where do people come up with this stuff? Excuse me." Just like that, she walked away, leaving Leo slightly shocked.

...Was Rob a former made man?

By the time Amelia joined him and they made their way to their room, Leo's head was spinning. He kept expecting Fred to corner him and accuse him of stealing the rare coins from the library, but his boss had merely stayed in the room and watched his employees with a line between his brows.

"Did you make any discoveries?" Amelia said when they'd locked the door to their suite.

Leo filled her in on the coins and on Trudy's reaction, to Amelia's utter amazement. He watched her face change from interest to shock to concern, landing on delight tinged with worry.

"Does Fred think we took the coins?"

"I don't know."

Amelia gnawed her bottom lip. "Someone's stealing from him."

"All this time, I half-thought Nadia had just lost her ring," Leo admitted. "And I figured Ari was lying about the watch, and he was really looking for the list we took."

"Me too."

"But with the coins gone, I think there is actually a thief among us."

"I didn't even notice the coins," Amelia said, frowning.

"You were too engrossed in your book." Leo had loved watching her read. He'd spent way too long staring at her as she gasped and giggled and lost herself in the story she'd picked up.

"The coins were next to the door, on the far side of the writing desk next to the window."

"What do we do?" Amelia tucked her legs up and wrapped her arms around her shins, resting her chin on her knee. "It was kind of fun snooping around before, but..."

"Now it feels serious?"

She nodded.

Leo stretched out on the armchair he'd chosen, threading his fingers together behind his head. He glanced at the couch cushion beside Amelia and set his lips in a grim line. "Let's call those numbers and find out what Ari's hiding."

EIGHTEEN

AMELIA WATCHED Leo fetch the list from beneath the couch cushion before grabbing his laptop. He settled on the couch beside Amelia, his knee touching hers as he arranged the laptop and the list on the coffee table.

She wondered if she was making a mistake. None of this was supposed to happen. She was supposed to learn some tips about how to get over her crippling awkwardness, pretend to be Leo's doting fiancée, then go on her way.

The worst part was Amelia was enjoying herself. She liked the way Leo glanced at her, eyes glimmering. She liked how he put his hand on her knee and squeezed gently, either to reassure her or himself.

Amelia licked her lips. "What do we do now?"

"Give me your phone."

She straightened. "Why my phone?"

"They might be able to connect my number to the company."

Amelia tilted her head from side to side, then tapped on the laptop a few times. "We'll use an online phone service. It's anonymous." She set it up, then tilted the laptop toward Leo. Her heart thumped. "It's ready. Who do you want to call?"

"Let's just go down the list."

The first two numbers had no answer. The third call was picked up by a woman.

"Heather Burton?" Leo said.

"This is she," an older woman replied. "Who am I speaking to?"

"My name is"—a panicked look at Amelia—"Rod...Todd," Leo lied. "I'm calling on behalf of Ari Ashfield."

Rod Todd, Amelia mouthed, incredulous. That was nearly as bad as Kitty Catelli. Leo seriously had to work on his fake name game.

There was a brief pause. Then, "Ari? From Goodhew? Our account is closed as of three months ago. My assistant confirmed it. What's this regarding?"

Amelia frowned, then listened to Leo lie through his teeth and ultimately accomplish nothing. They found no new information. Amelia slumped back on the sofa as Leo hung up the call. He scowled at the screen, then picked up the list to try again.

"Okay, hold up," Amelia said. "You need to take a breath and come up with a better fake name."

"What's wrong with Rod Todd?"

Amelia smacked him on the arm, laughing. "Stop it."

Leo didn't, in fact, stop it. He kept calling himself Rod Todd in every phone call, grinning at her the whole time.

It was the tenth phone call that netted them some information. The man on the other side of the call sounded like he was in his twenties or thirties, and when he heard Ari's name, he said, "Oh, great. I was going to give Ari a call, but I didn't think he'd launched the new company yet. I've got a friend looking to book a yacht in Miami for a bachelor party. Will he be booking events by August?"

Amelia straightened. New company?

"Great," Leo said, voice calm. How was his heart not thumping as hard as Amelia's? "I'd love to grab the details now, if it's convenient."

"Sure," the other man said, and he rattled off a name and phone number and a brief description of what they wanted for the bachelor party. Leo stayed calm through the call, then finally reached over and hung up the call on the screen when the conversation ended.

He met Amelia's wide-eyed stare. "Ari's poaching clients," he said quietly. "Either he's forgotten about the non-compete clause in our contract, he doesn't care about it, or he's trying to circumvent it somehow."

Amelia blew out a breath. Her mind was spinning. That must have been what Vanessa was upset about in the hallway. She didn't want to get in trouble when she needed to keep her job. But... "Why would he steal valuables from Fred? What about the watch?"

"Maybe he lied about the watch. Maybe he needs money to start his new company."

"And he's getting it by stealing?"

Leo leaned back on the couch beside her. His body was emanating warmth all down her side. He turned his head to look at her, then reached up to push a strand of hair off her forehead. "If he's willing to stab Fred in the back by poaching clients, he might be willing to do something worse."

"Twelve million dollars is a lot," she said. "Would he even need to start a new company? Couldn't he just go to Mexico and live on the beach for the rest of his days?"

"I don't know," Leo admitted. "Probably."

A knock on the door interrupted them. Amelia frowned, then stood up and opened the door. Fred and Percival stood on the other side. Both of them looked grim.

"Amelia," Fred said with a nod.

"What's up?" Amelia pulled the door a little bit wider, once Leo had shoved the list of names on the laptop keyboard and closed the screen.

Fred looked over her shoulder. "St. James." His gaze returned to Amelia as he stepped into their room, so chilled it made Amelia shiver. "Were you in the library today?"

Amelia nodded. "Yes. We spent a few hours reading."

"Was anyone else in there with you?"

Leo came to stand beside Amelia, his arm a comforting weight across her shoulders. "No. We were there from about one until four p.m. and no one else came in. George is the one who recommended we check it out."

Fred's lips compressed as his eyes narrowed. He shifted his gaze from Leo to Amelia, who stiffened in response. "Some valuable rare coins have gone missing. We're trying to determine a timeline. They were in the glass case on the southern wall, next to the writing desk."

"I saw them," Leo stated, his hand squeezing Amelia's shoulder. "Displayed on blue velvet, right?"

"That's right."

"Someone stole them?" Amelia squeaked, then regretted her question when it drew Fred's gaze back to her. His face was all hard lines and grim suspicion.

"Yes," he replied, an odd weight to the word.

"They were there when we left," Leo told his boss.

"I'll be calling the police," Fred said. "No one's to leave the grounds until this is cleared up."

"Of course," Leo replied.

The two men left, and Amelia closed the door behind them. When she turned back to look at Leo, her heart cracked at the look of devastation on his face.

"He thinks it was us," Leo said bleakly. "He's going to fire me."

"Hey." Amelia grabbed his hand and pulled him to the couch. She sat down beside him, still holding his hand. "He's just trying to figure out who took his stuff, same as we are. He didn't accuse you of anything."

"He knows we're lying, Amelia. Fred's not a fool. I saw the way he was looking at you." He rested his elbows on his knees and dropped his head, gripping his hair with both hands. He tugged, letting out a low noise. "*Fuck.* I never should have lied. This was such a stupid idea. Why didn't I just tell him I was single?" He scrubbed his face, then left his hands there, covering his expression. Amelia had the horrible suspicion he was trying not to cry.

Not knowing what to do, Amelia put her hand on his upper back and stroked him in slow circles. Leo had been so confident in their time together. She'd never seen him worried—not like this.

"This job means a lot to you," she said, and it sounded so pathetic in the heavy silence of the room.

Leo let out a bitter snort. He dropped his hands, letting them dangle between his knees. "I know what you're thinking. I just want to party for a living, and I'm sad the gravy train is ending."

"That's not what I'm thinking at all."

His lips twisted, but he didn't look at her. "Forgive me for not believing you. I'm the guy who gave chlamydia to his entire college. The guy who can't hold down a relationship. The guy who parties for a living because he can't let go of his glory days."

"That's not what you do for a living." The words came out heated—more forceful than Amelia had intended.

Leo finally turned his head to look at her. The green of his eyes was so bright, but his face was horribly drawn and tense. He said nothing.

She frowned at him. "You plan elaborate events for demanding clients," she told him. "You take in information from them, coordinate multiple vendors and subcontractors, and deliver on their expectations in high-pressure situations."

He blinked.

Amelia wasn't done. "You've told me only a handful of stories, but I know you don't party for a living, Leo. I just spent the last six months trying to get my sister's wedding to go off without a hitch, and I *know* how hard that was. The last three weeks of planning were pure hell. And I did it in Stirling, where weddings are basically part of the town's mission statement. It was still horribly complicated. I needed seventeen different spreadsheets to keep track of everything. So don't give me that stupid line about you being a brainless playboy wanting to party all the time. I know it's a mask, and it makes me angry every time you put it on. You're more than your stupid college nick-name, Leo, so don't be a coward. Stop hiding behind it."

Chest heaving, Amelia realized her tirade had ended shrilly, with her voice raised and her cheeks red. She glared at him and had the ridiculous, childish urge to stick out her tongue.

"You really believe that?" Leo grated.

"Believe *what*."

"That I'm more than my college nickname."

Anger rose in Amelia so fast she thought the top of her skull would fly off from the pressure. "Of course I believe that!" She poked him in the chest. "You're smart and hard-working and so stupidly beautiful it's hard to look at you sometimes. And, by the way, these are things *you* should be telling *me* because our agreement is meant to bolster *my* ego."

"You're smart and hard-working," Leo said, eyes intent, "and so stupidly beautiful it's hard to look at you sometimes."

"Har-har," she spat, making to get up off the couch. She shouldn't have been angry. It was silly, really. Didn't she know exactly how it felt to have her confidence dinged, even when it didn't make sense on paper? She knew what self-loathing felt like. She knew what shame felt like.

But it made her so *mad* to see Leo like this. And it made her even madder to think about the way Trish and Lauren and Rinn had giggled behind their manicured fingers about him. How much ridicule had he endured? How long had it taken for him to believe it?

So she had to get off the couch and go stomp around in the bedroom or down the hallway or out into the flower garden. She had to get away and calm down before she yelled at Leo some more, who didn't deserve to be yelled at at all.

Getting away from Leo was suddenly the most important thing, because beneath her anger was another emotion. One that had grown in her way too fast. One that would do nothing but hurt her in the long run.

But as she stood up, Leo caught her hand. She tried to tug it away, but Leo held on. He pulled, then caught her around the waist and dragged her down to his body, so she had no choice but to straddle his hips where he sat on the couch.

With one arm banded around her back, he lifted his other hand to cup her cheek. "I wasn't lying, Amelia. You're an incredible woman."

"Yeah, well, you're..." Her bitter words petered out. She wanted to push away from him, protect herself. Because that emotion in her breast was white-hot infatuation—or maybe something more.

His hand slid along her cheekbone and tangled in her hair, gripping tight. The arm around her waist was like a steel band. Immovable.

"Are we back to my spreadsheet now?" Amelia asked rudely, desperately scrabbling to regain control over the situation. Her body was heating under his touch. The pinpricks of pain on her scalp were quickly turning to liquid pleasure. She *liked* being held like this, being caught by him. "We could go over the intercourse section so I know what I've been doing wrong all these years."

A low, rumbling growl rattled Leo's throat. "This has nothing to do with your fucking spreadsheet," he said, then tightened his grip on her hair, angled her face, and kissed her.

She fought him for a fraction of a second, then lust went off like a rocket inside her. Fingers curling around the back of his neck, she pressed herself against his chest and let him control the kiss. It was a punishing embrace. His stubble rasped against her skin, the slight burn of it a delicious counterpoint to his soft lips, the velvet stroke of his tongue.

They kissed like they were fighting each other, with an edge of anger and aggression that Amelia had never felt before. It consumed her, the lust and fury and passion of it all. Hips bucking, she moaned against Leo's lips as the arm around her back slid down, his hand clawing at her dress. He finally reached up under it to grab a handful of her ass, kneading her flesh with his big hand.

"This dress has been driving me crazy all day," he growled, pulling away to look at the offending garment. One hand was still twisted in Amelia's hair, the other shaping her flank and bottom. Leo held her like that, then brought his mouth to her breast and bit her through the fabric.

She gasped, bucking her hips. Feeling his erection beneath her, Amelia moaned and ground down on it, drawing a hiss from Leo's lips. She liked that noise, so she did it again. The placket of his zipper covered his arousal, and she angled herself on top of it and rocked—

"Oh!"

A low groan escaped Leo's lips. He slid his hand out of her hair and gripped her hip. "That feel good?"

"Yes," she panted. "Yes."

"You like riding my cock? Thinking about how it'll feel once it's inside you?" His hand was still kneading her ass, and he moved it up to clamp on her other hip. Holding her firmly with both hands, Leo helped her grind down on top of him, right where she needed it most.

Another moan escaped Amelia's throat, her hands gripping Leo's shoulders for purchase. She could feel how big and hard he was, the ridge of his shaft giving her just the right amount of pressure—

"You're so beautiful, Amelia," he growled. "So fucking pretty when you're about to come."

When she was about to... "What?"

It was never this easy. She overthought things, became awkward, messed up when she was in bed with a man. Awareness prickled over Amelia's body, thoughts filtering through her mind like wisps of smoke.

Leo guided her movements with one hand, then used the other to wrench her bodice down. Plumping her breast, he brought it to his mouth and sucked. A bright, blazing sensation ripped through her nipple as he laved it with his tongue.

Those wisps of thought disappeared. All that existed was Leo. His big, hard body beneath hers. His mouth, tongue, and hands. His hard cock pressing against her clit with every rock of her hips.

When she came apart with a cry, he groaned in response. His lips coasted over her throat and up to her ear as he pulled her close, whispering dirty encouragement in her ear. Not letting her ease up, he used his hand to grind her hips over his clothed cock over and over again until she shuddered and bucked against his touch.

Dazed, Amelia pushed herself off his chest, curling her fingers into his shirt. She wanted more, like her orgasm had only stoked her lust instead of sating it.

"How was that?" Leo asked, a cocky grin curling his lips. His cock was still rock-hard beneath her core.

She affected a casual shrug and said, "It was fine," but the effect was somewhat diminished by the fact that her left breast was utterly exposed and still gleaming with Leo's kiss, and she was pretty sure her cheeks were red, her eyes glazed.

But Leo chuckled darkly. "Just fine?"

"Good enough to take a few notes down for the spreadsheet, I suppose."

His eyes sparked, and Amelia realized she liked teasing him. She liked poking at him, because it felt dangerous and exciting.

Her reward was a big hand between her legs, ripping her panties to the side. Without warning, he entered her with a finger, then immediately added another. "So wet for me," Leo said, grunting as he thrust his fingers inside. "My girl wants more, doesn't she?"

Amelia whimpered, and Leo added a third finger. They both groaned, Amelia's head falling back, her eyes closing.

"Fuck this," Leo said and took his hand away. Amelia didn't have time to protest, because she was lifted into his arms and carried into the bedroom. Tossed unceremoniously on top of the blankets, Amelia bounced once with a girlish squeak, then watched Leo climb up after her. He reached under her dress and ripped her panties off, tossing them across the room.

His hands were hot as they spread her knees, his eyes savage when they landed on her core. A bolt of self-consciousness went through her, but it was banished when Leo said, "You're so goddamn pretty, Amelia. Every part of you."

"No one's ever said that about my..." Her cheeks heated.

"About this beautiful pussy?" He pushed her dress up so it bunched on her stomach, then used his hands to stroke up and down her legs, his thumbs teasing closer and closer to her slit. It felt like fire coursing through her veins at every teasing touch. She wondered if she'd come apart from just this, from his hands on her thighs and his eyes drinking her in.

Then he made another pass, and when his thumbs got close to her core, a wet, squelching sound filled the room. Horrified, Amelia tried to clamp her legs shut. Embarrassment blazed through her. She squeezed her eyes shut, remembering the sneer on Josh's lips whenever she was wet enough to make those kinds of noises. One time he'd actually gagged and refused to have sex with her, asking her to give him a blowjob instead. It had been utterly humiliating.

But Amelia's knees made contact with Leo's body and she couldn't close them, couldn't hide herself. His hands paused on her thighs. "Amelia?"

"I'm sorry," she said in a small voice.

He froze. "About what?"

Her hands reached down to cover herself. "I'm too wet. I'm sorry. It's disgusting."

There was another pause, and Amelia didn't have the courage to open her eyes. She hid herself with her hands, cheeks hot, wanting the moment to end. All the lust that had blazed through her body vanished in an instant. Then the bed dipped, and her throat grew tight. Leo was leaving. And why wouldn't he? She'd ruined the moment, as usual. Was it even a surprise? This happened every time she got intimate with a man.

But Leo didn't get off the bed; he came to lie down beside her. Tugging gently on her arms, he gathered her against his chest and held her, one hand softly stroking her hair. Tension drained from her muscles, and after a few moments, Amelia gathered the courage to open her eyes.

Leo was watching her, his brows drawn. "I'm going to kill him, you know."

It was so unexpected that a laugh just fell out of her lips. "What?"

"That asshole who actually convinced you that your body was disgusting? I'll find him and kill him."

A whole new wave of shame crashed over her. "I feel so stupid," she said, dropping her eyes to his chin. She couldn't meet his gaze. "It's been so long. Six years. I should be over it. I just..." She took a deep breath. "Look, I understand that I ruined the moment. I'm sorry. At least now you know why I agreed to this arrangement in the first place. I'm a mess."

"You didn't ruin the moment."

She snorted. "Um, I'm pretty sure I did?"

He took her hand in his, kissing her knuckles. He placed her palm on his cheek, then ran his fingers down her arm, over her ribs, and down to her hip. "I'd like to touch you," Leo admitted. "Can I do that?"

The thought of making more of those embarrassing noises made her chest feel hot, but Leo's expression was so sincere. If she couldn't do this with him now, when would she be able to? They lived in a little bubble at this retreat, away from the real world.

And, though she didn't want to admit why, Amelia wanted to share this moment with *him*.

Unable to speak, she nodded. Instead of moving between her legs, his hand moved up to coast over her ribs, then to the back of her dress. He tugged her zipper down and helped her wriggle out of the garment. Then he pulled his own shirt off and shucked his pants off, giving her a clear view of his boxer-briefs —and the outline of his hard cock.

The sight of it shocked Amelia. He was still hard. He still wanted her. She let out a long, trembling exhale. He had his thumbs in the waistband of his underwear, but after a pause, left them on. Then he came to lie down beside her, his hands stroking over her naked body.

Kisses peppered her shoulder, her jaw, her lips. With every sweep of his warm, calloused palm over her skin, a bit of stress melted out of Amelia's body. His kisses were like a calming drug, slowly untangling the thoughts and worries that had gripped her mind.

Spending time shaping her breasts and tracing her nipples, Leo watched the movement of his hand over her body, occasionally letting out short, deep noises. "I love your body," he told her quietly.

"My boobs are on the smallish side, though."

He cupped her right breast. "A perfect handful."

A smile teased at Amelia's lips, which turned into a gasp when he pinched her nipple. Leo let out a low rumble and did it again. He kissed her, his tongue soft against hers, his arm curling around her head so they were pressed against each other, facing each other as they lay on their sides.

When her body was languid, melting into the mattress beside Leo, he let his hands slip lower and pushed her thighs wide. But still he didn't touch her center. He swept his palms up one thigh and down the other. He traced her hipbones down to the crease of her thighs, every touch feathery-light, teasing, until Amelia thought she'd lose her mind.

"I'd like to taste you," Leo said, low and quiet.

She stiffened. "No. I'm not—"

His hand slid up to her waist, soothing. "Okay."

"I'm sorry."

"Stop apologizing." He kissed her temple. "Can I touch you?"

She nodded, heart thundering. This felt different than what they'd done on the couch in front of the mirror, or the frantic orgasm he'd given her earlier. Amelia was exposed now, and not just because she was naked. There was an intimacy to their touches, a depth to their connection that didn't exist before.

Leo's hand continued its soft torture, over her thighs, brushing her mound, teasing her hips until Amelia's knees fell apart and she let out a low, keening noise. Then, with the barest tips of his fingers, he ran his hand down her slit. Amelia gasped, that soft touch rocking through her body until her hips bucked off the bed, chasing Leo's touch.

His exhale was ragged as he touched her again, a little bit harder. His fingers slipped against her wet flesh as he groaned, dropping his forehead to her shoulder, his body hard and trembling like he was holding himself back with every ounce of control.

Lips brushing her shoulder, he touched and teased between Amelia's legs until her thighs trembled. He slid his fingers inside her again and they both groaned in unison. He added a second, then a third. Amelia's hips bucked off the bed, her heels digging into the mattress as her breaths came short and sharp.

"Leo," she complained.

"Yes, love?"

"I want you."

His fingers dove into her again, the heel of his palm pressing against her clit. He ground down on her as she moaned, and when their eyes met, his gaze was dark. "What do you want?"

Amelia wasn't very good at dirty talk. She'd always been too self-conscious to ask for what she wanted in bed. She'd never felt comfortable enough to do anything but try to keep her whirling thoughts at bay. But now, with Leo, it was different. She ached for him, needed him, knew that he was right there with her. She felt safe.

"I want your cock, Leo," she whispered. "Want you inside me."

To punctuate her words, she finally gathered the courage to reach for him. Gripping him through his underwear, she squeezed his shaft as if there had been any doubt of what cock she'd been talking about.

Leo closed his eyes and gasped, then leaped off the bed and shucked his boxer-briefs off in less than a heartbeat. Then he pawed at his pants and came back with a condom. Watching him roll it on his shaft was erotic enough to make Amelia bite her lip.

Her heart thundered. Maybe it had been naive to think this wasn't going to happen. Hadn't she wanted to regain her confidence in bed with his help? Hadn't his skills in seduction been the whole point?

Somehow, Amelia had never pictured it happening like this. She hadn't thought his gaze would be so intent. She hadn't imagined his hands would be so reverent as they coasted over her waist, her ribs, her breasts. She hadn't imagined Leo would kiss her like this moment meant something to him as he notched himself between her spread thighs.

"You sure?" he grated, the muscles of his neck stark.

"Yes," Amelia answered, and she smiled because it was the truth.

He kissed her once, softly, then reached between them to position himself—and entered her.

NINETEEN

SHE FELT BETTER than Leo could have imagined. For an instant, as he pushed inside her, pure, blind panic overtook him. He knew this was different. He knew this would change him. He knew he could no longer lie to himself.

"Amelia, I—"

He stopped himself with a groan. He couldn't tell her how he felt. Not like this. Not when she'd essentially hired him, and he hadn't had the self-control to stop himself from touching her. Not when she deserved so much better than him.

She moaned, tilting her hips. Her sweet body was heaven beneath his. He cupped her breast, sliding his cock out and back in with a long, punishing stroke. His reward was another moan and a flush on Amelia's cheeks. She watched him with her pale gray eyes, looking utterly dazed.

"It feels so good," she whispered. "I didn't know it could feel this good."

Curving his body over hers, he kissed her long and hard as he fought to maintain control. He wanted to come already, just from feeling the warmth and wetness of her. She was perfect—perfect for him.

This woman would be his undoing, this beautiful fairy who'd trapped him with a scowl.

Her nails dug into his ass as she urged him deeper, drawing a ragged gasp from his throat. He braced himself on his arms to get extra purchase, driving his hips into the woman he loved. Her breasts jiggled, her eyes glazed over, and Leo was done for.

There was no coming back from this.

When she reached up and touched his cheek, he caught her hand—her left hand—and pressed a kiss to her palm. She wore his ring, hadn't taken it off. Right now, as their bodies joined in the most intimate of ways, that ring felt anything but fake. He wanted her to wear it forever. Wanted her to be his in truth.

Emotions tore at the very fabric of him. Sex had never been like this. Never so intense, never so fucking good. Trying to wrestle control back over his raging heart, Leo grabbed Amelia's legs and held them up over his shoulders. He drove his cock deep into her like he could thrust his way to making her understand what she meant to him.

"Leo," Amelia gasped. "Leo, Leo."

"I'm here," he replied, voice a bare rasp. He gripped her ankles, held them wide, nearly lost his mind. Sweat beaded on his forehead, dripped down his spine. He was gone. He was done. He was never coming back from this.

Stacking her legs to the side, he changed the angle until she moaned loud and long. Maybe if he showed her all his tricks, she wouldn't want to leave. Maybe if he made this good for her, she'd understand—

"Oh my God," she gasped, gripping the blankets. "Oh my God, Leo. You're so deep. You—" A ragged inhale. A whimpering exhale.

He turned her onto her stomach and thrust into her, then lifted her torso until her back was plastered to his front. "Grab my neck," he said, lifting her arms so they were curved behind her head, clinging to his nape. She tangled her fingers into his hair and pulled, like she didn't even know what she was doing. He bit her shoulder, losing his mind. Her breasts were lifted, nipples taut. He played with them until she keened and chanted his name, then let his hand slide down to rub her sweet, swollen clit. He dropped his fingers lower to feel himself entering her, unable to process the sheer bliss of the sensation.

Amelia—his Amelia, his woman, his love—wrenched his hand back up and pressed it against her bud. A feral smile curled his lips; he liked when she demanded her pleasure from him like it was her due. When she came, he felt like a superhero. She gripped his cock with tight inner muscles, and he gasped, wanting to make it good for her but quickly losing his grip—

He roared, the sound muffled by her skin. He bit her shoulder, holding so tight, so tight. She collapsed onto her hands, and he fell right there with her, his body draped over hers. After three or four ragged breaths, he pulled away from her and disposed of the condom. When he came back to the bedroom on shaking legs, she was on her side, limbs splayed, eyes half-closed.

"Leo," she mumbled. "What..."

Curling his body around hers, he ran a hand down her side

and over her hip. Her beautiful, soft body. He'd never tire of it. He pressed a kiss to her nape.

"What just happened?" she asked, voice dreamy.

He chuckled, curling his arm around her. "That good, huh?"

"Your ego will be totally unmanageable after this," she said in a slightly slurred voice. "But, wow. I didn't know it could be like that."

Neither did I, he thought.

They slept wrapped around each other, waking up an hour later in a daze. Amelia stumbled to the bathroom and he heard her electric toothbrush whirring, then she came back and collapsed in bed. When he took his turn in the bathroom, a part of him wondered if he'd be relegated to the couch when he came out.

But Amelia smiled at him and spread her arms, and he climbed under the blankets beside her. For tonight, at least, he'd be next to her.

AMELIA WOKE AT DAWN, her face mashed into the pillow. Leo's leg was a heavy weight across the backs of her thighs, his arm slung across her shoulder blades. She turned her head. His face was softened by sleep, his eyelashes dark against his cheeks. She couldn't believe she'd actually had sex with a man who looked like that.

It terrified her. Emotion filled her chest until it crowded out her lungs. She could barely breathe.

Somehow, in a week, she'd fallen for this man. As she

shifted, the rising sun glinted on her ring—but it wasn't her ring, was it? It was rented from a jeweler. She'd give it back to Leo in a little more than twenty-four hours. She curled her fingers and stared at the rock and its Art Deco band, dreaming of a world where she and Leo were in the same league.

She'd been stupid to agree to this, because now her heart was involved. She should have seen this coming.

"Morning." Leo's voice was rough with sleep, his eyes half-closed. With his arm still across her back, he pulled her closer and nuzzled his face into the crook of her neck. "I love the smell of your skin."

Maybe she could enjoy this for a little bit longer, Amelia reasoned. Maybe she could block out the outside world, forget about her spreadsheet, and pretend Leo's feelings were as tangled as her own.

"Morning," she said, trailing her hand over his chest. She liked the scent of him too, and the way it felt to wake up next to him in a big king bed.

His hands roamed over her body, and she liked that even more. Spreading her thighs for him, she let out a little whimper while her own hand went on an expedition south. Leo groaned when she curled her fingers around his shaft.

"I love it when you touch me," he told her, lips near her ear. "Your touch is so sweet, Amelia."

He wrapped a big hand around hers, guiding her to jerk him off a bit harder. Her heart stumbled. It had been so long since she'd shared a bed with a man, and it had never felt like this. She'd never felt so safe, like whatever she did, Leo would be right there alongside her.

Her eyes followed the movement of their joined hands, her head resting on his chest. Leo's other hand stroked her hair, the softness of his touch a complete contrast to the strong grip he kept on his shaft.

"You like watching?" he rasped. "You like seeing the two of us jerk me off?"

She nodded, her cheek rubbing against his chest hair. The hand he'd been using to stroke her hair smoothed down her spine and began plumping her ass. He let his fingers tease the cleft of her ass as they watched the movement of their hands on his cock.

"You make me so hard, Amelia," he told her, then pressed a kiss to the crown of her head. "Just knowing you're watching this is making me want to explode."

A fine tremor passed through her body. She rubbed her thighs together, and Leo let out a low grunt. He let go of his cock and rolled her onto her back, pushing her legs apart. Then his hand was there where she needed it, teasing, circling, penetrating. She arched off the bed, panting. "Leo."

"Come on my hand, Amelia," he commanded. "I want to watch you."

"I'm trying," she panted, which drew a laugh from him.

He pressed a kiss to her temple, her neck. "Yesterday was the hottest fucking thing I've ever done," he said, and Amelia knew he was just giving her lip service. A man with Leo's experience probably had a mental catalog of fantasies he'd watched come true.

But it was still a nice thought, to imagine that Amelia could make him unravel. That she had the power to undo him, as he had that same power over her.

He kissed her earlobe, breath ghosting over her throat. "I want you to grind that pussy on my hand the way you ground down on my cock yesterday. You made my jeans wet," he told her. "Did you know that? You soaked through your underwear and left a pretty little dark spot on my pants, and don't you dare apologize for it."

She gusted out her best approximation of a laugh, her hips bucking as he wound her tighter and tighter with nothing more than his hand and a few dirty words.

"I'm going to jerk off to that memory for the rest of my life."

"You are?" Amelia's eyes flew wide, and she realized that Leo had shifted so he could fist himself with one hand while he blew her mind with the other.

"No fucking question," he grated. "My girl making herself come, fully clothed, just from dry-humping my cock. I'll never forget it."

His girl. He'd called her his girl again. While Amelia's lagging brain tried to process it, Leo did something clever with his fingers, changed the angle, increased the pressure...and all thought fled from her brain. She came apart with a cry, her hands flying to his biceps. She held on for dear life as her body detonated. He coaxed her through her orgasm, wrenching every drop of pleasure until she pushed his hand away with a whimper.

Then the bed shifted, and she heard crinkling. Lust jumped in her—her body was buzzing from the orgasm. It seemed it would be like this every time with Leo; she'd always want more.

Before he could position himself between her thighs, Amelia pushed him onto his back and straddled him.

She could count on two hands the number of times she'd ridden on top. After trying it a few times, her ex had told her she was terrible at it and refused to do the position with her. She hadn't gotten far enough with other men to work up the nerve to try again.

But Leo was different. She could see from the heat in his eyes that he liked when she wrestled control from him. She felt safe with him. She wanted to try all the things she hadn't had the courage to explore with others.

"If I'm not good at this, just tell me," she panted, grabbing his cock to position it at her entrance.

"I'm not going to dignify that with a re—" Leo interrupted himself with a moan as she sank down on top of him.

A wicked smile curled Amelia's lips. Leo's fingers dug into her hips as she began to move, rocking up and down, then leaning forward to go forward and back. She gasped, and Leo tightened his hold on her.

"Grab the headboard," he said between breaths. "Use it for leverage."

Oh. Oh, wow. Amelia's breaths came short and sharp, then stopped completely when Leo bucked his hips in time with her movements. It took her approximately half a second to erupt, her second orgasm of the morning tearing through her body with such force all she could do was cling on for the ride and hope she survived to the end.

She felt the moment Leo came. His neck went taut, and a flush stained his chest and cheeks. He gritted his teeth and let out a rough grunt, the sight of all that tension, all that masculinity sending another wave of pleasure rocking through Amelia's veins.

She collapsed on top of him, wrapped up in his arms. While they were still joined, he rolled them over so he was on top, then kissed her long and deep, his hands cupping her face and jaw as fine tremors passed through both their bodies.

"Amelia," he finally gusted out, leaning his forehead against hers.

"I need to go brush my teeth," she said, dazed, and Leo began to laugh. "What?" Amelia complained, voice far away.

"A man needs a bit of coddling after that kind of performance. You should be petting me and telling me what a good job I did."

Amelia gave him a few cursory pats on the top of his head. "Good boy."

He laughed harder. "Don't worry," he said as he rolled off of her. "My ego is safe from overinflation around you."

She grinned, smacking his chest with the back of her hand. It took her a few more long minutes to work up the strength to move, but she did, eventually, make it to the bathroom for her morning ablutions. As she stared at herself in the mirror, she saw bright eyes, mussed hair, and flushed cheeks. She couldn't help but smile around her toothbrush.

Sex was *great*.

TWENTY

SATURDAY MORNING'S breakfast was another incredible spread, and Amelia decided to exercise restraint by only eating one of Camilla's pastries instead of three. She'd indulged enough over the past twelve hours. Leo's shoulder brushed hers, and she couldn't help the heat that singed her cheeks at the innocent contact.

She was in so much trouble.

Finding a seat next to Cora, Amelia smiled at the older lady who gave her a knowing look. Amelia blushed harder. Apparently, their night of hot sex was written all over her face. Whoops.

Leo settled next to her, then got up and poured them both coffees. He grabbed the sugar and cream from the center of the table and moved them in front of Amelia's plate without her asking, then dug into his food. Amelia blinked at the little jug of cream and the pot of sugar with the cute little spoon like they were aliens from another galaxy.

He'd noticed how she took her coffee? Not only that, but he'd made sure she had everything she needed without her even asking?

Leo's hand dropped onto her thigh as Trudy sat across from him and started a pleasant, casual conversation. Leo drank is coffee and spoke to the other woman while his hand warmed Amelia's thigh, as if that touch were the most natural thing in the world.

Meanwhile, Amelia's world listed like a boat about to capsize.

Maybe it was pathetic to be so rocked by casual touches and the fixings for her coffee, but she'd never been with a man who'd paid attention to her needs or cared enough to fulfill them. That little jug of cream with the cheery spout and swoopy handle was knocking on Amelia's heart and demanding to be let in.

With shaking hands, she picked it up and poured a dollop into her coffee. She watched the cream create puffy clouds in her coffee, her spoon suspended above it while her heart thundered.

"This morning is volleyball," Trudy told Leo after he asked about the schedule for the day. "Now that the dud prize is out of the way, I'm sure competition will be fierce." She winked at Amelia.

Amelia responded with a bland smile. It was all she could manage. Finally dipping her spoon into her coffee, she stirred the clouds of cream away.

Leo shifted his hand away from her thigh, propping it on the back of her chair. He ate a bite of his scrambled eggs and picked up a rasher of bacon, like having his arm around Amelia's shoulders while he ate breakfast was an everyday occurrence.

"You any good at volleyball?" Leo asked her, eyes shining.

"Shouldn't you know that about the woman you're about to marry?" Cora interjected.

"We haven't covered volleyball yet, but I still feel confident we're a good fit." Leo grinned at the older woman, sounding, to Amelia's ears, like he meant every word.

Or maybe that was just what she wanted to hear?

Trudy barked a laugh. "Funnily enough, in twenty-two years of marriage, Rob and I haven't covered volleyball either. You any good, babe?"

"I can spike like the best of 'em," Rob boasted as he took a seat next to his wife. "Just don't count on it getting over the net."

Laughter rang around the room, and Amelia sipped her coffee, trying to make everything make sense. It was pleasant, easy conversation, and she felt like she was losing her mind.

She wanted this. She wanted it so badly it felt like a demon scrabbling at the inside of her skin. She wanted a man's arm around her shoulders while he laughed with friends and acquaintances. She wanted someone who knew how she took her coffee without having to be asked. She wanted to wake up with a pleasantly sore body, confident in the knowledge that it would happen again and again and again.

No, Amelia realized with dawning horror, she didn't want a man; she wanted *Leo*. She wanted *this* man to sit beside her and make her feel seen. She wanted *him* to take her to bed, to wake up next to her, to spend his life with her at his side.

"You okay?" he asked, proving that he could see through every wall she'd ever erected.

She nodded, then lied through her teeth: "I'm good."

"Good." He squeezed her shoulder.

Ari sat down diagonally across from them and nodded to the group. Leo stiffened beside her, and Amelia remembered what they'd done the night before. So much had happened, she'd forgotten that Ari was trying to break away and start his own company. She'd forgotten about the ring, and Ari's watch, about the library's rare coins. She'd forgotten that Fred knew she and Leo were lying about something and that this whole mess might explode in their faces sooner rather than later.

Maybe the detonation had already started. Last night, they'd lit the fuse that would destroy them both.

Vanessa entered the room with her boyfriend Mark hot on her heels. She waved like a queen to her subjects. "Morning, everyone," she said as she glided toward the buffet tables.

Mark boomed behind her, "Morning! Did everyone see the cop car outside?"

Air was sucked out of the room as everyone inhaled at once.

"The cop car?" Trudy asked.

"Yeah!" Mark grabbed a plate and opened one of the silver food warmers. "It was unmarked, but I saw the police light sitting on the dash! Just like the movies when they stick it on the roof to catch the bad guys. Crazy, huh? Wonder what that's about? Hope one of you didn't steal Nadia's ring." He chortled while Vanessa glared at him. "What, babe?" he protested as he caught her look. "That thing's worth like twelve mil. I looked it up."

"Mark," she hissed. "Not now."

Amelia flicked a gaze around the room. Robert seemed nonplussed, focused on buttering his toast. Was he *too* casual? Trudy's brows were drawn. Gregory and George were in deep conversation at the far end of the table. Ari looked positively green.

She frowned at him. Leo followed her gaze, and the weight of their combined stares must have drawn Ari's attention. The other man stiffened across the table, his hands gripping his silverware so hard they shook.

"Ari?" Leo asked quietly. "You worried about the cops?"

"What?" Ari asked. "Are you accusing me of something?"

"Someone in this room hasn't been honest," Leo continued in a low voice.

Amelia sucked in a breath. Was he accusing Ari? Sure, they suspected he was trying to screw Fred over business-wise, but that wasn't the same thing as stealing a woman's ring right off her finger.

Ari's eyes blazed. He clung to his utensils for a moment, then visibly forced himself to relax. He set his knife down, then his fork, then smoothed the front of his shirt as if he were smoothing a tie. Unease trickled down Amelia's spine. Something was going on here, and she didn't understand what it was. Beside her, Cora shifted in her seat, then stilled. No one else moved.

In the silence, footsteps sounded down the hall. At least two people, probably three. The drumbeat of their steps rocked through the room like gunshots. Leo tensed beside her, and

Amelia tried to quietly fill her lungs in an attempt to calm herself down.

The steps drew closer. And closer. And closer.

The whites of Ari's eyes became more visible as his eyes widened. A bead of sweat trickled down the side of his neck. He was nervous. Tense. About to explode.

Without warning, Ari *lunged*. His chair clattered to the ground as he sprinted for the door on the far side of the room. Leo leaped from his own seat and tore through the door behind him, screaming, "Stop! Ari! Stop!"

Chaos exploded. Cora made a noise of dismay. Amelia jumped out of her seat and ran for the doorway, only to be jostled out of the way by Rob, who sprinted faster than she thought a man his age would be able. Utensils clattered. A glass broke. Screams and murmurs competed for attention.

"Leo!" Amelia screamed.

From the opposite doorway—the one where the footsteps had echoed—three men appeared. Fred and two gruff, grizzled men who could only be police detectives. They wore slightly oversized suits and deep scowls.

Amelia hugged the wall as Gregory and George froze halfway to the door, caught between stopping for the police and following the action.

"It was Ari!" Mark yelled, thrusting his hand toward the door where Leo had chased the other man. "He heard you were coming, and he bolted."

The detective to Fred's left took off like a shot. His brown blazer flapped around him as he ran, reaching for the gun holstered at his waist. Holy freaking moly. Amelia's eyes were wide as saucers, her palms flat on the wall. There were *guns* here now. Sure, they were in the hands of the police, but the danger of the situation had just ratcheted up a thousand notches.

She stepped into the hall to see the detective disappear around a corner, quickly followed by his partner. "Stay here," the man barked at her, then followed his partner into the bowels of the house. They were headed toward the backyard.

"Don't shoot Leo!" she yelled, like some kind of hand-wringing miss who didn't know what to do with herself. She realized she was, indeed, wringing her hands, and forced herself to hold her arms by her sides.

A stampede followed the second detective, with everyone from the breakfast room tearing down the hallway after the men, clearly unwilling to stay where the detective had told them to. After a brief hesitation, Amelia followed. She made it to the French doors at the back of the house in time to see Leo let out a gargled scream as he made a last, desperate leap toward Ari.

LEO'S ARMS clamped around the other man's torso. His lungs burned as he threw all his weight into the tackle, his muscles screaming from the long sprint. He yelled as he brought Ari to the ground, using the full force of his lunge to make sure the other man didn't get away.

They were halfway across the lawn when they landed in a heap. Ari screamed, his eyes wide with panic, and threw an unexpected right hook. It caught Leo in the eye socket. Pain bloomed across his temple as he yelped, loosening his hold on Ari's waist.

Ari punched again, but Leo turned his shoulder to block the hit. He jabbed at Ari's kidney, trying to get the other man to settle.

"You piece of shit!" Leo yelled, incensed, hitting Ari again.

Ari, in a feral rage, clamped his teeth around Leo's forearm and bit down hard. Leo shrieked, trying to fling the other man off.

It was only when strong arms clamped around his shoulders and pulled him off that he realized they had an audience. Panting, he looked up and saw every staff member, every guest, and Fred himself jogging toward them. Leo collapsed on the ground, breathing hard, and the world spun around him.

Ari had clocked him hard.

"What the hell is going on here?" Fred demanded.

"He did it," Leo wheezed, pointing a shaking hand at Ari. "He took the ring. The coins. Everything. He's trying to start a rival company by taking all your clients."

"*What?*" Fred's entire head turned flame-red.

Ari, who had been struggling against the policemen's hold, suddenly stilled. "What?" he demanded, eyes wide. "I didn't steal the ring! I didn't take anything! Someone stole from *me*. My watch is gone!"

"Cut the bullshit, Ashfield," Leo spat.

"I'm not a thief."

"You were stealing clients."

Ari's eyes narrowed. "You took my list."

"What kind of moron brings that to a company retreat? And

on paper? It's the twenty-first century. Ever heard of a computer?" Now he sounded like Amelia.

"Didn't want to get hacked," Ari gasped, his body jerking as the detective pulled him up to his feet with a rough tug.

"Hacked?" Leo scoffed.

"If one of you doesn't shut up and tell me what's going on, I'll have you both thrown in jail." Fred's voice was deep, and dark, and utterly terrifying.

Amelia approached, brows drawn. Sunlight glinted on her pale hair. Her quicksilver eyes were filled with worry. She cleared her throat. "We believe Ari is planning to launch a rival company and take some of your clients with him."

Fred gave her a heavy stare, then swung his head to face Ari. Ari shrank back against the police detective who held his arm, throat bobbing thickly as he gulped. "Is this true, Ashfield?"

"I c-can explain," Ari stammered. "It's not what it looks like." His gaze flicked from Fred, to Amelia, to Leo, then over to the gathered crowd. "I only wanted to make a bit more money, Fred. You take such a big cut of the fees, and we only get paid a salary, and—"

"And you thought you could turn around and *stab me in the back by stealing all my clients?*" Fred's roar sent birds flapping from the nearby trees. Amelia took a step back from him, her eyes darting to Leo.

Leo stood slowly, worried that a sudden movement would draw Fred's ire. His temple throbbed and when he darted his tongue out, he winced. His lip was split and bleeding.

Ari bristled. "You're a fucking billionaire, Fred. You can't pay your staff a decent wage?"

"You make multiple six figures! I offered you stock options in the company when you started, and you *refused*. Now you're trying to steal from me to make up the difference?"

"How was I supposed to know the company would do so well?" Ari protested. His eyes darkened. "You're just a greedy old man, Fred, and your time is *done*. I've already talked to three dozen clients, and they're done with you too. Done!"

"The only thing that's done is *you*, Ari. And as soon as you give me Nadia's ring back, I never want to see you again."

Confusion flittered over Ari's face. He shook his head. "What? No. I didn't steal the ring. Dumb bitch probably dropped it in the Blue Ro—"

For the second time that morning, Ari was tackled to the ground, except this time it was by a two-hundred-and-twenty-pound former linebacker with a receding hairline. Fred took Ari down, tackling both detectives in the process. Leo jumped in to try to drag Fred off and got a mouth full of knuckles for his efforts.

Vaguely, he heard Amelia cry out. He felt her hands on his arm and let himself be pulled away while Percival heaved Fred off the other man. The police officers turned Ari over and held him to the ground while they barked orders at everyone around.

Amelia's hands were patting his chest, his arms, his face, as if to make sure everything was still attached. Her eyes were full of concern...and maybe something more. As the chaos slowly abated around them, Leo found himself staring into her eyes.

"Are you okay?" she asked, voice soft.

"I'm fine." He reached up and tucked a strand of hair behind her ear.

"You scared me."

"Sorry, baby," he whispered, pressing a kiss to her forehead. He winced as pain splintered out from his lip and pulled away.

"Stop doing things to hurt yourself," she chided, clicking her tongue as she turned his face to inspect his lip, his temple, the bruise forming on his jaw. "That was so supremely stupid. He could have hurt you!"

"But then I wouldn't have you fussing over me like this," Leo noted.

Her smile was slight, but he saw it. Behind her, the men were hauling Ari to his feet, and Fred was calming down. Amelia turned to follow his gaze and set her hands on her hips. Her frown was beautiful, but Leo still wanted to kiss it away.

"If he didn't do it," Fred asked, jabbing a thumb at Ari, "who took my fiancée's ring?"

Amelia froze as a gasp crossed her lips. Leo saw her eyes widen as she scanned the assembled crowd. Under her breath, she whispered, "Holy shit."

Then she took off like a shot.

TWENTY-ONE

HOW COULD she have been so blind? How did she miss it?

Amelia berated herself as she sprinted, arms pumping, lungs wheezing. She knew who'd taken the ring. It had been right in front of her face from the first day they'd arrived on the property. She tore through the hallway where the whole gang had exited, feet pounding on the wide timber floors. Skidding to a halt in the dining room, she swore under her breath.

Empty.

Distant clattering alerted her to pursuers. They probably thought she was guilty and trying to escape, but there was no time to explain. No time at all. She had to *go*.

At the foyer, Amelia hesitated. Was it worth going upstairs to look for the thief, or would they already be gone?

The sound of many people running down the hallway echoed nearer and nearer. Upstairs or outside? Would a thief rush to get their things, or just bolt? The decision tore at her. A wrong one might get her in big trouble. It could get her shot if one of those detectives was trigger-happy. Chest heaving, Amelia started for the stairs—and changed her mind. She whirled, flying out through the first set of front doors, into the small, tiled foyer.

Through the diamond-paned glass of the front door, she saw Cora hobbling down the steps ahead, the old lady's big yellow purse banging against her side as she hauled her wheelie suitcase down the steps.

"Stop!" she screamed through the closed door, her breaths coming hard and fast.

The suitcase clattered as Cora dragged it down each step, rocking nearly off its wheels at each impact. It had been a different clatter that had helped Amelia figure out Cora's guilt. In the chaos of the breakfast room, Amelia had heard a lot of utensils clinking. It hadn't been until she was outside, watching Ari struggle against the cops, that she realized some of that clinking had come from *inside Cora's purse.*

She remembered the way Cora had shaken hands with her: grasping normally, then adding another hand on top. It seemed grandmotherly and warm at the time, but it was also distracting. Would she have been able to slip Nadia's oversized ring off with a handshake like that? And the day they were in the library, they'd met Cora in the hallway. Gregory had been the one to recommend they check out the beautiful old books, but Cora was there too. Had she been using them as cover to find items she could steal?

Cora had been robbing Fred this entire time.

She shoved open the front door and ran through. "Cora, stop!" Amelia lunged for the older woman, who glanced over her shoulder and dropped the suitcase completely.

And, wow. That old lady could *move*.

Cora sprinted onto the circular drive and headed for the distant front gates. She made it halfway around the fountain before Amelia caught up. Her fingers wrapped around the strap of Cora's purse, then slipped.

Cora turned and shoved Amelia with both hands. Amelia went stumbling back with a cry, nearly falling into the fountain. Distantly, she heard the crowd of onlookers arrive at the front door and spill onto the steps.

"You silly little girl," Cora spat, her face twisted into something horrible. "Look what you've done."

Amelia had spent nearly a decade making herself smaller. She'd had her confidence systematically stripped and destroyed. She'd survived an abusive relationship and come out the other side. She'd built her own business and had the courage to ask for help when she decided she was ready to date again.

She wasn't going to let some white-haired thief talk down to her. Not Cora. Not *anyone*. Amelia was done making herself small for other people. She wasn't a silly little girl. She was the only damn person in this place who'd figured out that Cora had been stealing from right under their noses.

Bunching her muscles, Amelia sprang. Her hands closed around the strap of the purse, and amidst the growing noise caused by their growing audience, Amelia tugged and tugged and suddenly she was in a Tug-o-War with a seventy-five-year-old woman.

A savage screech escaped Amelia's lips as she put all her angst, all her anger, all her old wounds into the effort. She gave one good, hard yank.

The purse ripped right down the middle seam, sending the contents flying through the air like they'd been fired from a slingshot.

Three forks and three knives and a couple of silver spoons glittered in the air before clattering on the gravel drive. Dull rare coins flipped like some strange game of Heads or Tails. Amelia stumbled back and fell on her butt, but not before she saw a gigantic pink diamond glittering in the sunlight. It twirled through the air in a graceful arc, heading straight for the burbling fountain.

Amelia screamed, pointing. "No!"

If the ring hit the water, it could get sucked into the pump. It could be damaged. It could be lost forever. All this effort, for nothing. She watched the ring fly through the air, spinning, spinning, spinning—

A large body appeared, sprinting past her. Leo jumped. He flew through the air toward the ring, grasping for it with both hands, trying to reach the jewel—then went tumbling right into the fountain.

Water sloshed over the edge of the fountain, spilling onto the gravel drive. Amelia found herself speckled with the spray, its chill shocking her into silence. The fountain's pool rocked back and forth, all that water displaced by Leo's big body splashing and sloshing over the edges.

Then—silence.

The world held its breath. The entire assembled crowd—Amelia, Fred, the cops, the guests, the staff, even Cora—sat silent for a long, long second, staring at the lip of the fountain.

Leo's hand shot up in the air, brandishing twelve million dollars' worth of vivid pink diamond between his thumb and forefinger. His upper body followed, face set in grim satisfaction. He met Amelia's gaze, and pride burned in his eyes. Then he turned to Cora and sneered.

"My watch!" Ari cried, staring at a spot on the gravel. "You stole my watch!"

"Oh, be quiet," Cora grumbled as one of the detectives lifted her onto her feet. Her jaw was set, but she presented her wrists like she knew the drill. "No one cares about your stupid watch. You're the one who tried to pull one over on Fred. Ever heard of a non-compete agreement, dumbass?"

"Dumbass? You're calling *me* a dumbass?" Ari looked like he wanted to explode, but the cuffs were still firmly manacled around his wrists. Cora soon got the same treatment.

Fred hustled over to Leo and took the ring, inspecting it. He let out a breath, relieved, and moved to help Amelia to her feet. Percival was already there, handing a fluffy white towel to Leo as he climbed out of the fountain. Water dripped from his clothing, his hair, and his skin, but he was smiling. Another staff member gathered the stolen silverware, the watch, and the rare coins.

Amelia was bustled inside. The scrapes on her hands and elbows from her tussle with Cora were tended to, and then the detectives came to interview her. She told them everything she knew and even admitted to going into Ari's room. They were grim, gruff men, and they were a little scary, but she squared her shoulders and told them everything she could.

She'd been serious before: She was done making herself small. She was done shrinking in the presence of others.

"Your name is Amelia Darcy?" one of them asked, pen poised above his notepad.

She nodded. "Yes."

"And what do you do for work?"

Well, this was it. She couldn't lie to the cops, so her and Leo's house of cards would soon come tumbling down. At least they weren't going to be accused of stealing millions of dollars—or dozens of clients—from Fred Goodhew. She answered honestly, and a long while later, she was released from the room where they'd interviewed her.

Leo, who had been leaning against the wall, straightened and came for her. "Everything good?"

"I think so."

"Are you okay?"

"I'm fine." She gave him a small smile. "Are you?"

"Haven't you heard? I'm a hero." He grinned, and Amelia's heart turned over. He was so handsome when he smiled, and when that smile was pointed directly at her. His hand coasted over her cheek, knuckles brushing her skin. "You're a lucky woman."

"Hey! I did all the work. I should be the hero. And *you're* the lucky one, mister."

His grin softened. "Don't I know it."

They walked to their room, and Amelia took the opportunity to take a shower and wash the sweat and crud and blood off her body. She stood under the spray and let out a long breath.

It was over. Cora had been discovered, and Ari had been exposed. Leo and Amelia were safe from false accusations. They had one more night of supposed team building, and then this whole debacle would be done.

As Amelia dried herself off and wiped the steam from the mirror, she stared at her reflection and realized she was sad.

Did this mean her relationship with Leo was over too?

DINNER WAS AN INTERESTING AFFAIR. The mood was a weird bubble of subdued excitement. Fred and Nadia both made an appearance, with Nadia's ring firmly on her finger once again. They both made a point to thank Amelia and Leo, which Leo appreciated.

He felt guilty for lying to everyone about having a fiancée, but he was in too deep now. If he came clean when Fred was still angry about Cora and Ari's betrayals, there was no doubt in Leo's mind that he'd lose his job. When Vanessa had admitted that Ari approached her about joining his new company, Fred had looked like he wanted to fire her too. She hadn't come down for dinner.

This job was the one thing he was good at. If Fred fired him, Leo didn't know what he'd do. Maybe if he just made it through this retreat—just one more night and one morning—he could figure out his next move when things weren't so volatile.

"Mm," Amelia moaned, wiggling on her chair as she took a bite of roast chicken. "This is incredible."

Leo couldn't help stealing a glance at her. It wasn't just sweets that put that look of bliss on her face. She dipped another bite of chicken into the jus on her plate and closed her eyes in ecstasy when it touched her tongue. Leo was half-hard just watching her.

"The mashed potatoes are unreal," George agreed from across the table, reminding Leo that now was definitely not the time to be lusting after his fake fiancée.

A waiter appeared between Leo and Amelia, refilling her wine before moving to Leo's other side to fill his. As the meal progressed, the tension slowly dissolved and conversation flowed more freely.

It was Amelia who finally broke the silence on this morning's drama. She turned to Nadia and asked, "How does it feel to have the ring back?"

Nadia let out a small gust of breath and smiled at Amelia. "So, so good. I can't thank you enough."

Amelia beamed. "I'm just glad we found it. Leo was the real hero." She jabbed him in the ribs for emphasis, which made him laugh.

"How did you figure it out?" Nadia asked, even though Amelia had been over the story a million times already.

"I heard the silverware clinking in her bag!" Amelia laughed. "If only I'd realized sooner."

The conversation grew in excitement, and Amelia beamed at all of Leo's coworkers. A bit of worry slipped out of him. Maybe everything would work out. After the retreat, they'd go back to regular life and all this madness about thieves and betrayals would be over. He could focus on work—and on Amelia.

Once they were out of here, he'd be honest with her. He'd tell her that he'd fallen head over heels for her, and he couldn't live without her. He'd get a place in Stirling and use it as his home base. He'd come back here between jobs, and ask Fred to give him Ari's old territory, which would have him home more often. He could show Amelia how much she meant to him.

"We're going to celebrate tonight," Nadia proclaimed. "Right, Fred?"

"Anything you want, baby," Fred told his fiancée with a soft smile. There were more lines on his face, and the man looked tired. Older, somehow. Like the two betrayals that had been uncovered today added a decade onto his age.

"Oh!" Nadia brightened and looked at Amelia. "We should sing karaoke!"

Amelia's fork stopped halfway to her mouth.

Leo shifted. "Amelia's voice needs to, um, rest...before, um, her next tour..."

"Nonsense," Nadia said. "I'm sure she's been dying to sing. It must feel like withdrawal to go so many days without practicing!"

"Well, not really. It's been okay," Amelia responded weakly.

"We'll do it in the theater," Nadia proclaimed. Her left hand was still bandaged, the broken fingers in a thick splint, but her arm seemed to be moving more freely. She stabbed a bit of chicken and chewed before smiling at Amelia and Leo.

"Percival," Fred said, leaning back in his chair.

"Sir?"

"Prepare the theater. We'll be singing karaoke after dinner tonight."

Amelia gave Leo a horrified stare. Then her gaze landed on her wine glass, and she downed it in one swig. She put the glass down, then faced Leo again.

"Uh-oh," she whispered. "This is not good."

TWENTY-TWO

DINNER HAD GIVEN way to dessert, and Amelia had only had two bites of it. Her stomach was in knots, which was a real shame, because they'd served an absolutely divine crème brûlée. Even downing three glasses of wine and getting a decent buzz going didn't help her anxiety.

All too soon, Nadia and Fred were leading the whole group down a new hallway and into a huge home theater. A karaoke machine had been set up near the big projector screen, with two microphones waiting, their cables like coiled snakes.

The wine in Amelia's belly turned sour. Throwing up was a real possibility.

But Leo's arm was around her shoulders, and she was gripping his waist. His body was a warm wall of strength and security, and she inhaled the scent of him to calm her rioting nerves. It helped, a bit. When she exhaled and took a seat in the second row of theater seats beside Leo, she figured she could make it through this evening without embarrassing herself. Probably.

"I haven't done karaoke since college," Trudy said. She was seated directly in front of Amelia, and she turned around to look at her and Leo. Her arm was on the back of her seat, and her face was bright with excitement. "Rob and I are going to do 'Ain't No Mountain High Enough.'"

"We are?" Rob asked dubiously.

Trudy laughed. "Better believe it, hun."

Rob pretended to grumble, but he still jumped up to help with the setup and write down their song choice. The first few turns filled up before Amelia could even settle into her seat, and she began to relax. Maybe no one would ask her to sing. Maybe she could sit here for an hour, enjoy some silly performances, laugh with her new friends, and let the stress of the day melt away.

This was just another team-building activity. Everything would be okay.

A staff member arrived with a silver tray bearing drinks, and she sipped the mojito she'd ordered earlier. Nadia started the party with a Britney Spears hit, and then Trudy and Rob were up. They brought down the house. Pretty soon, Amelia was giggling intermittently, leaning her head on Leo's shoulder. She was pleasantly tipsy, comfortable, and finally feeling a bit more at ease.

There was no more ring thief to uncover. No more risk of exposure. Nothing more to do but sit here, enjoy the company, and drink in the last few hours in Fred's beautiful mansion.

"Next up, Kitty Catelli!" Nadia screamed into the microphone. "Woo!"

The screen lit up behind her: *Man! I Feel Like a Woman!* By Shania Twain.

An anxious, exaggerated giggle left Amelia's lips as she shook her head. "No way," she laughed. "My voice. I need to save my voi—"

She was hauled up and cheerfully bullied to the front of the room. Nadia thrust the second microphone into her hands and then threw her good arm around Amelia's shoulders.

"You need to do this for me," Nadia protested. "As a thank you for finding my ring. You owe it to me."

"I'm not sure that logic is exactly right," Amelia said, and the room laughed. That's when she realized she'd spoken into the microphone and it was *very* loud.

Nadia leaned over, tapped a key on the laptop near the karaoke machine, and the first bars of Shania's masterpiece blared through the speaker. Amelia's eyes darted around the room. She saw Leo gripping his armrests, looking panicked. Everyone else was half-drunk and already singing along to the instrumentals. Fred was at the back of the room, chatting with one of his employees, paying no attention.

Amelia couldn't get out of this. She lifted the mic and in a dramatic voice, spoke the iconic first line.

When Nadia went wild, Amelia couldn't help but giggle along. It was so good to see Nadia happy again. She'd been morose at her few appearances during the retreat. Amelia couldn't blame her; it wasn't just the value of the ring. If Amelia lost the engagement ring Leo had given her, she'd never forgive herself. And if it had been stolen right off her finger? Well, that would be even worse.

Except her engagement ring wasn't even real.

Nadia wiggled her hips to the beat, and the lyrics appeared on the screen. Here went nothing. Amelia took a breath and sang.

LEO LEANED BACK. Amelia...wasn't great. She wasn't *bad*, exactly, but she wasn't a professional singer by any stretch of the imagination.

But she was laughing so uproariously, bringing Nadia and everyone else along with her, that Leo couldn't help but smile wide as he watched her. For a woman who needed a spread-sheet to tell her how much eye contact to make on a date, she sure was willing to let it all hang out when she finally let her guard down.

His heart expanded as the music filled the room, cheers and hoots coming from all corners. Amelia had to stop singing partway through to bend over and laugh. Nadia took up the slack, and at least she was a worse singer than Amelia. It meant their cover wasn't completely blown.

Not that Leo cared about their cover story just then. He was caught up watching the light fill Amelia's face. She brightened the room. She brightened his *life*.

He was hopelessly, desperately in love with her. She was everything he wanted in a woman, plus a whole host of things he hadn't realized he needed. She was a mediocre singer and an incredible woman. She was fire and delight wrapped up in a silver-eyed package.

She was the only woman he'd ever wanted to make his wife.

As the song ended, Leo stood. Amelia came to join him at their row of theater seats, and he wrapped his arms around her, then hauled her over his shoulder. She squeaked, wriggling, still laughing with every breath.

"Put me down!"

"No chance," he responded. "We're going to bed. Good-night, everyone."

Wolf-whistles chased them out of the room, and Leo barely heard them. His heart pounded as he carried Amelia to the steps, then put her down and dragged her to their room, both of them nearly sprinting. Inside their suite, he pinned her to the door.

"Didn't know karaoke got you so hot and bothered," she teased. "Might have to note that down for future reference."

"It ain't the karaoke's fault," Leo replied, then crushed his lips to hers. His hands came to her jaw as he deepened the kiss, emotions running riot inside him. She tasted like wine and Amelia. She was so perfect it made his whole body ache with the need to consume her.

He'd met her mere days ago, and he knew he couldn't live without her.

Hauling her legs up, he pinned her to the door and kissed her harder and deeper until she was tugging at his hair and begging him to strip her naked. They made it halfway to the bedroom before they collapsed on the floor. She was wearing another one of her knee-high dresses, this one black with a high neckline. He reached up beneath it and tore her panties clean in half, tossing the scrap of fabric over his shoulder.

"Oh, wow," she breathed, eyes glassy. "That was so hot."

His pants were in the way. He got them down to mid-thigh before he had to get a condom on so he could get inside her. His hands shook so hard he had to force himself to breathe just to get the little package open.

Then he was on her, *in* her, and it felt like coming home. She moaned, fingernails leaving lovely little indents in his biceps as she gripped them for dear life.

"You feel so fucking good, Amelia."

She made an unintelligible noise in response. Leo grinned and gave it to her harder. But it wasn't until he leaned down to kiss her that the moment changed. His movements became slower, deeper, more intense. She gasped and arched beneath him, urging him to give her more, more, more.

Leo lost his mind. Rational thought abandoned him completely, so that all that was left was the shell of his body and the beating heart that Amelia had resurrected. He gathered himself enough to reach between them and make sure Amelia found her pleasure before he lost control of himself entirely. She came, body arching, pink lips falling open on his name.

That's how he wanted her to come for the rest of their lives: falling apart at his touch, with his cock inside her and his name echoing in the room around them. She was so beautiful like that, so sexy he could hardly stand it for a moment longer. Then the tension snapped, and he joined her in ecstasy. Pleasure blasted through him, rushing up his spine, filling his body with heat. He clutched the woman he loved as he breathed in the scent of her hair, praying that this moment would last forever.

It didn't, but it lasted long enough. Leo peeled himself off of Amelia after they caught their breath, disposing of the condom in the bathroom and coming back to Amelia still starfished on the floor. Grinning, he gathered her in his arms and carried her to the bed.

"My brain is melted," she mumbled, staring at the ceiling.

"Good." He gathered her in his arms and pulled her close, spooning her so the lengths of their bodies were connected. His hand found its way to her breast like it was meant to rest there.

"No wonder you had five girls wanting to sleep with you in one night," Amelia said, half-dazed. "You're really good at that."

Leo stiffened, which made Amelia go still.

She turned around in his arms and frowned at him. "I'm sorry. That was a stupid thing to say, wasn't it? I didn't mean... I just meant you rocked my world, is all."

Forcing himself to relax, Leo pressed a kiss to Amelia's forehead. He rolled onto his back. "It's fine. I just...I don't want you to see me that way."

She lifted her head onto her elbow to look at him. It felt like she could see right through him. "What way?"

"As Pestilence."

"You think I'm hung up on some stupid nickname?"

He snorted, then sighed. "I didn't have sex with five girls in one night. You want to know what really happened?" He glanced at her, then had to look away. "I'd just been dumped, and I was a mess. We were at a house party, and I was drunk and emotional. Those five girls consoled me while I wept like a baby. We drank and discussed breakups, and one of them volunteered to start a rumor about how good I was in bed. It got all blown out of proportion because someone saw me come out of the room with all of them."

Amelia was quiet for a moment. "Oh. So the whole Pestilence thing...?"

"Oh, everyone got chlamydia. That's definitely true." He snorted, embarrassment making his chest feel hot. "And after that night, I slept around. I guess the rumors worked. So maybe the clap outbreak was my fault. Maybe it was Gerard Hill. Maybe it was one of half a dozen girls that were sleeping around. Everyone was having sex with everyone. It was college."

"Your college experience sounds like it was really different from my college experience," Amelia noted.

Leo laughed. He finally met her gaze. "Sex isn't usually like this," he said quietly. "The way it is with you."

She was quiet for a long moment, her expression unreadable. "Oh."

He caught her hand—the one that wore his ring—and started toying with her fingers, touching them with his own, holding her hand, braiding their fingers then sliding them apart. "The past ten years..." He exhaled. Should he be telling Amelia all this stuff? Wouldn't it just prove that he wasn't worthy of her, of any relationship?

"Who was the girl who dumped you?" Amelia asked, then added, "You don't need to tell me if you don't want to."

"Katie Rodgerson," he answered. "My first and only relationship." His smile was bitter, but he managed to keep going. "We met in freshman year. She was studying economics. I hadn't chosen my major yet, because I couldn't decide what I wanted to do with myself. My grandparents had died barely two years earlier, Marlon had isolated himself after basically hamstringing himself financially so I could go to college, and I was totally fucking lost."

She tightened her grip on his hand, and they lay in the bed, hands clasped, staring at each other.

"I don't know if it was real love," Leo admitted. "I was young. We both were. But I thought we cared about each other until she turned around and told me I wasn't driven enough for her. She was going to do big things with her life, and she couldn't hang around waiting for me to pick a career while I partied my way through college. It came as a total shock at the time. I don't know why her dumping me hit me so hard."

There was a long pause.

"Well," Amelia finally said, reasonable as ever, "your parents had basically dropped the ball, then you lost your grandparents, and you...drifted from your brother?"

Leo didn't want her to think badly of Marlon. "You have to understand, my brother took care of me for years. Growing up, he was the one who did everything for me when our mom couldn't. School lunches. Homework. Everything. You wouldn't think he was only two years older than me. He was my parent most days. Then we moved in with our grandparents and they weren't in great health, so he started taking care of them too. When they died, I think he realized he was just...burned out. Done. I didn't want to keep being a burden to him."

"But that still left you on your own." When Leo nodded, Amelia sighed sympathetically. "So he wasn't there for you, even if it was understandable. Your girlfriend was probably the only meaningful connection you had left. It's no wonder it affected you when the relationship ended."

Leo stared at her, with her liquid mercury eyes and her pale golden hair splayed over her shoulders, and he couldn't believe that she was here with him. It took her all of three sentences to explain a hurt that he'd never been able to rationalize. He'd always felt vaguely embarrassed to be so crushed by a relationship that had lasted barely two years and ended before he'd reached the legal drinking age. But his wounded heart had been injured by more than just Katie dumping him; it was every important person in his life leaving him to fend for himself. She was just the killing blow.

Amelia brought his hand to her lips and kissed his knuckles. "I'm sorry I made that comment about the five women," she murmured. "You know you're worth so much more than your bedroom skills, right? So much more, Leo."

Leo's throat grew so tight, he couldn't respond.

Amelia must have sensed the emotion choking him because with her lips curled in a witchy smile, she added, "Even though I *did* hire you specifically for those bedroom skills, and they are *quite* impressive."

He laughed, a wet, raspy sound, then grabbed Amelia around the waist and hauled her on top of him. He kissed his way across her chest until her nipple was between his lips. Nipping gently, he groaned. "I don't think I'll ever get sick of kissing you, Amelia."

She leaned down, her naked core nudging at his stiffening cock. It was intimate and erotic, and it made him want to fuck her until they both dropped from exhaustion. Her lips pressed against his in a chaste kiss. "That's good, because I'm a pretty big fan of kissing you too."

A shuddering sigh rattled his chest, then Leo wrapped his arms around the woman of his dreams and tried to use his body to show her what she meant to him.

It was, after all, what he did best.

TWENTY-THREE

STILL LAZY WITH the last embers of sleep, Leo lay on the bed and listened to Amelia move around the bathroom, humming to herself as she got ready for the day. He let a smile play on his lips as he closed his eyes, enjoying the quiet moment after the chaos of the last few days. His face was still sore from its introduction to Ari's fists, but enduring the pain was worth it. They'd found the ring. Cora had been taken away by the cops. He'd spent the night with the woman he loved, he'd opened up to her, and he'd made her cry out his name over and over again. All was well that ended well.

Today, Leo would drive Amelia back to her apartment and tell her he wanted more. He'd tell her what existed between them was real. He wanted every night to be spent beside Amelia, holding her in his arms. He'd work up the courage to tell her how he felt. He'd tell her that he knew he didn't deserve someone as intelligent and driven and beautiful as she was, but he was willing to become a better man for her. He'd move to Stirling to be nearer to her, and they'd make it work.

A ding drew him from his musings. He glanced at the bedside table and saw Amelia's phone screen light up with a new notification.

He wasn't snooping. Truly. He wasn't the type of person to go looking through someone's private things...but it was right there on the screen.

Ben's name.

Been meaning to ask, the barista wrote. *Would you like to grab dinner with me next weekend? There's a good tapas place...*

The rest of the message cut off. Leaning on his side, staring at the phone on the nightstand, Leo's heart thundered. Reality crashed into him like he'd lost a high-speed game of chicken with a concrete wall. He stared at the message until the phone went dark, then kept staring at the black screen.

He thought he would tell Amelia how he felt? Was he delusional? How could he ask her out when their relationship was built on this stupid exchange of favors? Could he even call it a relationship?

She had other prospects. Better prospects. She had a whole world of men who would soon discover how incredible she was, and Leo wouldn't come up to scratch. Sourness coated the back of his throat as the realization sank down, down, down to the pit of his stomach.

Whatever happened last night, the night before, or during any of the past seven days, the truth remained unchanged: Leo wasn't good enough for Amelia. Never would be.

The bathroom door opened and Leo straightened, his

mouth dry, his heart pounding. Panic and pain warred within him, closing his throat so tight he couldn't utter a word.

"Hey," Amelia said as she came closer. "Are you okay?"

She stood in front of him wearing nothing but a towel, her hair damp and hanging around her face. Leo straightened and she approached, putting her hands on his shoulders. The weight of them was slight, but they felt more solid than anything Leo had experienced before.

But he had no right to that touch. No right to ask Amelia to put the rest of her life on hold while he figured his shit out. She deserved a guy who could keep up with her. Whether or not that was Ben the Barista, Leo didn't know. But it sure as hell wasn't him.

"Leo," Amelia said, concerned. "Talk to me."

It was their last morning. These were the last few hours he had with her, the last time he could claim her full attention. Despicable man that he was, he let his hands curl around the backs of her thighs. "I'm fine," he grated, and he slid his palms up to the sweet little crease where her legs met her bottom. His thumbs rubbed her hips, and he relished the fluttering of her lashes. His touch did that to her. For today, at least, his touch brought her pleasure.

"We have an hour before we need to be downstairs," Amelia whispered, climbing onto the bed to straddle him. "Why don't we make the most of it?"

He shouldn't. He couldn't.

But he would.

. . .

A GASP WAS WRENCHED from Amelia's lips when Leo ripped the towel off. He tossed it aside like it had personally offended him and let his hands coast up her sides, moving up to palm her breasts with a rough, possessive touch.

"You want me?" he asked, voice dark.

A thrill shot through her as her lids fluttered closed. He was so sexy when he used that tone. She'd never tire of it. Her fingers dug into his shoulders, her core already growing wet for him. "Yes, I want you. So bad, Leo."

Who was this woman that was using Amelia's mouth to speak? Surely it wasn't Amelia demanding pleasure, confident enough in herself to straddle a man and grind herself against him? The thought made her lips curl. Leo hadn't followed her spreadsheet cell by cell, but he'd certainly shown her what was inside her all along.

"You like slumming it with me?" Before Amelia could answer, Leo flipped her onto her back, pinning her arms to the side. "You like getting dirty with a guy like me?"

Amelia's brows shot together. That didn't sound right. "W-what?"

Leo's expression was stark. She only saw it for a moment before he dropped his head to her neck and began to kiss her. His hand slid between her legs.

"Wait, Leo. What did you mean, slumming—"

Her words died when he slid a finger inside her, his thumb teasing her clit. She moaned.

"Love hearing those noises from you," he said, lips brushing her ear. "Love knowing I'm doing it to you."

"It feels so good." She spread her legs wider as he teased her clit before sliding his finger back inside.

"One last time," he whispered, almost too quiet for her to hear. His lips pressed against her neck, body trembling above hers.

She frowned, stilling, then pushed at Leo's shoulders. "One last time?" She pushed harder. "What are you talking about?"

Propping himself on his hands, Leo leaned above her and looked down. Amelia didn't recognize the man staring back at her. "After this morning, our arrangement will be done. You'll be free. You won't have to waste your time with me."

She blinked, then immediately clamped her legs closed. Ice water jetted through her veins as she tried to find the tender, loving man who had opened his heart to her last night. That man was gone. "Done?" Amelia whispered.

"Isn't that what you wanted?"

She shoved him away, wriggled off the bed, and picked her towel up off the floor. Whirling back to face him, Amelia clutched the terrycloth to her chest and stared. "No! What I want is for you to stop acting like some shameless playboy. I want the real you, Leo. The man who was with me last night. The man I got to know all week."

He sat on the edge of the bed and spread his arms. "There's only me, Amelia. Those two men are one and the same."

"No." She shook her head. "You don't get to push me away and put on that stupid persona. Not with me, Leo. Not after everything we've shared."

"We fucked, Amelia. That's it. Isn't that what you wanted?

You can think about this week and be confident that you're good in bed. Now go forth and find a man to make your boyfriend. Ben the Barista is just waiting for you to say the word."

His words *hurt*. He sat wearing pajama pants and nothing else, his bare toes curled into the rug on the floor, his green eyes pale and so, so bleak.

"What if I want you?" Amelia whispered.

For a moment, it looked like Leo's expression would crack completely. But he dropped his eyes and clenched his fists, then stood up. "I can't be the man you need, Amelia."

"Leo, stop it." Her voice was stern. "You're being ridiculous."

"I'm being *real*." His voice was harsh. She flinched, then watched him walk away.

She watched his broad back disappear behind the bathroom door, her whole body shaking. She'd thought... She'd thought what they had was the real thing. She'd thought they'd moved past the stupid fake fiancée deal days ago!

Leo thought he wasn't the man she needed, but he was wrong. *Wrong.*

But did it matter? If he didn't want to be with her, could she convince him otherwise?

Last night, she'd thought they'd connected on a deeper level. There had been no spreadsheet, no pretense. They'd shared a physical and emotional intimacy that she'd never experienced before.

To Amelia, that had been the start of something special— but maybe to Leo, it had been the end.

A tear left a hot trail down her cheek. She brushed it away with furtive movements, then sniffled once and pulled on her clothes. Her movements became more and more frantic until she was shoving her clothes in her suitcase and scanning the room for anything else she needed to pack. By the time Leo was out of the bathroom, his hair still wet from the shower and his lips set in a grim line, Amelia was zipping up her suitcase and placing it by the door.

"I'll wait downstairs," she said to the wall, then left Leo in the room and closed the door without looking back.

The next hour was torture. Amelia forced herself to paint a cheery smile on her face while she greeted everyone and subsequently said goodbye. By the time Leo came downstairs and the staff brought their bags to the foyer, her cheeks were sore from holding up her smile. She waved goodbye to everyone, hugged Nadia, kissed Percival's cheek, then got in the passenger's seat of Leo's car and slumped down in her seat.

It wasn't until they pulled up outside her apartment that she spoke. "Thanks for the lift," she said. Pulling the ring off her finger, she handed it over to Leo. "Here."

He was careful not to touch her fingers when he took the ring from her grasp. He didn't meet her gaze. He just nodded and said nothing.

Amelia waited a beat, then two. Maybe he would say something, apologize, fix this...

But he just lifted his gaze to hers. "Thank you for everything, Amelia."

His voice was painfully tender. His eyes were stark.

It sounded like goodbye.

Amelia's eyes watered as she got her bag out of the trunk, but she didn't cry until she was safely behind her apartment door.

TWENTY-FOUR

CHET the personal trainer barked orders, and Amelia rued the day she ever decided bootcamp was a good idea. Gasping for breath at the last whistle, she lay on the grass and stared at the blue sky, wondering if the past week had been a fever dream.

"Are you going to tell us what happened? You've been so quiet. You barely even showed up in our group chat all week."

Amelia turned her head to see Camilla's brows drawn together. Her coppery hair was piled on top of her head in a messy bun, her emerald-green headband somehow looking elegant and stylish even with her exercise-reddened face.

"Yeah," Lucy complained, flopping down on the ground on Amelia's other side, "you've been MIA."

Amelia grimaced. "It was a weird week."

"Weird good or weird bad?" Camilla flicked the mouthpiece on her water bottle and started sucking.

"Weird bad, I think," Amelia admitted. She'd been in a daze

since yesterday morning. Leo had dropped her off and just...left. As if they hadn't had a connection. As if what they shared hadn't been real.

Was Amelia delusional? He *was* Pestilence, after all, even if his nickname hadn't strictly been earned the way the rumors said. Had she totally played herself by falling for him?

"Do we need to shiv him?" Lucy asked. "I can start sharpening the end of my toothbrush."

"Who are we shivving?" a new voice cut in. "And can I join?"

Three heads turned to see a gorgeous, voluptuous woman with medium-brown hair pulled back in a high pony. She planted her hands on her hips. "Is it Chet? Because I'm down. That man is evil."

Camilla gave the other woman a wry smile. "He's not that bad."

"He's awful," Amelia groaned. "Anyone who tells me to do burpees automatically goes on my hit list."

"Amen," the new woman agreed, then grinned. "But I'll still come back on Wednesday for another session. I've seen you three here every week for a couple of months. Thought we should finally meet."

Amelia smiled in agreement, then introduced herself and her friends. "Sit down." She gestured to a patch of grass. "I'd say we should get up and go grab a coffee, but I need at least another five minutes before I can move."

"You're the new florist on Wilson Street, right?" Lucy asked, squinting.

"That's right. Scarlett Westbrook." She shook hands all

around then leaned back on her palms, tilting her head to the sun. "Gearing up for wedding season. I hear the summer and fall are crazy in Stirling for weddings."

Amelia couldn't help the groan that escaped her. "Please. Don't tell me about weddings. I don't want to hear that word again for a long, long time."

Scarlett arched a brow. "Bad experience?"

"Not exactly. But my sister just got married, and I'm in my early thirties so my social media feed is weddings, babies, and advertisements." *And I think I might be completely heartbroken.*

"Girl, don't even start." Scarlett laughed. "That's one of the reasons I had to move. My mother won't stop asking me when I'm going to give her grandbabies." She looked at the three of them. "The answer is never. But I want to hear about this shivving business. Who are we murdering?"

Amelia couldn't help the smile from curling her lips. She sat up and found herself relaying all the events from the bonkers company retreat. When she told her friends about yesterday morning, she was met with gasps of outrage.

"He just left you there?" Lucy asked, blue eyes wide. "Just drove away, hasn't said a word?"

Amelia pinched her lips and nodded.

"I think he's panicking because he cares about you," Camilla proclaimed.

Amelia groaned. "Don't, Camilla. I can't handle it right now."

"Can't handle what?" She reared back, offended.

"Your romantic heart. I feel..." Amelia shook her head. "I

feel scraped raw. He's gone, and I just need to deal with it. I fell too hard, too fast, and now it's over. The end."

Camilla frowned. She didn't agree, Amelia could tell. But she said nothing.

Scarlett plucked a blade of grass and started peeling it into tiny strips. "I once dated a guy for four years. We were a completely committed couple: holidays with each other's families, vacation plans, planning to move in together, jokingly discussing baby names for our hypothetical kids..." She met Amelia's gaze and gave her a grim smile. "Then one day, out of the blue...he ghosted me."

Amelia couldn't help her sharp inhalation. "What?"

Scarlett nodded. "Yep. I was freaking out. I thought he was dead. Finally, after two weeks, I got through to his mother and found out that he was perfectly fine, he just didn't want to talk to me anymore. His. *Mother*. He broke up with me through his *mommy*. That was almost worse than being ghosted."

Camilla had a hand over her mouth. Lucy's eyes were wide.

Amelia just stared at Scarlett and shook her head. "I'm so sorry."

"What did you do?" Camilla asked.

"I went through a major slut phase," Scarlett replied, eyes glinting. "*Major*."

Lucy giggled. "Well, that's one way of dealing with it."

"I might still be going through it," Scarlett admitted. "I haven't decided if it's over yet."

"Your sex life is going to take a serious nosedive if you stay in Stirling," Amelia noted. "The pickings are slim."

"Hey, it's an hour-and-a-half drive to Boston. I'll deal. I can always have an emergency sexcation weekend away."

The four of them laughed, and Amelia felt slightly better. As their giggles died down, she let out a long sigh. Camilla put an arm around her shoulders and squeezed.

"I feel so stupid," Amelia admitted.

"Are you going to go out with Ben?" Lucy asked, angling her head toward Amelia's phone, where it rested on top of her workout towel. Amelia had told them about his text message.

"I don't know."

"You have to!" Scarlett exclaimed. "Best way to get over someone is to get under someone else. I know from experience."

Amelia grimaced. "I don't know if I'm even into Ben. I had such a big crush on him and within half a conversation it just... died."

"You could just go and practice your new flirting skills, see if there's a spark. There's no harm playing the field," Camilla said.

"I recommend the slut phase approach," Scarlett added. "It's highly effective."

Amelia snorted. "I'm not sure I have it in me."

"Oh, you would have lots of things in you. That's the whole point."

Laughter burst out of them all. Amelia fell back onto the grass, slapping her hands over her face. Camilla wiped her eyes. Lucy's entire face was bright red. Scarlett just cackled along with all of them, then jumped to her feet and pointed to the coffee truck at the far end of the park. "Let's get some drinks. I need caffeine."

. . .

AN HOUR AND A BIT LATER, Amelia was back at home, showered, and gearing up to sit at her computer. It was strange to be back here, in her little apartment, sitting at her laptop. She had a mountain of work to do, with two potential new clients looking for a call with her to discuss their needs. It would be so easy to slip into her pre-Leo life, where her business was everything and data was her only companion.

But as she sat down and began to work, it was difficult to slip into that state of flow that used to come so easily. She'd start pulling data from clients' websites, and her mind would wander to something Leo said, how he made her laugh, how he'd slip his hand in hers like it was the most natural thing in the world.

This felt like a breakup, but that was ridiculous. They didn't know each other. Not really. They'd had a deal, and now the deal was done.

Why did that make her want to cry?

When all the numbers on her screen began to blur, Amelia sighed and pulled up Ben's message. She still hadn't answered. Her fingers hovered over the screen. Her indecision frustrated her.

Why was she so hung up on a guy who would treat her the way Leo did? What right did he have to toss her aside as soon as the retreat was done? They'd opened up to each other. Their time together had *meant* something. And he was just going to throw it all away?

A flash of anger had Amelia's fingers moving. She accepted Ben's invitation to dinner and asked him if he was free the coming weekend.

When his reply came through a couple of minutes later,

setting a time and place, Amelia let out a huff. There. She had a date. The deal was well and truly done.

She could move on from Leo, once and for all.

Clinging to that thought, she went back to work and tore through half of her to-do list. She only stood and stretched her body when the sun's rays told her it was late afternoon. Moving to the window, she watched the world go by, still feeling hot and angry and sad.

Little kids played in the park across the street, their peals of laughter ringing in the air. A moving truck pulled away from the curb, and Amelia wondered if she had new neighbors. A warm breeze shivered through the trees and ruffled her hair when she lifted the window sash, and Amelia inhaled the scent of late spring.

Life went on. This Monday was no different from last Monday. She'd had sex. She'd kissed a man. She'd realized that she could be attractive and sensual if only she got out of her own way.

The best thing for her to do was move on from Leo, from the drama at Goodhew Inc., from Cora and Ari and all the crazy people that had filled her week. She had a business to run. More pressingly, she had dinner to eat and TV to watch.

But in the very depths of her heart, Amelia knew the truth.

She missed Leo so much she ached with it.

TWENTY-FIVE

LEO LAY in his childhood bedroom, staring at the ring he held between his fingers. Light gleamed in the small stone, just like it had when it had been on Amelia's hand.

Where it belonged.

Dropping the ring on his bedside table, he scowled at the thought. The ring belonged nowhere near Amelia's finger. She deserved someone who wasn't known for spreading a sexually transmitted infection to half of his college population. She deserved a man who would treat her like a queen. Someone who was her equal in intelligence and integrity.

That man sure as hell wasn't Leo.

Dragging his carcass out of the narrow single bed, he stumbled to the bathroom and tried to wash the memory of Amelia off his body for the tenth time since Sunday morning. The ghost of her touch still lingered on his skin, sweet torture to remind him of all he never should have taken.

Downstairs, Marlon was sitting at the round kitchen table sipping from a gigantic mug. The aroma of coffee wafted toward Leo, and he grunted a greeting to his brother and made his way to the coffee maker. Leaning against the old laminate countertops, Leo sipped the drink and remembered mornings in the suite with Amelia, when she'd sip her overly sweet brew and light up his world.

"You look like you're in bad shape," Marlon noted.

Leo grunted. "I'm fine."

"Retreat didn't go so well?"

"The retreat was fine."

"Fine," Marlon repeated.

"Yes."

"I'm not sure you know what that word means."

Leo huffed. "It was a disaster, okay? Two people got fired. I dragged Amelia there and lied about her being my fiancée, so I'll probably be the next one to get chopped. And Amelia isn't—"

He stopped himself from saying how he really felt about her. That she wasn't ever going to talk to him again, especially not after he'd sent her packing like she meant nothing to him.

Marlon studied him. When he spoke, his voice was low. "You shouldn't have dragged her into this."

"You think I don't know that?" The words exploded out of Leo, and he dragged in a deep breath to try to calm himself. He stared at the ceiling for a beat, then let his gaze drop to Marlon's. "I don't want to hear this right now. Okay?"

Marlon studied him. He had thick, dark hair and a full beard. His skin was burnished bronze, and he had a permanent scowl etched on his brow. His eyes were hazel, bright amidst all that darkness. "She's Emory's sister-in-law, Leo."

"Marlon, just stop." Leo gripped his mug so hard his fingers went numb, and he tried to tamp down his temper. "Please, just stop."

His brother's chair squeaked on the tiles as he pushed away from the table, and Leo looked up to see Marlon put his cup in the ancient, yellowed dishwasher. Marlon hadn't changed an inch of this place since he'd bought Leo's half after their grand-parents died, other than clearing out some of their grandparents' possessions. It had the same old appliances, the same lace curtains, the same peeling paint and gingerbread trim on every eave and window.

It made the back of Leo's neck itch. They'd had good memo-ries here, the only good memories in a childhood filled with pain. But being back here made him think about all the ways he'd never been enough. He wasn't enough for his mother to love. Wasn't enough for his father to show up and step up. He'd been a hellion, nearly too much for his grandparents and brother to handle.

"Meeting the boys at The Shed tonight," Marlon said as he paused in the kitchen doorway. "You gonna join?"

Leo watched his brother's back. It was all so normal. Going to a bar with his friends, chatting shit, laughing and joking about all the same things. It made Leo want to scream. Instead, he said, "Yeah. Sure."

. . .

THE SHED WAS QUIET, which was no great surprise for a Tuesday night. He took a seat at the bar between Marlon and Cormac, nodding to both of them. Cormac had short brown hair and dark blue eyes. He and Marlon had a business together working in personal security, and, like Marlon, his eyes were always scanning. He'd positioned himself at the end of the bar so his back was to the wall and his gaze could roam the room.

"Heard you had quite the week," Archer said from Marlon's other side. His grin was a wide slash across his face. "Read an article about the police being called and a thief being arrested."

"Our payroll lady had sticky fingers," Leo said, trying to affect a casual grin. In reality, talking about Cora made him think about Amelia sprinting after her. Amelia figuring it all out. Amelia giving him that bright, blazing smile when he'd gotten up out of the fountain.

Then again, everything reminded him of Amelia. Coffee. Pastries. Cinnamon. Painted toenails. Red underwear. Computers. Sudoku. Had it really only been two and a half days since he'd seen her? It felt like he was gasping for breath without her.

"Marlon said you brought Amelia Darcy and pretended she was your fiancée." Archer popped a brow. "Emory know about that?"

On his left, Cormac leaned forward. Marlon turned and stared at Leo. Their stares pressed against his skin, demanding an answer.

Leo ignored his friends and motioned to the bartender. As the man walked over, he said, "Can we talk about something else?"

Archer let out a bray of laughter, slapping the wooden bar

top. Leo ignored him as he ordered a round for everyone, then scowled at his friend.

Archer threw his hands up. "Hey, don't look at me like that. But seriously, what were you thinking?"

Leo nodded to the bartender, who dropped a beer on a coaster in front of him. He stared at the golden liquid, feeling like a hot pile of garbage. "I don't know," he admitted.

"Have you spoken to her since the end of the retreat?" Cormac asked, his voice deep and resonant. Besides Marlon, Cormac was the one Leo was closest to. Probably because Cormac didn't feel the need to fill silence with pointless conversation and judgment.

Leo shook his head. "No. It's better this way."

"Hold on." Archer leaned his elbows on the bar and frowned at Leo. "You hooked up with her, didn't you?"

"I didn't hook up with her," he shot back. It had been so much more than that. He wouldn't lump Amelia in with all his other trysts. She was... She was *different*. She was special.

Archer frowned at him, his fingers wrapped around his glass as he stared at Leo. "What's going on? What aren't you telling us?"

"There's nothing to tell."

"There never is with you," Archer grinned. "Did you give her the Leo St. James special?" He made a vulgar gesture.

"Fuck off, Archer." Leo stood up, his barstool toppling to the ground behind him.

Marlon's hand appeared on Leo's chest. His older brother stared at him from under dark, furrowed brows. "I warned you about this," he said. "I told you to stay away from her."

"Yeah, well, I didn't. And I know I'm a piece of shit, okay? I know I don't deserve her. But she's fucking incredible, and I'm never going to be with her again. I had less than a week with the woman of my dreams, and now I'm supposed to just go back to my life and pretend none of it ever happened. How the fuck do you think I feel about that? About myself?"

Archer blinked, taken aback. "You... You really care about her?"

"Of course I fucking care about her!" Leo gripped the edge of the bar and let out a breath. In an attempt to quash his rioting emotions, he turned around and righted his stool. By the time he faced his friends again, the edge of his anger had worn down to something a little less jagged. He watched a bead of condensation cut a wet path down the side of his glass. "She's funny and clever and beautiful. She has this little smile that appears when she's saying something funny, like she can't quite contain herself from laughing at her own jokes. And she's *smart*. She built her own business. She looks at numbers and sees patterns. She did a sudoku in like, five seconds. And she frowns all the damn time. Like everything is a problem she just needs to solve. All week I'd just stare at her face like an idiot, trying to watch the moment her expression would clear. If she figured out a problem, she'd get this tiny little victorious smile for a second, and it made me—"

Abruptly, Leo stopped talking. The three other men were watching him with varying expressions of shock and confusion.

It was Cormac who spoke. "You love her."

Leo felt scraped raw. His throat was thick as he swallowed, then he jerked his chin down. "Yeah."

"Well, fuck," Archer said, turning forward again to stare at the bar. Marlon just let out a long sigh and scrubbed his face.

"Emory know about this?" Cormac asked.

"Emory is on his honeymoon with the woman of his dreams, who happens to be Amelia's big sister. No, of course he doesn't know about this. Amelia doesn't even know about this."

Marlon frowned. "You didn't tell her you cared about her?"

The pressure inside Leo's body was too much to bear. He gulped down half his beer and wiped his lips on his forearm, then growled in frustration. "I'm not an idiot, Marlon. What's a guy like me got to offer a woman like her? How am I supposed to even know if what I feel is real? I've never cared about a woman like I care about her. What am I supposed to tell her? 'Hey, I know I'm a total piece of shit who hasn't had a real relationship since I was nineteen years old, but I want to have one with you. I promise I won't fuck it up, except I probably will.'" He shoved his hands through his hair. "She has a date with another guy this week, and the thought of it is driving me insane. I want her with me all the time. I want her in my arms. I want her so damn bad, and I can't have her."

Silence settled over them after Leo cut himself off, lest he continue ranting all night. His heart thumped hard, and his breaths came heavy and fast. He wanted to scream and rip the room apart, or maybe just lie down and die.

"You should tell her," Archer said quietly.

Marlon grunted his agreement.

Leo scowled at them both. "How's a guy like me ever going to be worthy of a woman like her, Archer? Huh? What the hell do I have to offer?"

Archer shrugged. "The only way to be worthy of her is to be worthy of her. You want to be a better person, you just decide that's who you are, and live accordingly."

It wasn't until later that night, when Leo was once again in the single bed of his childhood room, that he really understood what Archer was telling him. In order to be a better man, he had to start acting like it, even if he didn't believe the change yet.

And he knew exactly how to take the first step.

TWENTY-SIX

THE GATES to the Goodhew Estate swung open silently, granting Leo access to the vast grounds they guarded. He drove onward, making it to the fountain, and cut the engine by the grand steps leading to the front door. Percival opened it a moment later, giving him a shallow nod.

He bounded up the steps and shook the man's hand. "Good to see you, Percival."

"And you. Fred is ready for you. He's in his study. If you'll follow me." The older gentleman swept into the big house, which felt cold and empty now that all the guests had gone. They marched down a long hallway and stopped at a closed door.

Percival knocked twice, then opened the door. Once Leo had stepped over the threshold, Percival quietly closed the door behind him.

He was alone with his boss, and he was about to have a very difficult conversation.

For a moment—just a second or two—Leo considered tucking tail and running. Wasn't that what he'd done all his life? He'd kept things casual with women because he'd been afraid of any kind of intimacy. He'd loved his jet-setting job because it meant he didn't have to be in one place for any length of time. He'd chased instability, if only to hide his wounds and fears from himself.

Leo gathered himself together and reminded himself why he was here. He was better than that now. He had to act accordingly.

"Sit," Fred told him genially, gesturing to one of the armchairs opposite his heavy timber desk. The older man leaned back in his chair and braided his fingers together, watching Leo with sharp eyes and an easy smile. "What can I do for you, son?"

Leo sat, tugging his cuffs, adjusting his shirt, wiping his hands on his thighs. Then he forced himself to still. "Thank you for seeing me."

"Of course."

Fred was a master negotiator who knew when to use silence. He wielded it like a weapon, and Leo felt its bite in the room right now. His boss wouldn't save him from the awkwardness of this conversation. Leo had to do all that on his own.

"I have to tell you something, Fred," he started, staring at a photo frame on his boss's desk. It was a picture of Fred and Nadia on a yacht, smiling as the sun gilded their features. Leo swallowed thickly. "I lied to you."

Fred's chair creaked, but the man said nothing.

Leo had to get it out before this got any worse, so he spoke in a rush: "I never had a fiancée. I lied about it from the start, because I didn't want you to think I was some party animal who couldn't hold down a relationship. But the truth is, that's exactly what I was. I wanted you to respect me, and I wanted you to trust me, so I made up the story about being engaged. That day you walked into the bakery and saw me with Amelia was the first day I'd met her. I'm so sorry, Fred. Truly. And in light of everything that happened at the retreat this year, I understand if you need to fire me for my dishonesty."

The words landed between them like bricks. It took long, long seconds for Leo to gather the courage to lift his gaze to meet Fred's, and when he did, it did nothing to quell his nerves. Fred's face was blank and stern. It gave nothing away.

But Leo deserved that, and more. He'd lied to the one man who had shown him real respect, the one man who had given him purpose. He'd taken the lie further than he should have and dragged Amelia down with him. He had savings; he'd be able to find another job. He probably wouldn't get a letter of recommendation, but maybe he could tap into his network, or go back to college and study something else, or he could—

"I know, Leo."

Leo's whirling thoughts came to an abrupt halt. He blinked at his boss, then frowned. "What?"

"I always knew you were lying about the fiancée. I mean, come on. Kitty Catelli from The Nymphomaniacs? I do have access to Google, you know."

"But. But, I... You never..." His heart pounded so hard he could hardly breathe. "I didn't..."

"I was trying to put you on the spot in the bakery, get you to come clean. Then you showed up at the retreat with Amelia, and—well, how did you convince her to go along with it, anyway?"

Leo grimaced. "It was an exchange of favors. She wanted help getting a date with a barista." He spat the last word like it was made of bile.

Fred let out a long, low chuckle. "Oh, Leo. You done fucked up, son."

Leo dropped his head in his hands. Humiliatingly, his eyes began to prickle. This job was everything to him, and now it was over. "I can hand over my current projects to Vanessa or one of the other event directors. I always keep notes, so it shouldn't be too much of an issue to transition. And I understand that you won't give me a reference, so I won't ask for one, but—"

"I'm not firing you, Leo."

He jerked his head up. "What?"

"Are you quitting?"

Leo blinked, then blinked again. "I... No. No, I'm not quitting."

"Good. So there will be no talk of handovers and transitions. You have Thelma Vonn's seventieth party coming up, and she was very insistent about two dozen Chippendale dancers. Last I checked, that hasn't been confirmed, and we'll need to lock them in by the end of the month. And Quincy Boorhouse's kid's party on the hundred-foot yacht needs another once-over. You'll need to contact the coast guard to get it all buttoned up before they can do anything." Fred tapped his computer and frowned at the screen. "I've just gotten an inquiry about a vow renewal in Fiji, and with your experience in the South Pacific, I think you should get the project."

"You're not firing me?" Leo asked stupidly.

Fred arched a brow. "Do you *want* me to fire you?"

"No, I just...don't understand. With Ari and Cora..."

Fred sighed and rubbed his forehead for a moment before answering. "I've had a couple of days to think about them, and their betrayals still hurt. They lied to me. They stole from me." He lifted his gaze to Leo's. "You didn't. You just acted like an idiot who forgot the internet exists, and that fact-checking isn't that hard when you're talking about public figures like lead singers in a fake band."

Leo's neck grew hot. He snorted, embarrassed. "Were you just waiting for me to come clean this whole time?"

"I knew it'd happen eventually. You've got too much integrity to live with something like that," Fred said casually, like that simple line didn't shoot a spear through Leo's chest. Fred flicked his hands. "Now go. You've got work to do."

Leo stood, then extended his palm. "Thank you, Fred."

The other man stood and shook Leo's hand across the desk. His grip was firm and sure, and Leo felt his heart settle. He still had a job. He still had this man's respect. It didn't fix everything, but at least his life wasn't in complete shambles.

"Say hi to Amelia for me," Fred said as he took a seat again, his eyes back on his computer.

Leo walked to the doorway and paused. "We're not in touch

anymore," he admitted. "I think I messed that up worse than I did this."

Fred lifted his gaze and watched Leo for a beat. "I wouldn't be so sure, son," he answered quietly.

The words rang in Leo's head all the way back to his car, and during the entire car ride back to Stirling. By the time he was back at his grandparents' place—at Marlon's place—Fred's words had settled somewhere deep in Leo's heart.

And he made a decision.

TWENTY-SEVEN

AMELIA ADJUSTED her purse and squared her shoulders. She locked her apartment door and did a double take when she saw the door open to number 303, with a young couple trying to fit a couch through the door. They dropped it halfway through the threshold and scowled at each other.

"Are you relations of Mrs. Gordon?" Amelia asked. She pointed to her door. "I'm her neighbor."

"We're moving in," the man said, wiping sweat off his forehead. "I'm Eric. Nice to meet you."

"Kayla," the woman said.

Amelia shook hands with the two of them, frowning at the slice of apartment she could see through the door. It was utterly bare of Mrs. Gordon's knickknacks. "I didn't even know Mrs. Gordon moved out," she said, feeling oddly hurt.

Yet another person leaving her stranded. It wasn't that she

loved Mrs. Gordon, but the old lady had been a constant in her life since she'd moved into the building.

"The old bitch disappeared overnight," Mr. Petrovski said, poking his head through the open door. "Didn't even take her cat. Now Her Majesty is shaking her rear at my Winston all hours of the day and night."

"She didn't take her cat?" Amelia gaped. "Did she die?"

"One can only hope," he replied, then slammed his door.

Amelia turned back to the new couple and grimaced. "He's actually really nice. His cat is great."

Eric and Kayla exchanged a glance, then gave her a polite smile. She left them to maneuver their couch and jogged down the stairs, head spinning.

The restaurant loomed ahead, inside which Ben probably waited. Unless he was late. Should she text him to tell him she was nearly there? Was she being too eager by being on time? But being late was so rude. On Maggie's wedding day, when Leo was late—

No. No, Amelia wouldn't think about Leo. Not tonight. Not when she was the new-and-improved version of herself, the version that dated and flirted and smiled coquettishly.

Stomping down the sidewalk, she opened the door and bared her teeth at the hostess, who blinked in response. With a deep breath, Amelia rearranged her face into her best approximation of a smile. "Hi," she said, "I'm meeting someone? Ben?" Why did her sentences keep coming out as questions?

"Of course," the hostess said with a professional smile. "Follow me."

The rapid beat of Amelia's heart drummed against her ribs.

As she kept her gaze on the woman's swinging ponytail, she reminded herself of all the things Leo had taught her. She just had to be herself—truly. If she felt attraction, all she had to do was let it show. And if all else failed, she could touch Ben's arm and compliment his shoes.

Ben stood when she approached his table. There was an awkward moment when they looked at each other, unsure of how to greet each other. A hug? A kiss on the cheek? A handshake? A high five?

Deep breath. Emboldened, and determined to make this date a success, Amelia cut the tension and reached over for a half-hug and a cheek kiss. It was moderately awkward, but it was fine. When they sat down across from each other and asked for water from the hostess, Amelia's nerves settled slightly.

"I'm glad we got to see each other," Ben told her. "This place is supposed to be great." He gestured to the menu.

"Oh, it's all small share plates, is it?" That meant discussing the food and coming to an agreement about what to order, which was good because it was natural conversation, and also awful because what if they didn't agree on what they wanted to eat?

Stop overthinking.

Amelia studied the menu for a moment, seeing nothing. Her nerves ratcheted tighter and tighter until all she wanted to do was run away.

But she hadn't gone through a week with Leo St. James and the utterly ridiculous heartbreak that followed just to fail at the first hurdle. She'd kissed him and had sex with him, and it had been good. It had been great! Sure, right now, she had no desire to get physical with Ben. But she *would not* run away from this. Maybe she was awkward and uncomfortable, but she'd been awkward and uncomfortable on her first sales call when she launched her business. This was no different.

Gathering her courage, Amelia glanced under the table. "Oh, different shoes today," she noted. "I like these ones too."

Ben beamed. "Thanks! I got them on sale."

So he'd bought this pair himself. That was encouraging! Amelia asked him where he'd bought the shoes, and the stilted conversation became a little bit smoother. She relaxed, and then the waitress was filling up glasses of water and asking if they wanted to order drinks or appetizers. They laughed about not having even glanced at the menu yet, then began discussing options. Conversation flowed.

This was better than Amelia could have expected. She even worked up the courage to reach over and touch Ben's hand when he suggested they get the grilled corn, cooing about how much she loved the idea, really laying it on thick. Ben looked pleased.

Then conversation turned to work, and before they knew it, the food was arriving. It was a perfectly pleasant conversation. Amelia even found herself enjoying it. There was no spark, of course, and she found herself comparing Ben the Barista to Leo at every turn—and why was she thinking of him as Ben the Barista now, instead of just Ben?

When the waitress came over to clear two of the small plates they'd finished, Ben peered at her curiously.

"What?" she asked. "Why are you looking at me like that?"

"I don't want you to take this the wrong way," Ben started.

"But..."

"But I feel like you're not really sensing any chemistry between us."

Amelia froze for a moment, then relaxed her shoulders. "Is it that obvious?"

"Not at first," Ben answered, smiling softly. "But I have the feeling I'm being friend-zoned."

"Can I just say, I hate it when guys use the word 'friend zone' as if it's some fate worse than death? You should be glad to be my friend!"

Ben laughed. "If you were to call me your friend, I would be glad, Amelia."

She narrowed her eyes. "You're not feeling a spark either, are you?"

He shrugged. "Sorry."

"Can't force it, I guess."

"Nope." He stabbed a potato with his fork and chewed it, then said, "I had high hopes for this date. I've always thought you were really cute, but I figured you were too good for me."

Not again. Amelia stared. That was crazy talk. "That's crazy talk."

Ben chuckled. "Come on. Beautiful, talented, clever, and runs her own business? What guy *wouldn't* be intimidated?"

The words rang through her like the peals of a massive bell. She frowned, mulling over the words, thinking about that last day with Leo in the car. "Intimidated?"

"Of course." He ate another potato.

Amelia sipped her drink as her heart began to pound. Here she thought Leo had pushed her away because he wanted to keep living the single life, playing the field, sowing his wild oats. But that was the opposite of everything she'd learned about him. Leo craved companionship and closeness. Was it possible he'd been *intimidated...by Amelia?*

"Who was that guy you were with at the bakery a couple of weeks ago?" Ben asked, going in for a third potato. In his defense, they were delicious.

"Huh?"

"The one who sat with you when you came to pick up your sister's wedding cake."

"Oh," Amelia answered, already knowing who Ben had been talking about. It wasn't like there were many guys who sat with her at Camilla's bakery. "That's Leo."

"And you and him...?"

She let out a long sigh. "I don't know."

A sad smile tugged at Ben's lips. "You and I never had a chance, did we?"

"I'm sorry," Amelia exclaimed. "I shouldn't have agreed to this date, but everything's so confusing, and—"

"Hey, don't worry about it," Ben cut in. "I've wanted to try this restaurant since it opened. This gave me the perfect excuse."

"You're not mad?"

He shrugged. "Nope. Might be time for me to enter the hellscape of online dating, though."

Amelia laughed. Relief swept through her, cool and sweet. Sure, the date had been an utter failure as far as romance went, but she'd come here, and she hadn't messed up. She hadn't been unconscionably awkward, and she hadn't scared Ben away.

"So you and Leo. What's going on there?" Ben asked.

Amelia grimaced. "Nothing, unfortunately."

"You like him?"

She let out a sigh. "Yes. A lot. Too much. He was clear with me about what he wanted, which was nothing serious, and I went ahead and opened my heart to him anyway. It's my own fault for feeling heartbroken about it."

"Did you tell him how you felt?"

"No, but thanks, Dr. Ben."

He grinned, hair flopping down over his eyes as he leaned forward to grab a little crispy piece of chicken skin that had been pushed to the side of one of their plates. The food had been truly divine tonight, so that was another bonus. The evening hadn't been a total waste.

"I think you should tell him," Ben said.

"He's probably gone by now." Amelia tried to gulp away the lump in her throat. "I probably won't see him again."

Ben chewed, his gaze drifting over her shoulder. Eyes widening slightly, he swallowed and said, "I'm not so sure about that."

"Amelia!" a familiar voice screamed. Murmurs grew behind her, and Amelia spun in her chair, heart thundering.

Leo stood in the restaurant doorway, shirt askew, hair mussed, eyes wild. He blew past the hostess and ignored the wide-eyed stare of the other patrons, eyes stuck on Amelia as he stomped across the restaurant toward her.

Heart a trapped bird in her chest, Amelia put a hand to her breast and tried to catch her breath. Her voice was gone—completely disappeared. She couldn't say a word.

In the restaurant's windows, Amelia saw three faces pressed to the glass: Camilla, Lucy, and Scarlett. They must have told him where she was. But why?

Leo came to a stop beside her table. He gave Ben a short, withering glare, then turned back to Amelia. They stared at each other for a long moment, the tension in the air shimmering until Amelia could hardly breathe.

When she was sure she couldn't stand another moment, Leo dropped to his knees beside her and said two words on a gust of breath: "Marry me."

TWENTY-EIGHT

THE WORDS FELL out of Leo's mouth before he could stop them, and now they were out there, between him and Amelia, impossible to take back.

But how could he want to take them back? What he wanted was Amelia by his side, forever. Every night. Every morning. Every day. He wanted her laughs and her scowls. He wanted her sudoku skills. He wanted her pleasure-drunk expressions when she ate the center swirl of a cinnamon bun.

He was desperately, foolishly in love with her.

"What?" she answered, blinking rapidly.

He fumbled in his pockets and pulled out the ring. He didn't even have a box for it, useless man that he was. He just held it between his thumb and forefinger and thrust it at Amelia's chest. "Take it. It's yours."

"Leo, slow down."

"This is so romantic," the hostess swooned behind him. A smattering of applause sounded around the restaurants, quickly hushed by Amelia's friends as they crept closer, listening in.

Leo didn't know how he'd convinced Amelia's friends to tell him where Amelia was. He'd banged on the bakery door and waited for a startled Camilla to show up, then he'd poured his heart out to her. Somehow, she'd been swayed.

Now he needed to do the same thing once more—but the stakes were so much higher.

"Amelia," Leo said, voice raw. "I love you. I love you more than I thought was possible. I'm so sorry I pushed you away. I know I acted like an ass. I asked you to come to my company retreat with me and then I left you at your door like nothing had passed between us, but I was lying to you—lying to myself. I fell in love with you. I fell in love with your eyes and your eyebrows—"

"You fell in love with my eyebrows?"

"And the way you laugh. Kissing you is a revelation. I've never felt the kind of connection I feel with you. You make me want to be a better man. If I were decent, I would wait until I could prove to you that I've changed, but this is me, and I have to tell you how much I need you. I love you, Amelia. I love you so much I'm in pain when I think about it. I love you so much that I wish I could tear my heart out and give it to you. So take this." He thrust the ring at her chest again. "Please, Amelia."

"Leo, we've known each other two weeks."

Gasps echoed around the room.

Panic nipped at Leo's chest. "I know." He sighed, then scrubbed a hand through his hair. "Shit. I don't—"

A soft palm slid over his jaw. Amelia tilted his head up so she could meet his gaze again. "I can't marry you, Leo. Not when we don't really know each other."

His heart cracked, a deep fault line he knew would never heal.

"But," Amelia continued, voice tentative, "I...I love you too. And you don't need to change yourself for me, because I love you exactly the way you are."

"But you won't marry me?" His voice was small and thin.

Amelia's lips curled into a smile. "Well, we've known each other two weeks. How about you wait two more and ask me then? And if I still say no, you could wait two more. Give us time to think about it. Get to know all my horrible habits."

Happiness was a nuclear explosion in Leo's chest. "I love your horrible habits."

She laughed. "Slow down, cowboy." Her eyes were glassy. With a tremulous smile, she brought her lips to his and kissed him softly, tenderly. When she pulled away to the sound of polite (if slightly confused) applause from other patrons, Amelia wiped a tear from her eyes. She glanced down at the ring in his hands. "You kept it. Did you go back to the jeweler and buy the ring just for this?"

Leo sighed. He might as well come clean about it. "This is my grandmother's ring," he admitted. "It's one of the only things I kept after Marlon bought my share of the house."

Amelia's eyes widened. "And you let me wear it all week?"

"It belonged to you the moment you put it on, love," he whispered. Gulping, he grabbed her right hand. "How about until you officially say yes, you wear it on your right ring finger?"

As tears coursed down Amelia's face, she let out a little squeak. "Okay," she whispered.

"You just have to promise not to shake hands with any old ladies."

Snort-laughing, Amelia let him slide the ring on her right ring finger. "And stay away from squirrel-chasing chihuahuas."

Once the ring was firmly back where it belonged, Amelia flung her arms around his shoulders. He stood, holding her, feeling like he was floating on air.

She felt perfect there, in his arms, exactly where he needed her. He inhaled the scent of her skin, her hair, then pulled away and kissed her long and slow and deep, not caring that they were in the middle of a restaurant and he'd just interrupted her date.

"I love you," he whispered against her lips.

"And I love you," she answered. "You nutter."

Laughing, Leo turned to Ben. "Sorry, buddy. She's mine."

Ben grinned. "We already decided to friend zone each other."

"But in a nice way," Amelia added. "It's a compliment."

"Yeah." Ben nodded. "We're happy about it. And I'm happy for you."

Leo assuaged the tiny twinge of guilt in his heart by paying for the dinner Amelia and Ben had eaten. He shook the other man's hand, then wrapped his arm around Amelia's waist and led her out of the restaurant. They enjoyed the cool evening breeze on their way back to Amelia's building, only stopping six times along the way for impromptu kisses and makeout sessions on street corners.

Leo's heart soared. He touched her like a man starved. He held her face, stroked her skin, wrapped his arms around her waist, and tugged her close. She was his—she would be his—forever.

"I love you," he told her for the thousandth time, which made her laugh.

"You mentioned that," she teased.

"And I'll keep saying it."

When they got to Amelia's building, she paused at the front door. Keys in hand, she gazed at him curiously, then touched the ring on her right hand. "This proposal," she started, "it's not just a ploy to continue your cover story, is it?"

Leo's heart ached. He'd put those doubts in her head. This was his fault. Sliding his hands over her cheeks, he lifted her face until their eyes met. "I came clean to Fred this week," he admitted, "and Fred already knew we weren't really engaged."

"And he was okay with it?"

Leo grinned, smug. "He could tell you were in love with me the whole time."

"Oh, wow, I just got a call from NASA, and they said they can see your ego from outer space."

Laughing, he slid his hand to her nape and pulled her in for a hard kiss. She tasted perfect and sweet and his. Heart soaring, he curled his other hand around her waist and pulled her tight, only coming up for breath when his chest heaved.

"I did, you know," Amelia whispered.

"Did what?"

"I loved you the whole time. I know you think you need to change who you are to become worthy of me, but that's just bullshit, Leo. It's like what you told me when I was trying to learn how to flirt. I like you because you're you. And you're more than an old nickname, more than your past. You're a strong, complicated man who makes me laugh, who sees the real me no matter how much I try to hide."

A shuddering breath escaped his lips, and he wrapped his arms around Amelia and held her tight. Finally, she wiggled free and opened the door. They rushed upstairs and into her apartment, and they made it all the way to the sofa where they'd first kissed before falling in each other's arms.

Leo made sure to show Amelia just how happy he was to be with her again until the only word she could speak was his name.

BONELESS, Amelia stared at the ceiling and let out a happy sigh. Leo's fingers trailed over her arm, up and down, soothing. She was collapsed on his chest, both their bodies sticky and sated.

Sex with Leo was explosive, passionate, and perfect. She'd never tire of it.

Pressing a kiss to his chest, she snuggled against him as he reached for the remote and flicked on the television.

"I'll get up in a bit," he promised. "I just need a minute."

"Same."

"Hey, Amelia?"

"Mm?"

"Will you marry me?"

"I said two more weeks, not two hours," she mock-grumbled, trying to hide her smile, but her gaze slid to the ring snug on her third finger. It was still on her right hand, but she already knew she'd move it to her left sooner rather than later.

EPILOGUE

SIX MONTHS LATER, Amelia and Leo were married. The morning of their wedding day, Amelia found herself surrounded by her girlfriends, her sister, and her mother, reclining in a luxurious hotel suite as she sipped champagne and got ready to become Mrs. St. James.

The air rang with laughter and easy conversation, happiness filling Amelia from head to toe. At first, her sister had been totally against the marriage. Maggie had come back from her honeymoon to the news that Leo and Amelia were together, and she'd actually brought a fireplace poker to Amelia's apartment, shaking it menacingly at Leo.

Amelia hated that they thought so little of Leo, but he just put his arm around Amelia and kissed her temple, telling her to be patient with everyone. It would take time, he told her, to show them he'd changed. He acted like he deserved their derision, which made her so angry she wanted to scream.

It took a couple of months for everyone's opinion of Leo to truly improve. Every time Amelia heard a comment about Pestilence, she grew apoplectic, which seemed to amuse Leo. Eventually, he reasoned, people would understand that he was more than the reputation he'd encouraged. And if they didn't, they weren't worth the time or worry.

Amelia was less Zen, but her sister did finally come around. Camilla and Lucy had already been convinced by his initial proposal, what with their soft romantic hearts swaying their opinion without any encouragement from Amelia. Apparently, he'd banged on Camilla's bakery door and begged to know where Amelia was when he hadn't had any luck finding her at her apartment.

Scarlett seemed happy for Amelia, but she did lament the fact that Amelia would never experience a true slut phase. Joking, mostly, Amelia thought.

It was fast. Amelia knew it, Leo knew it, all their family and friends knew it. But six months had been enough for Amelia to realize that she didn't want to live without Leo. Six days had been enough.

Now, as they all helped her get ready to marry the man she loved, her family and friends knew just how important Leo was to her. They knew that he was hard-working, loving, and utterly devoted. Amelia even caught her sister sighing when she saw Leo tuck a strand of hair behind Amelia's ear.

"Oh, look!" Lucy waved her phone around. "They're saying Meredith's trial date has been set." Cora's real name was Meredith Brown. Her name and picture had been splashed all over the local news for three months straight after her arrest.

"Did they ever find her accomplices? Didn't they find evidence that there was a whole operation?" Camilla leaned over Lucy's phone to look at the article.

"Was there?" Amelia tilted her head. "I never heard about that."

"You were too busy making cow eyes at your fiancé," Scarlett said, grinning. "Not that I can blame you."

Amelia stuck her tongue out at the florist, who laughed. They'd grown close over the past six months, and Amelia appreciated Scarlett's no-nonsense nature.

"Yeah, they had shopfronts on all the major online stores like eBay and whatnot. Look." Lucy tapped her phone, then spun it around to face Amelia.

It was an archived version of a website, where dozens and dozens of items were for sale. All of them stolen. Very few of them recovered by the police.

Eyes wide, Amelia scrolled through the images and shook her head. "She seemed so nice. I can still hardly believe it." She scrolled some more, then frowned. Her eyes bugged. "Wait."

"What?" Scarlett leaned over to look.

"These candlesticks. These were in Mrs. Gordon's house!"

"Your neighbor?" Maggie frowned, a tube of lip gloss held halfway to her mouth. "Didn't she die?"

"No, she disappeared."

"What, like Mob-style?" Camilla's eyes were wide. "She's swimming with the fishes?"

Amelia laughed. "No, just moved out all of a sudden. There's been a young couple living in her old place since May."

"One of Cora's aliases was Gordon," Lucy said, filling up

her champagne flute, utterly oblivious to the wide-eyed stares everyone gave her.

"*What.*" Amelia sat up.

Lucy met everyone's gaze, frowning. "Yeah. It's in the article. Just click the back button and you can read it. Gordon, Fitz, Rossi... She used all kinds of names."

Amelia stared at the candlesticks on the screen for another moment, then turned back to the article. "Holy crap," she breathed. "Cora's sister was my neighbor. And wait!" She pointed to a grainy CCTV image of a man. "That's Mrs. Gordon's grandson! She kept trying to set me up with him!"

"Your neighbor..." Scarlett whistled. "Life in Stirling isn't so dull after all."

"Enough about thieving old ladies," Amelia's mother said, swatting her hands at the phone. "You need to get your hair and makeup done. We have two hours until my baby gets married, and I won't have her dreaming up conspiracy theories when she should be celebrating her marriage. Up! Come on. Get in the chair. The makeup artist is just coming up the elevator."

Laughing, Amelia complied. She gave Lucy her phone back, head still spinning about her grouchy old neighbor. She'd lived in Amelia's building for years. Had they been using it as a base of operations? She had so many questions!

Meeting her mother's gaze in the mirror, Amelia grinned. She could ask those questions later. For now, she was going to get married to the man she loved.

Along with the hair and makeup artists, Nadia appeared in the suite's doorway. She squealed and greeted everyone, hugging Amelia tight. "It's so perfect! I poked my head into the reception room, and everything looks amazing!"

Amelia laughed along with the other woman's positivity. Over the last few months, they'd had a number of double dates, and Leo was quickly becoming Fred's unofficial protégé. Amelia, for her part, enjoyed Nadia's company. The other woman was utterly without guile. Nadia loved the finer things in life, but she appreciated simplicity too. She was just as likely to gush over a taco bought from a street vendor as she was a Michelin-starred restaurant. She loved her twelve-million-dollar ring, and she proudly displayed the blazer she got on sale for twelve dollars. It was hard not to love her.

"Leo's spreadsheet must have helped the whole wedding planning process," Nadia noted. "I was so impressed when he finally sent it through!"

Amelia grinned. "I may have helped with that."

"Amelia is absolutely feral for a good spreadsheet," Scarlett noted, popping a tiny hors d'oeuvre into her mouth. She chewed, swallowed, and said, "It's unnatural."

"You didn't seem to mind my spreadsheets when I was helping you put some order into your shop's accounts," Amelia nodded.

Scarlett just winked. "I didn't say being feral was a bad thing. Or being unnatural, for that matter."

"Amelia, sit still," her mother barked. "That hair isn't going to style itself."

Smiling at her mother's bossiness, Amelia settled. She was pampered, plucked, and groomed, and finally slipped on her wedding dress. It was an elegant silk dress with long sleeves and a small train, in a subtle off-white ivory color that made her skin look vibrant instead of deathly. Her veil was embroidered with scalloping along the hem to match the sleeves and neckline of her dress. When she slid it into her hair and looked at herself in the mirror, her eyes glazed with tears that would surely mess up her makeup.

Camilla beamed at her in the mirror. "Leo is going to lose his mind."

AND HE DID. When Leo saw his bride walk down the aisle toward him, he couldn't help the hand that rose to hide his trembling mouth. His heart hammered, his throat worked to clear its obstruction, and his legs turned to jelly.

She was so gorgeous, and she was all his. When her father handed her over and he finally got to take her hands in his, Leo could hardly see through his tears.

"You look beautiful," he whispered.

"Not so bad yourself," she whispered back, squeezing his fingers.

The ceremony was a blur. He said his vows into a microphone and thought they went over well, but the memory was vague. All he remembered from it was the light in Amelia's silver eyes, and the shimmery pink on her lips as they curved into a blissful smile.

When they shared their first kiss as a married couple, Leo thought he'd died and gone to heaven. It wasn't possible that a guy like him could've been so lucky. It was too good. He'd never deserve this kind of joy.

But all he could do was take it day by day, shed his past identity, and be the man he wanted to become, for himself and for Amelia. His goddess. His love. His wife.

CAMILLA PLACED the top tier of Amelia's cake on its pedestal and let out a breath. The cake was decadent chocolate with raspberry filling and rich Swiss buttercream icing. She'd spent hours crafting and decorating it to Leo's and Amelia's specifications. They wanted a simple enough cake, but Camilla took pride in her work. She arranged fresh flowers on the cake boards at every tier, then took a step back.

Her hands trembled as she curled her fingers into her palms. Wetness gathered in her eyes, and she didn't even know why she felt like crying. She should be happy for Amelia. She *was* happy for Amelia. It was just... There was a lot going on!

The stress was getting to her, and now that Amelia's cake was done, she could cross one thing off her list.

"It looks incredible, Camilla," Leo said behind her.

She turned and smiled. "Only the best for my besties."

Leo approached and put his hands on her shoulders. His green eyes were solemn. "I don't know if I ever thanked you properly for telling me where Amelia was that day."

"The day you proposed?"

"The day I got her back," he replied. His hands squeezed her shoulders. "Thank you."

"How could I say no to those eyes, hmm?" She grinned at him. "You looked so pathetic. Like a puppy who'd just gotten kicked."

"Yeah, yeah," he laughed. "I wasn't that bad."

She leaned in and hugged him tight, then pulled away. "The way Amelia talked about you after she got back from the retreat, I knew there was more to you than met the eye, and I knew you'd be great together."

He swallowed thickly, nodding. "Thanks, Camilla."

She had the impression her words meant a lot to him, and she smiled. She shouldn't be worried about her own life's problems; those would get sorted out eventually. She was here to celebrate her friend's wedding to a truly great man.

Leo gave her a sharp nod, then turned for the door. Camilla took a deep, cleansing breath and squared her shoulders in preparation to follow.

She froze when he said, "Why do you have an air mattress?"

"Oh, I, um... It's for...a friend."

He spun around, frowning. "What?"

"Okay, it's for me." She grimaced. "My landlord didn't renew my lease, and with the rental market the way it is... I didn't have time to buy an air mattress earlier and I remembered when I went to grab the flowers from Scarlett's place, so I ducked into the hardware store. I meant to drop it at the bakery before coming here, but..."

Leo frowned, eyes narrowing for a moment before growing wide. "Are you sleeping at the bakery?"

"It's temporary," Camilla rushed to explain. "And it's fine, really. I'll shower at the gym, and there's enough room at the office to fit the air mattress, so it's no big deal. I'll be finding a new rental as soon as possible, Leo, so—why are you looking at me like that?"

"Come with me." He grabbed her wrist and tugged her forward.

"Leo! Stop! You just got married! You should be dancing with Amelia! Or greeting your guests."

"Amelia's primping before our grand entrance, and all our guests are drinking and nibbling happily in the bar. I don't need to be anywhere."

"Still. Don't worry about me. Go do...wedding things! I need to go up to Amelia's suite and make sure she has everything—"

"Amelia's fine. She has this event figured out down to the minute, with the spreadsheets to prove it. She's sending me a warning text exactly five minutes before I need to be by her side for our entrance."

"Leo, let go of me." She tried to sound stern, but he was utterly immune.

He marched her down the hallways of the hotel, from the kitchen all the way to the cocktail lounge. There, he stopped in front of the knot of groomsmen who laughed and chattered boisterously. Leo cleared his throat.

His four groomsmen—Marlon, Cormac, Archer, and Emory—looked up at him.

"Leo!" Archer exclaimed, smiling wide.

Leo gave him a short nod, then turned to his brother. "Marlon. This is Camilla."

Marlon was a great beast of a man, with thick, coarse hair and a full beard. His features were strong, his brow low over beautiful, deep-set hazel eyes, his jaw strong and square. If

Camilla were honest, she'd admit that he was a little bit scary and a little bit thrilling.

He arched a brow and said nothing, his eyes flicking over to Camilla and back to Leo again.

Leo nodded once, like that was all the communication required. He reached into his pocket as he spoke. "Camilla will be taking my old room." He pulled out a set of keys from his pocket, clipped off his car fob, and slapped the set into Camilla's hand. "She's moving in with you, starting tonight."

WANT TO FIND OUT WHAT HAPPENS IN CAMILLA AND
MARLON'S STORY?
GET BOOK 2: CRAVING AT THE LINK BELOW:
HTTPS://GENI.US/CRAVING

EXTENDED EPILOGUE

AMELIA SPRINTED across the vast green lawn, a giggle bursting from behind her lips. She skidded to a stop at the tree-house on the Goodhew Estate, flinging her arms around Leo. He held up the phone, snapping a picture of their cheesy grins.

"Quick," Amelia urged him, breathless. "Upload it."

"Done. Okay, next is the back gate. This way."

Her feet pounded on the beaten dirt pathways through the forest until they reached a small cast-iron gate set in the estate's tall boundary walls. They took another selfie, and while Leo posted it online, Amelia scanned the list.

"That's everything outside," she said, panting, then paused. "Hold on. Look."

Leo glanced at where she pointed, frowning. "What does that say?"

There was small print on the second page of the scavenger

hunt list. It was printed in a pale color, so it was easy to miss on the white paper. "'Bonus Points: Get Fishy,'" Amelia read.

"What does that mean?"

Amelia snapped her head up, eyes on the distant horizon. "The fountain!"

She laughed, tearing off through the trees again. They ran around the house, skidding to a stop on the circular drive. Leo took a photo of her sitting on the lip of the fountain, almost exactly the spot where he had dived in after Nadia's ring a year before. She grinned, then jumped up to keep hunting.

They tore through the house, finding specific sculptures, stained glass, old books. They took pictures with them all, breathless and red-faced, until time ran out. When the siren sounded, Amelia threw her arms around Leo and hugged him tight.

"Much better than last year," he murmured in her hair.

"I don't know," she hedged. "Last year was pretty fun too. Especially the part where you picked me up and shoved me against the wall."

Leo growled, and a bolt of lightning went straight down Amelia's spine. She pulled back, feeling frisky and flirty and adventurous. "Maybe we should visit our favorite shoe closet before we join the others."

"Please don't," Vanessa's deadpan voice sounded behind them. She rolled her eyes and strutted past them, her boyfriend Mark trotting behind her, a big dopey smile on his face. He waved at them both, his grin widening.

"Guess we've been caught now," Leo said in Amelia's ear. "But we can visit the closet later."

Amelia flushed, then took Leo's hand and headed for the back patio. Waiters milled with cool drinks as the scavenger hunt's participants arrived in twos and fours. Amelia took a seat on a gliding wicker rocking chair, feeling utterly content.

"How'd you do?" Fred asked, coming to sit beside her.

She showed her list, all items crossed off save two. "Pretty good. Better than last year."

"You were busy with other things last year," Fred said, smiling. There was still an edge to his eyes, though, and Amelia wondered if he was still hurting from his employees' betrayal. "Hopefully the retreat will be less eventful this year."

"Agreed," Amelia said with a nod. She dropped her glass on a passing waiter's tray, then leaned back on the plush cushions. "Thank you for having us again. Despite everything that happened last year, I loved the time we spent here."

"I think that has more to do with St. James than any activities my team planned," Fred replied with a grin.

Amelia laughed, conceding the point.

Fred glanced down at his left hand, where a gold band sat snugly behind his knuckle. He and Nadia had been married at the beginning of December in a beautiful, lavish ceremony.

"So," Fred said, his tone changing ever so slightly. He turned to look at Amelia with steely eyes. "Your business has grown in the last year."

How did he know that, and where was he going with this? She nodded. "Yes."

"I've been keeping an eye on your progress, and I've heard lots of good things from your clients."

"Okay..." Amelia frowned. "Thanks?"

"With Cora—Meredith—gone, I've had to hire new administrators, and it's become painfully obvious that our systems are out of date. I hadn't realized C—Meredith did a lot of our payroll manually. I was thinking with your skillset, you might be willing to consult on how we could best organize some of our data."

He'd said the magic word. *Data!* Amelia perked up. "Really?"

"We need a complete overhaul of our processes from onboarding new clients to the final reckoning of the financials, and I need someone with a good head for numbers. I'd like to know if anniversaries are more lucrative than corporate events. Or if bachelor parties are worth the insurance risk. Or if we should be focusing on the older crowd or really leaning into the corporate side of the business. Is that something you'd be interested in doing?"

Amelia had to reel in her immediate response, which was *omg yes, yes, yes, yes!!* to something more sedate. She gave him a slow nod. "I think I could help you with that. You mentioned I'd be working as a consultant?"

Fred's eyes gleamed. "Let's discuss the particulars after the retreat. I'm glad you're interested." He got up off the chair, and Amelia did a little wiggle. Fred Goodhew was going to hire her as a consultant! How fabulous! If she did a good job, she'd be able to get a testimonial from him and hopefully tap into his network.

"What's that look about?" Leo asked, coming to sit beside her. He put his arm around her shoulders and tugged her close.

"Fred wants to hire me on as a consultant. He wants me to

help set up all new systems for his company." Her eyes shone. "This is huge!"

Leo's smile was bright and proud. He curled his arm to bring her close, then slid his free hand over her cheek. "My beautiful, smart, amazing wife," he murmured, and then he kissed her.

Kissing Leo felt like tumbling headlong into love all over again. She clung to his shirt and kissed him back, not caring where they were or who might see. He lit her body up, teasing the embers of her desire to a full blaze from one heartbeat to the next.

Distantly, she heard wolf whistles, and when she came up for air, the teasing intensified.

"Young love," Trudy said, hands clasped at her chest. "Why don't you kiss me like that anymore, Rob?"

Rob put his drink down, grabbed his wife by the waist, and dipped her like they were in a ballroom dance competition. Then he kissed her, and her arms came up to wrap around his neck. When they straightened, Trudy's face was flushed and laughing, and Rob looked smug.

Leo laughed. "Think that'll be us in a decade or two?"

Amelia smiled at him. "I hope so."

Before too long, Percival appeared. He had a few extra grays in his hair this year compared to last, but he was his same unflappable, gracious self. He nodded to Fred, and everyone gathered to hear if they'd won the prize.

Amelia found Leo and vibrated next to him. She curled into his side, loving the way he slung his arm around her shoulders.

He did it automatically, without hesitation. It made her feel like in his arms was exactly where she belonged. Being beside him still made her head feel loopy, like his touch disconnected a few wires in her head. Or maybe that was just a symptom of their earlier kiss.

Either way, when Fred announced her and Leo's names as the scavenger hunt winners, it took her a few seconds to understand. It was when Leo laughed, hugged her tight, and lifted her feet up off the ground that she finally let out a loud *whoop* and began to laugh.

They'd won! They'd *won*!

When the gilded envelope appeared, Amelia's stomach was aflutter. She hopped from one foot to the other, bursting with excitement.

"Vienna, here we come!" Amelia exclaimed, waving the envelope around.

"Hell, yeah!" Leo laughed, leaning over to kiss her temple. "Open it up, babe."

With trembling fingers, she broke the seal. The paper inside was thick and luxurious, slightly rough to the touch. Her heart thumped. Before she unfolded it, she glanced up at Leo, who was smiling down at her.

"Love you," he said.

"Right back atcha," she whispered in response, then she unfolded the sheet of paper to claim their prize.

And scowled.

Leo read over her shoulder and began to laugh. He took the paper from her clenched fingers and spun it around to show the other scavenger hunt participants. "Pizza party tonight, anyone?"

WANT TO FIND OUT WHAT HAPPENS IN CAMILLA AND
MARLON'S STORY?
GET BOOK 2: CRAVING AT THE LINK BELOW:
HTTPS://GENI.US/CRAVING

ALSO BY LILIAN MONROE

For all books, visit:

www.lilianmonroe.com

The Four Groomsmen of the Wedpocalypse

Conquest

Craving

Combat

Calamity

Manhattan Billionaires

Big Bossy Mistake

Big Bossy Trouble

Big Bossy Problem

Big Bossy Surprise

Later in Life Romance

Filthy Little Midlife Fling

Dirty Little Midlife Crisis

Dirty Little Midlife Mess

Dirty Little Midlife Mistake

Dirty Little Midlife Disaster

Dirty Little Midlife Debacle

Dirty Little Midlife Secret

Dirty Little Midlife Dilemma

Dirty Little Midlife Drama

Dirty Little Midlife (fake) Date

Brother's Best Friend Romance

Shouldn't Want You

Can't Have You

Don't Need You

Won't Miss You

Protector Romance

His Vow

His Oath

His Word

Enemies to Lovers/Workplace Romance

Hate at First Sight

Loathe at First Sight

Despise at First Sight

Secret Baby/Accidental Pregnancy Romance

Knocked Up by the CEO

Knocked Up by the Single Dad

Knocked Up...Again!

Knocked Up by the Billionaire's Son

Yours for Christmas

Bad Prince

Heartless Prince

Cruel Prince

Broken Prince

Wicked Prince

Wrong Prince

Lone Prince

Ice Queen

Rogue Prince

Fake Engagement Romance

Engaged to Mr. Right

Engaged to Mr. Wrong

Engaged to Mr. Perfect

Mountain Man Romance

Lie to Me

Swear to Me

Run to Me

Doctor's Orders

Doctor O

Doctor D

Doctor L

Made in the USA
Monee, IL
23 June 2026